'We don't so much read *Mountain Road, Late at Night* as live it with these troubled characters and the child, Jack, robbed of his parents by the shocking car crash on a lonely mountain road. This is a complex, deeply moving novel, given completely to the interrogation of its witnesses. An extraordinary debut for an extraordinary new talent'

Frederick Barthelme, author of
There Must Be Some Mistake

'Written in chapters that alternate between the character's perspectives, this is a subtle examination of the effects of trauma and sudden loss, as well as a tense conflict between different views of parenting, what's in the best interests of an orphaned child, and how it is influenced by one's own upbringing. Through sharply drawn characters, Rossi achieves a clear-eyed and poignant view of a family in crisis'

Sydney Morning Herald

'*Mountain Road, Late at Night* is a wondrous thing and deserves to win prizes ... Rossi's narrative burns off the page – I kept thinking of it as a stream of lights, of cat's eyes, illuminating each new stretch of the road it travels, offering partial but transformative glimpses of what is to come ... impossible to forget'

Nina Allan, author of *The Dollmaker*

'A deeply compelling novel'

David Shields, author of *Reality Hunger*

Mountain Road,
Late at Night

Alan Rossi was born in 1980 in Columbus, Ohio. His fiction has appeared in *Granta, Missouri Review, Conjunctions, Agni* and *Ninth Letter,* among others. Rossi was named the New England Review/Bread Loaf Scholar for 2017 and his stories have been awarded a Pushcart Prize and the O. Henry Prize. He lives in South Carolina with his wife and daughter. *Mountain Road, Late at Night* is his first novel.

MOUNTAIN ROAD, LATE AT NIGHT

Alan Rossi

PICADOR

First published 2020 by Picador

This paperback edition first published 2021 by Picador an
imprint of Pan Macmillan
The Smithson, 6 Briset Street, London EC1M 5NR
EU representative: Macmillan Publishers Ireland Limited,
Mallard Lodge, Lansdowne Village, Dublin 4
Associated companies throughout the world
www.panmacmillan.com

ISBN 978-1-5290-0236-2

The epigraph on p. ix is from *The Wasteland* by T. S. Eliot, it appears
here with permission of Faber and Faber Ltd.

The Publishers acknowledge the following for copyright material:
The Way of the Bodhisattva: Shantideva, translated by The Padmakara Translation Group,
Shambhala, 2008; *The Mountains and Waters Sūtra: A Practitioner's Guide to Dōgen's 'Sansuikyo'* by
Shohaku Okumura, Wisdom Publications, 2018; *The Dhammapada,* translated by Eknath
Easwaran, Nilgiri Press, 2007; *Realizing Genjokoan: The Key to Dogen's Shobogenzo,* by Shohaku
Okumura, Wisdom Publications, 2010; *You Have to Say Something: Manifesting Zen Insight,*
Dainin Katagiri, Shambhala, 1998; *The True Dharma Eye: Zen master dōgen's three hundred kōans,*
translated by Kazuaki Tanahashi and John Daido Loori, Shambhala, 2011.

1 3 5 7 9 8 6 4 2

A CIP catalogue record for this book is available from the British Library.

Typeset by Jouve (UK), Milton Keynes
Printed and bound by CPI Group (UK) Ltd, Croydon, CR0 4YY

Visit **www.picador.com** to read more about all our books
and to buy them. You will also find features, author interviews and
news of any author events, and you can sign up for e-newsletters
so that you're always first to hear about our new releases.

To Emily

Beings are numberless, I vow to save them all.
Delusions are inexhaustible, I vow to end them all.
Dharma gates are myriad, I vow to enter them all.
Enlightenment is unattainable, I vow to attain it fully.

—THE FOUR GREAT BODHISATTVA VOWS

Thinking of the key, each confirms a prison.

—T. S. ELIOT

NATHANIEL

May I be a guard for all those who are protector-less,
A guide for those who journey on the road.
May I be a boat, a raft, a bridge,
For all those who wish to cross the water.

For all those ailing in the world,
Until their every sickness has been healed,
May I myself become for them
The doctor, the nurse, the medicine itself.

—SHANTIDEVA

Nathaniel observed – alternating between varying degrees of clarity and confusion, doubt that resolved into certainty, which in turn morphed into questioning – his central role in the numerous discussions among the family members about where the boy should live, who would best serve as replacement parents, who had the necessary parental acumen, who had the finances, who would be dedicated, whose lifestyle the boy would most easily fit into, who was young, who was old, who had been parents, who hadn't, who was willing to do it again, who wasn't, who knew the wishes of the boy's parents and who only thought they knew, who was closest to the now-gone family itself – the parents both dead in a car accident – and finally, who would make the boy immediately feel safe. None of these discussions yielded clear answers for Nathaniel, the dead man's brother, or anyone else. All the accumulated arguments were like an uncertain sea of information, Nathaniel thought, one point swelling into a wave of what felt like fact only to have another point wash out that wave with its own relevance and truth. In this way, rather than revealing who could best help the boy, the debate among the family members in the first days after the accident left the continual, implied, unasked, but deeply felt question: what did the boy want and need? The answer was both too simple and too impossible to approach: Jack wanted his parents. Nathaniel felt that all that these conversations were doing, and what they would continue to do, was serve as a way for the family to act out their scripted roles without any of them seeing what was right in front of them.

Nathaniel received a phone call from his dead brother's mother-in-law the day before. She called to tell him that she had started driving Monday night and would continue for the next four days, since it was over a thirty-hour drive from Boise, and that she would arrive on Friday. She was sorry she couldn't be there sooner, but see no one thought to tell her, you know, the *mother*, that her *daughter* had been in this accident, and plane tickets were way too expensive at this point, to which Nathaniel wanted to explain that there'd been a mistake, that he believed she'd been notified by the police, but before he could say anything this Tammy woman had said, It is what it is and it doesn't matter now. She said she was on her way and would pick up the kid on Friday afternoon in order to drive him back home, asking Nathaniel to please have a suitcase packed with a week's worth of clothes, whatever toys Nathaniel felt the boy needed or would want. He could ship the rest to her later, and then she ended the phone call by saying that she was appreciative of Nathaniel taking the time out of his sched-ule to look after the boy, appreciative of Stefanie as well, please tell her that, she knew that children weren't in their plans so it was really great that for the past week they'd moved in and stayed with the boy in the house he knew, but not to worry, she'd be there soon and they could go back to their apartment and their lives. Nathaniel had then explained to Stefanie, his wife, that Tammy – a woman he had met only once and with whom he had never had a real conversation before – this woman didn't even say *hello*, she just began *talking*, telling him that she was coming to pick up the *kid* with barely any acknowledgment that Nathaniel was even on the line, and *then* she gave him *instructions* for packing. Nathaniel told Stefanie that the mother-in-law basically patronized *both of them* by implying that these few days with Jack had been a burden for them. He told Stefanie that his brother's mother-in-law conveyed this information to him with such flippant urgency, almost an annoyance at having to convey it to him, so that he'd felt reproached and stupid, like he should've somehow known this information, and he hadn't known how to react and therefore hadn't reacted, except to say, Okay, that all sounds great. Thanks, Tammy.

Now, a day after that call, thinking about when to call this Tammy woman back and what he would say to her, Nathaniel watched Stefanie looking through the cabinets for what she said was 'a strainer.' They were in the kitchen of Nathaniel's brother's cabin-like home. They had driven nearly three hours from Charlotte where they lived and worked, driven into the mountains, to be there with Jack in the home that Nicholas had built. Besides the appliances, the kitchen itself – the wood floors, the wood cupboards and drawers, the counters of poured concrete – had been constructed, like the rest of the house, by Nicholas. Every place Nathaniel looked, every space he occupied in the house, he felt his brother. He didn't know how many times he'd cried. He remembered being in the bathroom a few days ago, and how he dropped his toothbrush and was reminded that he'd helped Nicholas lay the tile and how Nicholas had eventually kicked him out of the bathroom because it was too small for both of them to be working in, and when Nathaniel had stood up in an annoyed hurry, he'd smacked his head against his brother's chin as he was standing, hit his brother's chin so hard with the top of his head that he could hear the clack of Nicholas's teeth and when Nicholas uncovered his mouth and spit into his hand, Nathaniel had seen both blood and maybe a quarter of Nicholas's tongue. They had to go to the ER, where a doctor sewed the tongue back on. When he had dropped his toothbrush all this moved through his mind, making him see something other than what he was seeing, which was also what he was doing now standing in the kitchen with Stefanie – seeing something other than what was right in front of him, being somewhere else. In order to correct this, instead of thinking about dropping the toothbrush and remembering how that caused him to remember Nicholas's tongue, now, in the kitchen with Stefanie, he tried to look at everything without letting it remind him of anything, to just see what he was seeing.

Out the windows above the kitchen sink, a constant rain fell, a sound that was at once one sound and many: a padding sound on the grass, a tinny sound on the roof, a thudding sound on the wood of the porch. Stefanie had failed in finding the strainer and was now cleaning potatoes at the sink, potatoes she had picked from the garden, scrubbing them with a little wire brush which caused mud to streak through the running water in the porcelain sink. For the first couple of days, they'd gotten by on sandwiches, but now she wanted to cook. She told Nathaniel, while she scrubbed the potatoes, that he had to call this Tammy woman back. He said he couldn't call her back, what was he going to say? I can't remember a single time I've ever addressed the woman by name, he said. I've only met her once at Nicholas's wedding, where she told me that her daughter had almost married a guy who lived in California. Some guy named Desmond, who was now in the Secret Service. She told me she had no idea why April had chosen to be with my brother, but she had, so she was going to support her daughter, though, Come on, she'd said: Secret Service or anthropologist? Stefanie shook her head, her dark hair, which was in a ponytail, swinging.

Jack, Nathaniel's four-year-old nephew, was napping in his bedroom. Nathaniel walked down the hall and looked into the boy's room. Jack was still sleeping, his breath deep and steady, his body turned away, covered, his black hair messed from sleep. Out the window, a stream flowed beside the cabin. The steady rain that fell from the slate grey sky muffled the sound of the stream, so that Jack, if he woke, wouldn't even notice the sound of the running water, Nathaniel thought. Nathaniel felt the privacy of the rain, like a blanket enclosing the cabin. A half mile away, there was a barn where his dead brother did his carpentry, had once done, Nathaniel thought, and further along the property, a greenhouse and larger outdoor garden, all of which Nathaniel, standing at Jack's bedroom door, had forgotten about to some degree until arriving – it felt nearly impossible, how exactly Nicholas and April and Jack lived – but more than anything, Nathaniel had forgotten how quiet his brother's place could be, how quiet the nearby town was. Even the rain, the reverberating thunder, felt as though it emphasized the quiet of the mountain rather than negating it.

He went back down the hall to the kitchen and stood at the kitchen island, leaning against it, watching Stefanie cleaning potatoes. He could hear, just under the rain, the stream that passed by his brother's cabin, and as the rain lessened, the two different sounds of water created one sound, both seemingly issuing from the underlying silence, and Nathaniel felt he was on the verge of sensing something significant: how that one watery sound – the combination of the rain and the stream – meant something else entirely. The stream trickled and gurgled over rocks, over logs, through grasses, numerous sounds creating the sound of the stream, and the rain that fell into the stream also contributed to that watery sound he was hearing, almost a humming sound, and the many things the stream once was went down the mountain as one thing, where it became a larger river, and merged with another river that ran through the town, which then came out of the mountains, and moved toward the coast, where it became the Atlantic. Many things changing into one thing. One thing changing into another. Or was it simply that the river was already the ocean? Nathaniel's mind tried to grab onto something – he didn't know what – as he stared out the window. He'd been doing this, he'd noticed: his brother was dead, he had to take care of Jack, but he kept thinking of other things. Now it was this: what was he feeling about this mountain rain? Was he feeling the force of coming from the city to the countryside? He knew the natural world was there, but he'd forgotten it, somehow. Mountains and fields and rural life, clouds moving in the still cold spring wind, and trees, just budding, obscured in fog each morning, and rain falling or simply materializing as mist in the air, and the air itself cold and crisp in the morning, slowly warming during the day, still damp, and then temperatures dropping again at night, everything wet, muddy, just becoming green again, everything in balance with itself, a peacefulness that was undercut by something quietly haunting and dreamlike, all of which Nathaniel felt at the fringes of his perception, like he was just a child, learning how the world worked again.

Stefanie finished cleaning the potatoes and said, Okay, back to the original mission, and after opening a few cupboards and moving pots and bowls around this time, she found the strainer. A *colander*, she now said, it's called a colander. She went back to the sink, grabbed a potato from the counter, and peeled the skin into the colander. Nathaniel stopped looking out the window, turning off the natural world like turning off a switch, and watched Stefanie, the potato skins making a quiet slapping sound as they occasionally missed the colander and hit the sink. Stefanie reiterated that Nathaniel needed to call this Tammy woman back and explain to her that this wasn't how things were going to go. I don't like that solution to this particular problem, Nathaniel said. Because it involves me confronting a person and you know I hate doing that. Nathaniel asked if maybe he should get a second opinion, and Stefanie rolled her eyes and said, Go ahead, call your parents. That's not fair, Nathaniel said. No, that's completely fair, Stefanie said. You and your family have to have little conferences before anything gets decided. Your parents call you with detailed travel plans before they visit us. They outline down to the hour how long they'll stay. You call them with questions about your work, your financial situation, and now you're going to call them about this woman. It's not a judgment, but my family isn't the same. That's what you learn coming from divorced parents. You're on your own. You guys are a little committee. Except Nicholas. The one that broke away. That's so hyperbolic I can't tell if it's mean or not, Nathaniel said. You know you're going to call them, she said. He looked at her and said, yeah, he was.

He picked up the phone and thought for a moment of this Tammy woman driving from – where was it again, Omaha or something, somewhere in Idaho, was Omaha in Idaho? – and how she was so sure she was going to be picking up Jack in just a few days. What was he going to say to her? Then he realized that maybe his father would know how to approach the situation, like he knew how to approach so many. When his father answered, Nathaniel said that he wanted to talk to him and to Mom, forgetting, of course, that his mother had decided to take a vow of silence earlier in the week. Before he could say anything, his father was explaining, once again, solemnly, that it'd just have to be him because his mother was still deep in her grief about her son's death – his father actually used the phrase 'her son's death,' which was the kind of overt formal use of language that his father often employed in moments of seriousness, but which also, especially in this moment, came across as insensitive, as though Nathaniel didn't know that his mother's other son was dead – and she was currently going through a period of total silence, no talking at all, which she'd conveyed on a notepad a few days ago, writing out that she wouldn't be talking for some time in order to fully experience her son's leaving this world. Nathaniel said that his father could stop, thanks, he'd just forgotten, and he remembered now, Mom wasn't talking. He thought of how his mother had essentially remained in the hotel in town, not visiting the cabin, and that alone felt distancing, and along with the complete silence, she felt even more cut off from him and the rest of the family. At the same time, it all also felt like a kind of performance, the exact sort of thing his mother would do. The performance of being alone with her sadness: not only was she not leaving her hotel room, she was also now not speaking, and how profound, Nathaniel thought, immediately disliking that he'd thought such a thing. She's still writing little notes and communicating though, his father said. So I guess she might text you. But she won't speak. Right, I know that, though I don't understand the difference, Nathaniel said. His father immediately replied that neither did he but it wasn't for either of them to understand, this was how she was grieving her son's death. Nathaniel knew that what this actually meant was that his mother was grieving her *favorite* son's death and wanted to fully experience her *favorite* son's leaving this world. Then, again, Nathaniel felt mean for having such a thought, even though it wasn't particularly untrue. Nicholas was the son who had left home, who had made his life entirely different from the life of his parents and from Nathaniel's, and who was not only a craftsman, but also an intellectual – teaching botany and anthropology courses at a liberal arts university about thirty miles from his cabin – while Nathaniel was just a chef, didn't have beautiful and ardent thoughts about life, and had once been, for a period of time that was now over, a burden to his parents, who had to bail him out of jail twice for admittedly minor indiscretions, but still, and had to help him finish his high school degree, and then had to support him after college when he decided to forgo grad school and go to culinary school, which had nothing to do with his communications major, and which he knew they had doubted he could really be successful at, but he'd done it. He was not his brother, but he was doing okay: he was married, was an up-and-coming chef, according to a local magazine, and owned a condo with Stefanie. On the phone, after his father was finished talking, Nathaniel explained what had happened with Tammy and what Stefanie thought he should do. He asked if his father thought that was a good idea or not, if he should call Tammy back. Stefanie stopped peeling potatoes and was looking over her shoulder at Nathaniel. His father said, Stefanie's right, you need to call the woman back immediately, to which Stefanie, who apparently could hear his father, mouthed to Nathaniel, Told you, then went back to the potatoes. His father began to say something about how he wanted to talk to Nathaniel about another issue, though, if he had a minute, and Nathaniel replied by saying, Dad, no, I don't have a minute. I have to call this crazy person back.

Stefanie had stopped peeling the potatoes and Nathaniel felt her looking at him. He went to the door, grabbed his jacket, and stepped out onto the porch. He was struck by a sort of fungal, muddy odor of plant and land. He was so accustomed to the sterilized environment he was usually in, or the intensely pleasant smells of garlic and onion and oil and herbs or intensely unpleasant smells of garbage where he worked, that he often forgot the world could have this odd, not bad, smell of dirty freshness. He surveyed the land and mountains as a way to survey his thoughts, annoyed that his father had confirmed what he already knew his father would confirm, that he had to call Tammy back, and now had to figure out how to say what he had to say. He thought of the fact that his dead brother and his dead wife had chosen this town, and this place in particular, for its remoteness. He looked down the mountain as though looking through the trees and fields to the town itself, which he couldn't see, but which arose in his mind as a series of images, like a PowerPoint presentation: a small town of nine thousand people in southern Appalachia, home to a liberal arts university of around a thousand students, beside which was the town proper, a little crosshatch of streets: Main and Church and Broad, all parallel, crossed with Spring and Henry, many of the old buildings still in place, one cobblestone road a reminder of some other period, like an expression of the town's memory. Whenever he and Stefanie visited, they walked downtown with Nicholas and April and Jack, almost always in the summer, almost always with Nicholas or April pointing out things about the town, though he and Stefanie had visited before. Jack would always walk next to Nathaniel, making faces at him, his blue eyes contrasting with dark hair, his striking little boy's face, a face of playfulness and sincerity that wanted the sincerity of playfulness returned, and Nathaniel returned it: listening to his brother, and making adult 'hmm' and 'oh' sounds while giving Jack, in asides, weird, exaggerated faces that Jack giggled at.

Nathaniel was always eventually pulled into his brother's world, and he couldn't help noticing that since moving to the town, his brother had changed. He was someone Nathaniel didn't recognize. He was at once more distant and more open, Nathaniel thought. Nathaniel couldn't tell if this was because of the place, if the remote cabin and the forest and the mountain had changed his brother, or if his brother had changed first and had felt himself out of place in the city where Nathaniel still lived. His brother walked through the town, pointing out spots – family doctors and pediatricians, dentists, two chiropractors, a holistic healing doctor, a yoga studio, one meditation center (also one on a farm outside town), a new/used bookstore, several restaurants – but more than the actual places, he said that the doctor was Dr. Shelly, she was a good one, lots of homeopathic stuff, and the chiropractor was Dr. Nick, the meditation center run by a little Cambodian guy who everybody called Ted because it was easier to say than his name, the manager of the restaurant was Davis, etc., etc. Nathaniel had never known his brother to have any interest in other people, his brother barely had any interest in Nathaniel. And the fact that he lived with his family alone on the mountain seemed contradictory. Did he really know these people? Nicholas would eventually tell them that the town was associated with three nearby state parks, and along with a small art community that arose from the liberal arts college, there was an aspect of the community that was interested in outdoor sports, hiking, kayaking, rock climbing. He'd explain that there was no mall, no nearby fast food places, two gas stations, two garages, a body shop, a farmers' market twice a week that brought in the rural community who lived outside the town proper. When Nathaniel had asked him why this place – Jack tugging on his hand to tell him a joke or get him to listen to what he had to say – his brother had said the college gave him a tenure track job, and when Nathaniel said he knew his brother could've

14

gotten a job at a big state school and made more money, so why here, Nicholas had said, I like it here because there's space to be a person alone and a person not alone, and that's what April and I want for Jack. And when his brother said this, Nathaniel had at first laughed, then saw his brother wasn't joking and wondered if Nicholas was aware of the contradiction of wanting to be alone and yet somehow suddenly having more friends, or acquaintances or whatever they were, than Nicholas ever had in the city.

Standing on the porch, Nathaniel could see the town in his mind: the old buildings set in the Blue Ridge Mountains, a part of Appalachia that was just slightly distanced from authentic Appalachia, a place mainly for middle- and upper-class white people, a destination for travelers who wanted sweeping vistas of blue mountains in the summer, achingly beautiful trees shifting shade in the fall, snow-capped peaks in the winter, and relatively few foreigners, brown people, Nathaniel thought. Nathaniel and Stefanie both noted that when she was in town, she was looked at: dark hair and dark skin and while it was overt, it wasn't malicious. White tourists visited the mountain town for its smallness, its safe quaintness, its Americana-ness, which Nathaniel hated a little, but which Nicholas seemed to have bought into. The two major streets of the town offered a view of Bear Mountain rising in the distance, blue and fog-cloaked, and then on the other side of Main, the river valley and rolling hills stretching away toward the piedmont. Nathaniel understood the idea of giving Jack some remoteness from city life, or just life in a fast-paced suburbia, but he didn't understand the wanting to be near rural depression, or limiting cultural experiences, in particular, for him,

15

like food. Where was Jack going to eat real Indian, Italian, Cambodian, Vietnamese? Sure, there were a couple of Thai restaurants, but those weren't real, and where would he interact with the people who made these foods? At the time Nathaniel had felt sad that this chance to interact with people from all over the world, through food, and through him, Nathaniel, wasn't going to be part of Jack's growing up. It was disappointing that Nicholas had done much of his research in South America and still didn't feel the need to give something more to Jack than a privileged view of white rural-ness. But Nicholas was his brother, and Nathaniel knew there had to be something else Nicholas wasn't fully saying. He wondered if Nicholas's friends at the school knew what it was. He wondered how many of them were thinking of Nicholas now.

It seemed that almost all of the inhabitants of the town knew of the car crash. At the grocery store, the coffee shop, a restaurant he and Stefanie went to, people offered heartfelt condolences. Over the course of a couple days, Nathaniel noticed that the townspeople shared more than just condolences: they shared their knowledge of Nicholas, of April, of the boy. They seemed to want to let Nathaniel know that they knew his brother, understood him even. They told Nathaniel information that was not necessary for him to hear: we all loved Nicky so much, did you know his book about plants from the rainforest, I mean, you're his brother, you must know, but apparently his book about nature containing a hidden intelligence was a big hit. A woman said he was like their mini-celebrity. He performed public readings of the book, not just in the town, but in other actual cities. Chicago and New York. I had no idea he lived in Peru until I read his books. It must be wonderful having such a fascinating brother. Oh god, I'm sorry, the woman had said. I'm so sorry I said that. I wasn't thinking. Another had asked, Have you looked his books up on Amazon? They have hundreds of reviews. He's gonna be here even after he's gone. That's important to remember in this trying time. It made Nathaniel feel odd, even lonelier, this try at connection, this mock understanding of his brother, and it made him sense that he couldn't be for Jack anything close to what Nicholas was, not only not a biological father, but also not a person of interest. Because of the smallness of the town, Nathaniel realized after a few days, because many people knew of his brother before he died, knew of his family, the townspeople felt they had some ownership. They liked talking about Nathaniel's brother as if he was theirs. They seemed to like talking about all of it because it was such a tragedy, and it was *their* tragedy, part of them now. Nathaniel, now sitting on one of the porch rocking chairs, wondered if they'd also like talking about it even more once they learned that there was a custody battle going on, that this Tammy woman, the mother-in-law, was staking her claim. He thought the phrase, The mother-in-law is staking her claim. Fascinating and sad, they'd say. And the poor inept brother having to handle it all. But maybe they'd think good things about the situation. He imagined the townspeople, as they conveyed to each other – at decriminalizing marijuana meetings, after Hot Yoga, as discussion for meditation class, in the faculty cafeteria at the liberal arts university, at the two Thai restaurants, amid the folk rock of two small music venues, quietly in a used bookstore, too loudly in the coffee shop, in the aisle of the organic grocery, at the vegan café, among the art of local art galleries, on the trails of the state park, and at various other meeting places in their Blue Ridge mountain town in southern North Carolina – some version of the idea that it must've been so hard for the family, for the boy, of course, but also particularly for the brother, Nathaniel, who instead of simply missing his brother, had to clean his brother's house, go through his brother's and his sister-in-law's things, box up those things, set up the services, call people, accept condolences and engage in what probably felt like rote, empty sentiment, and in addition to all this, somehow find some place in himself that wasn't grieving and wasn't distracted from grief for his brother's four-year-old boy, Jack, his nephew, who the townspeople knew the brother loved so much, they'd seen him visiting often, more often than the grandparents on either side of the family, and how hard for the brother, and also for his wife.

Nathaniel looked at his phone, the phone number from the Tammy woman. He didn't want to call. He thought that if he just waited something would occur that would allow him not to call, though he knew this was not an actuality and that he'd have to call. He enjoyed imagining how the townspeople saw his own suffering, though he knew it was a selfish thing to consider at the moment, yet he did like it, there was a weird pleasure there, knowing that people knew you were going through something painful and doing it gracefully, and in thinking this thought, Nathaniel thought that he wasn't doing it gracefully, he was imagining what people were thinking and saying and his brother was gone. Yet even this realization did not stop him from further imagining a townswoman, a person who'd served him at the coffee shop, named Meredith, and what maybe she was saying to friends and family about Nathaniel, Nicholas and Jack, the situation itself. Maybe she was saying that the boy must have found it totally confusing that his aunt and uncle were now living in his family's house, sleeping in his mom and dad's bed, cooking in their kitchen. Maybe she'd tell people that she had seen the uncle and the boy at the grocery store, the uncle probably just taking the boy out so he could feel normal, and the uncle had picked Jack up, the once-happy boy now with a fearful and stunned look in his blue eyes, a sadness through his whole being. She'd explain all of this at the pro-marijuana-legalization meeting, telling the members at the meeting how she'd seen how the boy did not want to be away from the uncle, who'd ordered himself a coffee and Jack a hot chocolate, and told her something so sad. Nathaniel remembered explaining it to her: this Meredith woman had asked how the boy was doing and Jack had sort of hid from her behind Nathaniel's leg. He'd told her that Jack was sleeping next to him in his brother's bed during the night, always holding onto him very tight and often clutching his t-shirt. During the day, Jack's thumb was almost always in his mouth, and he followed Nathaniel through the house, his small hand gripping Nathaniel's pantleg even when they sat down to read a book. Nathaniel had told this Meredith person all this and imagined her now telling it to others, and he found himself thinking of how others saw his suffering, his care, his possible neglect, ineptitude, and wondered if they knew anything about him, if Nicholas had ever in conversation conveyed what a fuck-up Nathaniel had once been. He wished he hadn't said anything to this woman, but he'd kept talking, telling her that Jack not only did this holding on thing with him, he also did the same with his aunt, holding onto the black curls of his aunt's hair when she held him, or her skirt, and not only that, but Jack had actually crawled under Stefanie's skirt one afternoon when a friend recognized the boy in the bakery and came by to offer condolences and tried to say hello to Jack, had tried to say, Hi Jack, do you remember me? Ms. Katie? I'm a, I was, I mean, a good friend of your mom's. How are you?, and Jack had at first hid in Stefanie's skirt and then had actually crawled inside it, between Stefanie's legs, and the Ms. Katie woman had apologized, quietly, in a whisper, and said she hadn't meant to say that, she didn't know what possessed her to say that, and she actually began crying in the bakery, and Stefanie had told her it was fine, also in a whisper, and the woman had left, and Stefanie had had to get her order of bread and croissants from the baker by walking up to the counter with Jack clinging to her legs. Nathaniel imagined this Meredith person passing this information on to others in the town, and he knew they all probably were looking at this tragedy askance, like not wanting to turn your head to look at what you know is just a coat on a chair but feels like the silhouette of a person watching you. And though they maybe felt like they were looking at it – both the deaths of the parents and Jack's heartbreak as well as his yearning for some kind of safety, certainty – directly, inwardly, unconsciously, he knew that if they paid too much attention to these clear expressions of not wanting to lose anything more, of learning to hold so tight on to what he didn't want to lose, that it could keep them from doing anything. Because they would see the uncertainty in their own lives.

Just as he himself felt in those moments when Jack held on to his pantleg or gripped his shirt in bed, that he couldn't do anything either, couldn't possibly know what to do amid such clear and powerful impermanence. When moments like talking to this Meredith person arose in Nathaniel's mind, he sensed his distance from himself, as though he was trying to judge his actions and suffering from some outside perspective, which he knew wasn't helpful in any way, and which he also knew was a kind of romanticizing of the pain he was in, the romanticizing serving to distance himself from it, to turn it into a story he could tell himself and understand and pity, rather than doing what he should be doing, though he didn't know exactly what that was. Jack was asleep, after all.

The wind picked up, Nathaniel felt a spray of rain on his face, and he noticed a deep, damp cold move through his body. He pulled his unzipped jacket together over his chest and then went back inside, gently opening and then closing the front door so as not to wake Jack. Stefanie was dumping the potato skins in the trash. He knew that his main job here should be to find some way to help Jack, but when he thought of how he might do that, he didn't know how: was he supposed to help Jack understand where his parents were now? Were they anywhere? Did he invoke God? Was that something his brother had talked to Jack about? Did he go with a more scientific view that in nature energy cannot be created or destroyed, it can only change forms, and so Nicholas and April had simply changed forms, and were, actually, everywhere? Jack wouldn't get that though. Or would he? Would Nicholas have said something more like that? It sounded a little like Nicholas, though he and his brother had stopped having those conversations years ago, and recently, in the last year or two, what they mainly talked about, or what Nathaniel mainly questioned Nicholas about, was when Nicholas was planning on returning to the real world, which Nicholas almost always deflected. They occasionally got into arguments, matters of perspective, with Nathaniel claiming that Nicholas had retreated from life, not just from society and thus community, which Nathaniel argued Nicholas could make change in, but also from the problems of the world: you've created your own little utopia in the mountains while everyone else suffers, Nathaniel had told Nicholas. Nicholas claimed, in his cryptic, unrevealing way, that he didn't feel that was the case at all, that he wasn't looking for some separate peace, that this was his attempt to speak from his inmost intention, for his inmost intention to manifest as action, to which Nathaniel had said that it seemed selfish, and that, actually, it had all been April's idea anyway, and he was only following it out and seeing how some different life might feel. Nicholas had then quoted some old Japanese writer to Nathaniel, had actually sent Nathaniel an email, which had said, I think this explains my position best, though it hadn't explained his position at all. Nathaniel had not understood and still didn't, though he thought of it often and looked at the email often, looked at the quoted words like they were foreign objects from some other universe whose purpose and meaning he glimpsed intuitively, but with clear thinking he could not see: 'Because the blue mountains are walking they are constant. Their walk is swifter than the wind; yet those in the mountains do not sense this, do not know it. To be "in the mountains" is a flower opening "within the world." Those outside the mountains do not sense this, do not know it. Those without eyes to see the mountains do not sense, do not know, do not see, do not hear this truth. They who doubt that the mountains are walking do not yet understand their own walking.' Nathaniel had read the passage so many times he had it memorized, and he had asked Nicholas about it several times, only for Nicholas to respond that they'd talk about it in person when Nathaniel visited next, but that never occurred. Was it something about knowing nature, being close to nature, Nathaniel thought now? Something about people's oneness with nature? He thought of Jack, again, of what Nicholas would say to Jack now. It was impossible to know his brother's mind. Could he say to Jack that his parents had gone away, but they would return, in another form, as grass or trees or a dog, or as the mountain, born again? But that didn't make sense. What did *he* even think? To him, his brother was just gone, so was his brother's wife, April, who Nathaniel liked in theory, but not always in practice. That's all he felt – both were just gone. And he hated it, he didn't want them gone, especially his brother, but that's all that was left in their place: a goneness. The cabin, the cupboards of this kitchen, the small farm his brother had made, all of it was just things. Was he supposed to simply help Jack let go of them, his parents? But how could he do that, he wondered, when he knew that all he wanted to do was also hold on to his brother? Something tightened in Nathaniel's chest when he realized he had no idea what to do with or for Jack, and now, standing in the kitchen watching Stefanie rinsing some carrots, he tried to refocus on getting everything done so that he could understand clearly how to help Jack, and to begin doing it, because so far it felt a little like he'd been putting it off.

Nathaniel thought that all week he'd had to ask Jack to go away, when all the boy wanted to do was hold on to Nathaniel: telling Jack he wanted him to play with Stefanie in the backyard or could Jack go to the greenhouse to get some basil or sage, fill this basket, telling him these things so that Nathaniel could have a few moments alone on the phone with a local estate attorney, with the funeral home, with the bank, who he had to call twice, because he didn't have the death certificates, calling the department of health to ask how to get the death certificates, on the phone with his brother's school to figure out what insurance he had so that Nathaniel could figure out how life insurance was supposed to work, and also setting up cancelation dates for things like utilities and the postal service, all phone calls that required him to say that he was calling on behalf of his brother and sister-in-law, who had recently passed away, which he didn't want Jack hearing over and over again, and all of which he wanted finished so that he could just focus on Jack. Yet now, standing in the kitchen with Stefanie, wondering why she was cleaning carrots and potatoes at ten in the morning, Jack napping because he'd gotten up so early and had worn himself out, there was now his brother's mother-in-law, Tammy, in addition to everything else, and after listening to Stefanie tell him again, now slicing the potatoes, that he needed to call this woman back right now, no more waffling, that this was the most important thing, more than anything else now, he said he got it and told Stefanie that okay, he understood, he had to call.

From the boy's bedroom, he heard Jack begin to make half-crying noises as he woke up. They looked at each other, unmoving for a moment, as if some game, waiting for the word that would unfreeze them. They had learned that these half-crying noises didn't mean he would wake up fully. He would cry some, then talk a little at the mobile that Nicholas had made, which hung above the bed, the mobile fashioned out of wood, little birds that Nathaniel's brother had carved that bobbed up and down on three separate 'branches' of the mobile. After talking at the mobile for a few minutes, both Nathaniel and Stefanie listening, Jack stopped and fell asleep again, and, it felt to Nathaniel, he was free to operate in the world, and in his mind, again. Again, the stream and the rain emphasized the quiet around them, and after Jack was quiet, Nathaniel decided to do it.

He told Stefanie, in a moment of clarity, that he was going to call Tammy on speakerphone and he wanted Stefanie to grab her phone and record the call, so he could share it with his father, the lawyer, to see if this woman had any actual legal rights. He tapped the woman's last incoming call on his phone's screen and then hit the green button. He reminded himself to speak in a low voice, not quite a whisper, so that he wouldn't wake Jack. The mother-in-law answered her cell phone, and Nathaniel said hello, it was Nathaniel, to which he and Stefanie heard (Nathaniel's phone was sitting on the counter. Stefanie also had her phone out and was holding it close to Nathaniel's phone on the counter in order to record the call), I know who it is, what's up, which made Nathaniel pause. They could hear her driving, that monotonous sound of static behind her voice – the hollow white noise of a car traveling over road, and then behind that sound, Nathaniel heard what must've been rain. It was raining where she was too. Nathaniel took a short breath and continued by saying that he was sorry to call back, to be bothering her here, but he maybe hadn't heard correctly, but did she say that she was coming to pick Jack up on Friday? She told Nathaniel he had heard her one hundred percent correctly. She was on her way, and it was what, Tuesday now, so she would arrive Friday morning, and then would drive Jack back that afternoon or the next day. They could arrange for all of Jack's things to be boxed and shipped to her whenever was convenient for them, but not too long, because she wanted Jack to feel at home with her. Stefanie's eyes went wide and she shook her head when she heard this information, as though hearing it for the first time. Nathaniel said that he didn't want to be rude, but he wanted to ask why Tammy thought that she would be taking the boy. Well then ask it, the mother-in-law said. What? Nathaniel said. You said you wanted to ask it, the mother-in-law said. So ask it. Okay, Nathaniel said. Why are you—. I'm just fucking with you, the mother-in-law said, and sort of snort chuckled at this and then said, in an annoyed and almost vacant voice, Who else is going to take him? You? I know neither of you wanted kids. April and I talked. Spoke words on the phone. Conveyed information to each other. Plus, I talked to April about it all when Jack was born. He's coming with me. Nathaniel and Stefanie made confused-looking faces at each other, and Nathaniel leaned into the phone resting on the counter, and said that that was, you know, he didn't think certain, you know, things pertained, since, actually. He stopped, composed himself, as if finally realizing the reality of what he was encountering, and said that look, all that sounded odd because he was told that in the event that both Nicholas and April should pass away, that guardianship would pass to him and Stefanie. Nathaniel heard himself saying this in his most cordial, most warm voice, a voice that, he felt, asked for understanding. The mother-in-law said that that's not what she was told and that wasn't what was happening anyway – she knew about both of them and there was no way Jack was going to *live the rest of his life* with them. I mean, do you get that: you think he's going to live until he's an *adult* with you, Nathaniel? There was a pause, as though the universe was stretched on a taut line between the past and future, the present suddenly unavoidable in its tension, and this tension was expressed, Nathaniel felt, in the way she had used his name, as though he himself was an indictment of himself. He asked if Tammy had any documentation of her guardianship, or did she only *speak* to April, see, because that wouldn't constitute *legal* guardianship. Stefanie was nodding, her eyes still wide, her hand still holding her own cell phone and recording the call. The mother-in-law said that she didn't have any *documentation*, no, but that even a *will* wasn't binding, only a court could grant *legal guardianship, Nathaniel,* though if there was a will, she'd abide by it, and actually, she thought that there probably was one, and it most likely showed that *she* was to be the guardian, and she was really sorry, here, but the truth was she knew she was meant to be the guardian and knew that probably pissed off Nathaniel and Chiquita Banana over there – Stefanie stepped backward, as though the absurdity of the remark contained a physical force, and threw her arms up and let them flap at her sides in apparent disgust – but they'd just have to get over it because this is what April wanted, she knew that for a fact, *Nathaniel*, and it was better for Jack anyway to have an experienced parent. Just because he and his brother were Mr. Educated didn't mean she was a moron or that he could push her aside, she had her rights, she knew them, and she was on her way to pick up the kid, and unless he could prove otherwise, she was just really sorry, but *she* was the guardian here.

Nathaniel had begun to say that well maybe they'd have to talk about this together when she arrived, and would she, but as he was saying it, Stefanie was shaking her head, indicating that Tammy had hung up. Nathaniel looked at her, his mouth slightly open, and Stefanie said, Chiquita Banana. Really? Because my dad is from Mexico? That doesn't even make sense. Nathaniel nodded his head and said they needed to remain calm here, which was what he believed Nicholas might say. He continued by saying that it was very important not to do anything rash or emotional that could jeopardize Jack's chances of being with them, which was the sole goal here, suddenly a very important goal that Nathaniel hadn't even thought was going to be a goal or even thought was going to be a real problem he had to deal with. The problem had somehow not felt *actual* until being confirmed by his brother's mother-in-law, this Tammy woman. I'm not not calm, Stefanie said. I'm just saying that woman is a racist bitch. I think that's exactly right, Nathaniel said calmly, aware that he was acting calm. He added that he supported the notion that this Tammy woman was obviously a racist, there was definitely no questioning that, though maybe bitch was too much, he said, feeling it was a very composed thing to say, but that wasn't the point here, he went on, the point was about Jack, they needed to figure out how Jack could stay with them, and, Nathaniel wondered, there had to be a will or something somewhere in here, so they'd just have to start going through some of the boxes they'd packed, go through the boxes again, and see if they could find it. He said he'd call his father – the *lawyer*, he said in a deep baritone that was supposed to be funny but elicited no response from Stefanie, probably, Nathaniel thought, because he shouldn't be joking – who had been coming over each day for a few hours to help pack, and see if he wanted to come and help them with this new problem, this woman.

He went down the hall to his brother's small office, really just a guest room, with a desk and a twin-sized bed, which he and Stefanie had squeezed into when they visited in the past. They'd packed up much of the room, and now Nathaniel began looking through the papers again, to see if he could find a will. Rain was still falling outside the cabin, a steady, calming sound. A mutter of thunder moved over the cabin. He'd looked through all these papers already, knew the will wasn't there, but he shuffled through a box again, not really paying attention to what he was doing. He opened an accordion folder and looked through the papers there. Drawings that Nicholas had made of plants and trees, with short descriptions, scientific and common names. Their mother had liked these drawings, and had had several framed and hung in her office at the university where she taught, as well as in her home. Nathaniel listened to the rain falling on the trees of the early springtime mountain, and thought that the rain, based on the radar he'd looked at on his phone, would soon move to the town proper some ten miles southeast. There it would become more sporadic yet maybe somehow drearier.

His brother had once told him of a group in town called CALM-AA, and he'd actually met a member of the group before, who was in one of Nicholas's grad classes, a woman named Maddie Dobenstein. CALM-AA stood for Citizens for A Less Materialistic and Apathetic America and met in the basement of the Unitarian Church, and at first Nathaniel thought it sounded like some kind of joke, but apparently it was real, they met and had conversations much like the pro-marijuana group. Nathaniel thought that even those who felt apathy and ambivalence toward all things would be moved to note that the deaths of the boy's parents, and the situation with the rest of the family, was particularly poignant. He put some folders back in a box and thought that Maddie Dobenstein might comment on the sad affair at the next group discussion. He knew from Nicholas that the members of CALM-AA shared either their emotionally numb responses to the state of the materialistic culture they lived in and their disappointingly materialistic part-hippy part-bohemian part-bourgie lives, or noted, with hope, that they were again feeling something, could see beyond the sad materialism and rote-ness and vapidity of their American lives, and he wondered what they would think of this. He pictured all the members of the group suddenly feeling a kind of interest they had not felt in some time when Maddie, normally one of the most bored of the group, asked if everyone had heard about the boy's parents who had died on Smoky Mills Road, which would draw nods from the circle of CALM-AA, and which would then allow her to relate that she had heard about the mother of the dead son. Had anyone heard about her? None of the members had heard, Nathaniel imagined. All of them shook their heads, though Tom, who some suspected of being not really apathetic, deluding himself about his uncaringness, would say No, he hadn't, what about her? Listening to the steady rain, Nathaniel thought of Maddie telling how she'd heard that the mother of the dead son, the grandmother of little Jack, had taken a vow of silence. This mother would not speak again until she had fully accepted the fact that her son was dead, was what Maddie would convey, and that this process could take who knew how long, but the mother had not spoken for a week. Nathaniel saw this Maddie person explaining that she herself had seen the mother one day, ordering sandwiches from the Vegan Café, and in order to do so, this mother and grandmother had written her order on a legal pad she carried with her (which was some-thing that Nathaniel's father had told him his mother had done, which embarrassed Nathaniel, but which he knew he shouldn't be embarrassed about, or maybe simply shouldn't be concerned about his embarrassment), and what devo-tion, Maddie would tell the group, didn't everyone think? What a reverence for things, what an act to make. Nathaniel could see this Maddie Dobenstein person saying something like she had to admit that she found this particularly moving, one of the most moving things that she had witnessed in a long time, one of the most real things, and she hated the way people used this word, real, that people said things like 'it was real' or whatever, as though there were a certain number of moments in one's life that were real moments and that all the rest were just unreal capitalistic, consumer-ist bullshit moments, like somehow watching reality TV, which was clearly fake, was somehow less real than say staring at a tree. The problem, Maddie might add, was that every moment, every life, was immersed in complete and total reality, and it was just that people didn't want to deal with that, that was too hard. They didn't want to experience the actual reality of watching a reality TV show, which was that it was a complete waste of time, a numbing, in the same way that a drug addict doesn't want to see the reality of their life, which is that it is a waste, in the same way we here at CALM-AA don't want to really look at the reality of our apathy, which is that it's pointless, and so what people do is they construct 'real' moments and call the rest bullshit, and Maddie really hated that. But watching this mother was such a real thing, Nathaniel could see this Maddie person saying about his mother, like his mother had chosen some real way to express her suffering. This mother's actions felt completely and wholly real, as if everything else around it was only sketched, and that was because this woman, this mother and grandmother, was attempting, Maddie would explain, to live out every moment as though it was completely real. What this mother highlighted, Maddie would explain, was that the people around her did not want to do this. They didn't want to take part in reality in this way. They only wanted to take part in a capitalistic process covered over in some faux-peaceful hippy philosophy, and Nathaniel, in what he understood as the sweeping final drama of this imagining, saw Maddie now saying that in particular she was going to stop going to her yoga classes because going to those classes was not about yoga, it was about who was getting something, who was being something, who was more devoted, who was better, and who was going further and pushing harder, and what bullshit, more fakery, but this mother, Maddie would say – this woman wasn't bawling her eyes out as was popular when sons died on television, she wasn't frantic or hysterical with grief, she wasn't displaying her grief for anyone, she wasn't making it about who had more grief or who suffered more or who was feeling deeply in their lives. This woman, Maddie would explain, she wasn't doing anything for anyone else or anything else, not for other people and not to fit into some prescribed form of progressivism or liberalism. She was simply allowing herself, as far as Maddie could tell, to feel something fully. Allowing herself the time and the silence to do that. Nathaniel saw this Maddie person, now crying a little in the CALM-AA meeting, say it was like a great lightness opened in herself and she'd cried and felt things, all kinds of things, that she couldn't remember feeling in just a long, long time, and in imagining this, Nathaniel felt himself moved, and then remembered that his brother was gone, that this thing he had made up was a fantasy, and his brother was gone. Just gone. And who knew what his mother was doing anyway? He wasn't even sure why he was doing this imagining – it was just something he'd always done, he'd always imagined people's responses to his food, his failures, his appearance, his family, trivial things and meaningful things, like how they saw him right now, if they believed he was being unselfish, self-sacrificing, a good brother, son, godparent, in the same way he wondered what they felt about Stefanie, about his mother and father – and he knew he should stop, but he began thinking of other members of CALM-AA, members who might feel that his mother was actually being deeply narcissistic, show-offy, and therefore selfish, but before he could continue he heard something from the kitchen and he realized he didn't know how long he'd been in the room, staring vacantly at some papers, not really looking at them. Out the window, the rain had stopped and patches of blue began to show in the sky through the grey and white cumulus.

Nathaniel closed the box full of papers and folders that he wasn't really concentrating on, though he hadn't seen a will, he was pretty sure he hadn't seen one, and walked to the kitchen to investigate the sound he'd heard, but then was overtaken with the thought that the rain had stopped and the eastern side of the mountain would be a patchwork of sun and shadow, making it appear, if one were viewing the side of the mountain from the valley, as though the trees were slowly undulating toward some new destination, moving wavelike, heaving slowly forward. He'd witnessed this once when driving up the mountain to Nicholas's place. The small cabins that populated the mountainside appeared to be moving under the shifting shade and sun. He knew that if one were looking at the cabins on the mountainside, Nicholas and April's place would be seen as a glint of sun off the tin roof and solar panels. The property was well-maintained, trails clearly visible overhead, the barn also tin-roofed, the garden and greenhouse well-kept, a stream running by the main cabin. All would appear exactly as it should be, and it was nothing Nathaniel himself could have constructed, and the life inside the cabin, before Nicholas and April had died, was not one he could ever recreate for Jack, he thought. From a certain point of view far away from the cabin, Nathaniel knew that none of the discussions, the analysis of the situation, the reanalysis, the hesitation about what to do, the lack of hesitation, the need for clarity amid the uncertainty, none of what was occurring on the inside of the cabin would feel a part of reality at all, and no one looking at the cabin would know anything different was occurring there, but it was, he thought.

In the kitchen, Nathaniel focused on what he should be focusing on, telling himself to pay attention, and asked Stefanie if maybe they were acting a little too impulsively here. If maybe it wasn't a great idea for Jack to be with them. After all, Nathaniel wasn't exactly in a good place financially. When are you ever? Stefanie said. Oh, haha, Nathaniel said in a mock-annoyed manner, to which Stefanie did an aware-of-how-stupid-the-joke-was-toothy-grin. But seriously, he told her, his job didn't pay enough, did it? To support a child? How much did children cost, exactly? They hadn't thought about that. He could Google it but his brother didn't have internet on the property, and while there was a cell signal, it was weak. Not only this, he said, but he also wanted, no, he needed his own restaurant, it's what he'd been working for for so long, and certain things were finally coming into place. They had a little money saved up, and he didn't want to be working for a rich family his entire life. He wanted to, you know, make an impact, he said. A food impact, Stefanie said. Jamie Oliver shit, she said. I mean, sort of, he said. Whatever. The job itself as a private chef for this ridiculous family was already difficult, he thought. He drove nearly an hour on Thursday, to Greensboro, stayed at the Camerons' Thursday night in the guest house so that he could prepare Friday's dinner, then stayed again Friday night so that he could wake up and prepare Saturday's dinner, and then stayed again Saturday night so that he could wake up very early on Sunday to prepare brunch for the entire Cameron family, a group of around twenty people, depending on the weekend, so that he often arrived home Sunday evening so tired he couldn't do anything other than stare at the television, and then it was back to work on Monday prepping at the country club, a second job that he truly hated – a rote menu with rote flavors. And yet cooking, the simple act of it, not being a chef, but being a cook, was not only finally something he was good at, but also something that he felt made an actual impact on the world. People need to eat, Stefanie said. And they need to eat high-quality local foods prepared rustically. Okay, the mocking thing is hurting my feelings a little, he said. She walked over to him in the kitchen, squeezed his arm, and said, I love your food, don't be so uptight. Nathaniel said but that was exactly the thing: he was uptight. He was a seriously uptight person. He was so uptight that his brother died a week ago and he was worrying about his job in relation to his nephew – that was the definition of uptight. He was hating himself a little bit that he was thinking about himself here and his career, which was an admittedly superficial concern, he knew that, but it was something he had worked on for so long, and he didn't like how he was saying all this, that he might be implying that Jack was somehow going to mess that up, that's not what he was implying. What are you implying then? Stefanie said. Because it sounds like all you're doing is being worried about things you can't control. I'm worried we won't be good parents to Jack, he said. And you're right, maybe that's not a thing we can control, but we should think about it. We have to, he said. For Jack's sake. Because maybe what he had failed to acknowledge, maybe what this Tammy woman had *revealed*, was that while he loved Jack, maybe they weren't exactly in a position to take him, maybe Tammy was right, maybe this was an opportunity they should really look at?

Stefanie looked at him as she was putting the sliced potatoes and carrots into a Tupperware bowl. She put on the lid and then put the bowl in the refrigerator. After a moment she asked if maybe he thought he was doing more than thinking about just Jack's welfare here? Maybe he was being actually selfish. She went to the front door and put on her raincoat and told him that if he really wanted to continue this conversation, they could, but he knew the answer was pretty simple. I don't know that the answer is simple at all, he said. She said that he knew what Nicholas wanted, she herself knew what April wanted, they were the godparents. Even if this wasn't public record, Nicholas and April had asked *both of them*, at the same time, at Jack's first birthday actually, if they would be the guardians. Simple. She put on a pair of rubber boots she kept outside, near the door. Nathaniel was hobbled over, getting his boots on as well. The bottoms of both pairs were covered in mud. Nathaniel looked at their bootprints of dried mud, that moved off the porch, down the steps, and then into the yard, which wasn't a yard, but was just the mountain. The traces of their coming and going. And we accepted, Stefanie said.

She stepped off the porch with Nathaniel following, Stefanie walking fast, her arms crossed across her chest against the wind, which was moving the clouds above relatively quickly across the sky. Her body's quick movements, quick pace, conveyed her slight irritation toward him. Nathaniel caught up to her and pulled on her coat a little and she glanced at him, relaxed her arms. They walked side by side to the garden, a mile away on the property. Stefanie held her phone in her left hand, and on it, a feed from Jack's room monitor. She showed it to Nathaniel and made a he's-so-cute face – it was both audio and visual, but was extremely pixelated and blurry because it was connected to such a weak cell signal, but they could still see the boy in his bed, in black and white – the image seeming almost like a negative of a photograph – sleeping on his side in his bed, with what they both knew was a blue blanket bunched up near his chin and face, his left hand cupping his left ear, a thing the boy did when he slept or in moments of what they deemed 'worry.' The cat slept on a chair in the corner. Stefanie put the phone in her pocket – the phone would vibrate if he moved – and said that Nathaniel didn't need to bring his self-doubt to this. Please don't do that, she said. He brought it to everything else. He brought it to his life with her, he brought it to his job, he brought it to his existence as a person, and every time he did, it made her feel like shit, because it meant in some way that he wasn't content with her.

Their boots made squishing noises on the dirt, now mud, path. It was still cold in the mountains, spring defrosting rather than warming, and yet small wildflowers, the size of bees, grew along the trail. They were in a pocket of sunlight that broke through the trees and was highlighted by mist rising from the ground, then they were in the shadow of a quick-moving cloud. Nathaniel told her that he didn't want her to feel that way. He didn't mean to bring any doubt into this, he just wanted to know if Stefanie really wanted to do this. No, that's not it, she said. You understand that this is going to be a fight of some kind, and you want to run from it. You don't want to engage in it because you think that you're above it in some way. You're just like your brother in that respect. For a moment, neither of them said anything. Nathaniel felt the force of the absence of the dead brother, of April, too. As though his name conjured both his presence and his absence at once, and the confusion between those two things. Here and gone, Nathaniel thought without willing himself to think it, like the thought wasn't his. Where did a thing come from and where did it go? All this in his mind in the space of a moment felt like the reality of the moon reflected in water: the moon is there, in the water, and also not, and in the same way, these thoughts existed in his body and also not, and you were here for a short time in the world and then you were gone, and this coming and going seemed to contain some hidden message, like the coming and going itself was attempting to say something, as though everything was trying to tell itself something, though he didn't know what. He thought of Jack and felt a pressure rise through his chest and into his head and stopped himself from crying by biting his cheek hard. Stefanie said she was sorry – she shouldn't have said that about his brother. Her hand briefly touched his and in the touch, he felt a small release. Nathaniel shook his head and quietly said it was okay, it was fair, she was being accurate. He did think Nicholas ran away to some degree – that was the meaning of his moving out here. His brother couldn't deal with certain things. They were the same in that regard, they didn't like to fight. Even when younger, they didn't fight as kids. Or rarely did. Not like other brothers he knew. After a moment he said that he missed Nicholas. Stefanie moved her body close to his and in the way bodies communicate their own actuality, he accepted wordlessly, and they held each other standing under the trees on the trail.

Nathaniel said okay, okay, and they continued walking and after a moment he thought that Stefanie was right, that he didn't want to fight with this Tammy woman. So much of his existence was fighting. His career took getting good reviews and getting noticed and creating new things not solely because he wanted to be creating dishes, but because that's what the industry demanded, and there was a certain kind of 'new' that was acceptable, there was a certain kind of creation that was immediately obvious as creative, and in this way, he'd realized over time, he was in a kind of box – there were things he had to do, this wasn't purely creative – and it made the thing he did less in some way, corrupted in some way, and Stefanie was right, he was a little like his brother, he was tired of fighting so much for what he wanted. Had he not proved himself? Did he even need to? He'd worked under one of the best chefs in the city, he'd helped open two new restaurants, he'd been featured in the local magazine as a chef to 'watch out' for, and yet he couldn't get help starting the kind of restaurant he wanted to start. It was like he was going backward. He was a private chef. He knew he was selfish. He was selfish and idealistic about his job, which was a thing he didn't think he should have to fight for, the fighting ruined some part of it, and he knew that she knew this made him, often, like now, feel shitty. Like maybe he wasn't actually good at what he did – maybe he was just lucky even to work for the Camerons. And because of all this, he thought, maybe the clear answer here was to just let Tammy have Jack because he already had to go back home in a few days and deal with the fallout from a mediocre review of his spring menu at the country club, a review which had called the menu theoretically interesting, but almost too interested in the small things, in pure tastes, so that everything was a little bland. As though Nathaniel had any real choice in that menu. He had to go back home and deal with that on top of the ever-pervasive stigma about vegetarian food in the first place, as though good vegetarian food can't be rustic and elegant, can't be simple and complex, can't taste great and be affordable, that it's either plates of mush or salads. Nathaniel said, I don't know, maybe this is wrong, maybe we can't do it. How are we supposed to raise Jack and live our lives? Stefanie stopped walking and asked him what were they supposed to be talking about here? Fuck, he said. I know. See, that's evidence itself though. All I do is think about myself. I've been having these terrible moments where I imagine what the town is thinking about all this. She told him to stop. She didn't want to hear about the existential crisis of his career or whatever right now, she didn't want to hear his food philosophy again. She knew his food philosophy. She was on board with it. She didn't need to hear it again. He said that she was right, he was done, sorry, he just had to get that out.

They came to a part of the trail that crossed a stream – Nicholas had built a wooden bridge some years before, complete with a handrail. He'd built it, Nathaniel remembered, when he had moved himself and April to the property, before he had cleared part of the woods for the garden and greenhouse. Nathaniel had helped him construct the bridge, which basically meant that he held boards in place while Nicholas hammered and constructed. They walked across, the bridge now bowed, moving gently above the rushing stream. Nathaniel thought of the things Nicholas could do well, things which came easily to him while he himself could barely do one thing well, he could barely be a good husband to Stefanie, be a decent chef, be a somewhat involved son, and also do other things he cared about like working in some hiking and tennis from time to time, he could barely even approach the idea, he was so busy, about how to actually be a decent person, so how was he going to be a parent? In an effort to stop thinking this, he said that what it came down to was that he was very anxious now that this Tammy person had said her piece. Stefanie agreed.

The garden emerged, through trees and fog, set in a large clearing. It had recently been planted, small green sprouts coming up in places, the neat rows of dirt still noticeable. In the back of the garden, some larger plants, winter vegetables. Nathaniel watched Stefanie walk around the garden to where potatoes and carrots grew. She began to dig up carrots and turnips from the ground. She seemed so capable of doing, of completing tasks, he didn't know how, though at the same time he thought that there was no reason to be out here getting vegetables. She'd peeled and cut up potatoes and carrots already. What did they need more for? As the carrots and turnips came up from the wet dirt, Nathaniel collected them where they lay. She told him that his problem, which had always been his problem, was that he had lost his original intention in all of this, he had allowed himself to be influenced by others and by himself. She said that that was the difference between their two families: his family was a family of people who overthought everything, though his parents had improved now that they were nearing retirement, as he himself had described, and Nicholas had apparently entered some way of life that was unfathomable to them both, but Stefanie had parents who taught her to just do things. When you have a father in Mexico and mother in Dallas, you learn to just do what you have to do. She said that wasn't he happiest when he was just making food, making a dish, creating, wasn't that the thing? Why add all this extra onto it? She didn't like the phrase 'man up' because they were living in a culture that was still stupidly patriarchal, and obviously 'grow some balls' was insensitive, so maybe she'd use the thing the pilot says in *Raiders of the Lost Ark*, 'show some backbone.' Seriously, she said. Show some backbone. Nathaniel was gathering the vegetables and he said, Okay, okay, yeah, I got it, you're right, and Stefanie was saying that she knew she was right. She knew she was right because she was the kind of the kid who got left at home when her mother used to go to the bar. She was seven and had to make dinner for herself. She was eight and had to set her alarm, make her lunch, and walk to school by herself. She took care of her father when she was twelve and thirteen and he refused a hospital. She didn't want to do it. But she also didn't get to think about it. She just did what she had to do. Nathaniel was picking up the vegetables behind her, now saying, I think that's enough, that's plenty of carrots. Didn't you already cut a bunch of carrots up? Stefanie pushed the spade into the dirt and looked at Nathaniel. I'll say when there are enough carrots, she said in a mock-dad voice. He stood up and nodded his head and said she was right, he got it, and said,

I'm done, I'm over it. We can do this. She quickly kissed him on the cheek and said, That's better.

They walked back to the cabin and when they arrived, Jack was just waking, and when he was fully up from the nap, Nathaniel watched him walk from his bed toward him and immediately grab his pantleg. He sort of combed Jack's black hair into place, Jack's wide blue eyes briefly looking up at him and then back down. Want to read a book? Nathaniel said. Jack put his thumb in his mouth and nodded. They went down the hall and into the small family room. Nathaniel picked Jack up so he could choose a book from what was a sturdy, probably oak bookshelf that Nicholas had constructed. Jack pulled a book about a bear in a toy store, whose overalls are missing a button. The bear, convinced that a new button will help him find a home, has an adventure at night in a department store. Nathaniel had read the book to Jack what seemed to be countless times since they arrived – and when reading it the first time, unfamiliar with the book, he felt so moved he almost wasn't able to complete it without his voice wavering and had to take several breaths and then cough in order to compose himself. Now Jack held the book while Nathaniel held him and when Nathaniel sat him on the sofa, then sat next to him, Jack immediately stood up on the sofa, and sat on Nathaniel's lap, holding, with his left hand, the sleeve of Nathaniel's shirt. Jack handed him the book, and Nathaniel said, Okay, you turn the pages, and Jack opened the book, and they began, and Nathaniel tried to be fully there for Jack, but he was thinking about how Jack might be thinking of how Nicholas read the book, or how April read it, how they probably read it with different inflections, how they emphasized parts that Nathaniel maybe didn't know to emphasize, and along with this, since he'd now read the book several times, he knew to distance himself from the sentimental story he was a reading, a story about a bear wanting a family, feeling outcast, left out, alone, a story which would be trite and amusingly, maybe even warmly, clichéd at any other time, but that was now, Nathaniel couldn't help but feel, exactly what Jack was feeling, a book chosen because it mirrored Jack's own feelings, and was probably Jack's way of indicating, over and over and over, in a child's way, his longing to be with his family, to have a family, and if Nathaniel allowed himself to think about it too much, to consider this barely coded message and to really be there with Jack and therefore with the book, he would start crying. So he read it distantly, thinking of the Tammy woman, of how to figure out that situation, while Jack turned the pages. When he finished, and Jack closed the book – he always closed it – he turned it over and looked at Nathaniel and said, Again. Nathaniel said, Yeah, one more time, then we need to eat lunch, and when he said it, Jack sat up higher in his lap and hugged him around the neck briefly, then opened the book again.

After reading, Nathaniel fed Jack lunch and played with him on the kitchen floor and in the afternoon they went on a walk. The day passed quickly, quicker than Nathaniel was used to. Jack was quiet and sullen, but Nathaniel so sensed a wish in his small body for physical expression. Nathaniel played a wooden block game with him, he kicked the soccer ball with him in the muddy yard, they read another couple of books, thankfully not the bear book. Nathaniel watched Jack, his play withdrawn, and Nathaniel thought his play seemed to be more of an attempt at play than actual play, which if he allowed himself to think about, just like when he thought about the story the boy wanted read to him over and over, made it impossible for Nathaniel to engage, so he tried to stop thinking about it.

That evening, Nathaniel made pan-roasted chicken, with the vegetables on hand and a mushroom cream sauce. For Jack, homemade mac and cheese. They ate quietly in the kitchen, Jack watching them and looking away in the same way Nathaniel felt he was observing Jack. Nathaniel watched Jack, and watched Stefanie, thinking about how he could never be Nicholas, how Stefanie couldn't be April – they would always and only be substitutes. He thought of April, how when he first met her, he didn't know how to talk with her, she was so quiet. It unnerved him. She watched. Yet when she finally spoke, he found her easy, kind, and also full of her own anxieties that he hadn't seen. She wasn't this observant, perfect person, and this understanding – Nathaniel remembered now while eating dinner, watching Jack brush his long hair out of his face while spooning mac and cheese to his mouth – endeared her to him, and thinking of it now, it made him feel like maybe he and Stefanie could do this, that their flaws weren't an inescapable problem. There was a piece of macaroni on Jack's face and Nathaniel reached across the table with his napkin and wiped it off, as though symbolically proving to himself that he was capable, that he could do this. He ate a piece of chicken and thought of April, knew from Nicholas that people found her odd, and he did, too, at first, and though he wasn't sure he liked her, he did feel an odd admiration of her, that she was okay being considered odd and wasn't going to change herself to fit some more prescribed idea of normal. She didn't do any social media, didn't even look at the internet, had influenced Nicholas not to look at the internet, almost never drank, though she claimed she didn't dislike drinking, and was impressed when Nathaniel told her he was a vegetarian chef, but was also distant when he revealed he himself ate meat, as though she was judging him, but he'd learned, over maybe a half a year or so, that she wasn't, she was only observing. Nicholas had told Nathaniel that the townspeople thought April was odd, he told Nathaniel he could just see it. Nathaniel imagined that probably no one disliked her, no one thought she was a bad person or that there was anything malicious in her, they just thought she was strange, maybe they mistakenly thought she was a little dim, all that quietness: Nicholas had explained that her fellow teachers at McComb Montessori had learned that, along with the weirdness surrounding technology, she had a shaman she met with occasionally, and that while this was not terribly strange for their town (many people in the town had gone to one of the two Peruvian shamans for a cleansing), what was odd was that April invited the shaman to her and Nicholas's cabin on the mountain. The shaman had stayed for several days. This was all sometime in her sixth month of pregnancy, and while the shaman himself didn't reveal any of what had gone on during those days, April did, Nicholas had told Nathaniel. She had told her friends, or supposed friends at the school, that the shaman took the whole family on a cleansing journey. Nathaniel remembered how Nicholas explained that the other teachers asked April what she meant by whole family, since it was just her and Nicholas at that point, and she'd replied that she meant

Jack, too, of course. Nicholas just knew that the other teachers at McComb Montessori glanced at one another, out of comedic suspicion, because apparently this woman believed that her unborn child had also entered the dream dimension with her and Nicholas, and sure, the whole shaman thing was acceptable for adults, many of the townspeople would've thought, but it was of course just a psychological trick, a way of meditating maybe, all that drumming meant to bring one into a trance-like state which could thereby allow a person to see into their own idiosyncrasies and flaws and be accepting of those things, possibly learn from them, or, alternately, if there were drugs involved, the drugs opening a person to some unseen aspect of themselves, but to think that an unborn child also experienced this journey was a little superstitious. Nicholas had said he could just see that to the Montessori teachers this all was a little superstitious, and also sort of dumb, and therefore, he'd said, that's how they saw April.

Stefanie was cutting some of her chicken for Jack, Nathaniel noticed, and though he'd been aware of Jack asking for some chicken, he hadn't actually been seeing what he was seeing because of his thinking, though now he saw it because the pieces of chicken seemed too big. Cut it a little smaller, Nathaniel said. Stefanie looked at him. They're small enough. Jack do you want the pieces smaller? Nathaniel asked him. Jack looked between the two of them and Stefanie said, They don't need to be smaller. They're fine. Don't be so controlling, I know what I'm doing. Nathaniel looked at her and tried to convey with his eyes that he wasn't trying to be controlling. The boy took the pieces from her and began eating them without any trouble.

Nathaniel saw, for a moment, that this was what it would be like: he would have one idea of how to care for Jack, Stefanie would have another, and they'd be at odds, the gap would only get bigger. In the same way that, when April claimed that she had seen her unborn son's face in whatever astral-dreamscape the shaman had brought her to, the other teachers couldn't help but laugh, already constructing stories for their spouses and friends, and she'd been at odds with them. In the same way that the Tammy woman thought she knew what was best for Jack, and now Nathaniel and Stefanie were at odds with her. Everyone was always thinking they knew the right way to live, Nathaniel thought, eating some of his potatoes. The other teachers at McComb Montessori thought they knew better than April what was the right way to live, that her way was strange, stupid, and this was what caused isolation. Nathaniel knew from Nicholas that April didn't talk much with the other teachers, the shaman thing being one of the first stories she'd told after moving to the town. Nicholas had told him that all April had wanted from this journey with the shaman was to open up a calm, loving space for the child to come into because she was experiencing some anxiety about the pregnancy. This was what Nicholas had told Nathaniel on the phone, this was what Nicholas told Nathaniel that April wanted, a simple thing, and Nicholas said he knew the story had gotten around, and though he didn't care, he cared that it was isolating April and making her feel like her worries weren't real. She was thirty-six after all, and this was their first child. She and Nicholas hadn't been able to get pregnant before, and now she was able to, and what might that mean? She was a little scared, sometimes more than a little,

Nathaniel remembered Nicholas telling him, but how could you make that clear to people? You couldn't. And so, Nicholas had explained, he knew that the story had gotten around town, and all he could hope was that when people gossiped about how she wouldn't allow plastic toys in her house, how the family didn't have television, how there was no internet connection on the property, how they grew and ate their own vegetables and built their own house, which they all probably thought was commendable and sustainable, but also a little wild, and how weird they all thought the shaman thing was, maybe they would also think, initially out of guilt and shame but then out of actual conviction, that she was just trying, you know. Like us all.

Jack asked to be excused, and Nathaniel looked at him. His plate was partially finished, and Nathaniel felt a small guilt for not paying attention while eating, not talking to Jack, but then Stefanie hadn't either. Come here, Nathaniel said. Jack came over and grabbed Nathaniel's pantleg. Ice cream? Nathaniel said. Jack smiled, and Nathaniel stood and picked him up. They had some dessert and by the time Stefanie put Jack to bed, and Nathaniel read him one more book, Nathaniel's mind felt full of a cloud-like feeling, stuffed yet also empty, and when he got into bed he couldn't remember falling asleep or thinking anything on the way to sleep which was what normally happened at home in their condo.

The next day was Thursday, the day before Tammy was supposed to arrive, another day of intermittent cloud and sun and rain, the temperatures very cold at night, in the high thirties. The cabin was warmed with wood burning from the two iron stoves, the insides of the stoves glowing and hot and sending out a smoky cedar smell, still cold in the early morning when Nathaniel made Jack pancakes from scratch and used the syrup that Nicholas harvested from the maple trees on his property, Nathaniel's mind just beginning to orient, as it did every day, into rain-like, unremitting thought. While cleaning the dishes and pans from breakfast, Nathaniel observed Stefanie reading Jack a book, holding him on her lap, and he tried to assess the boy's mood, if it was improved, if he was even the slightest bit happier, all while feeling the futility of the attempt. After reading, Jack followed Nathaniel around the house wherever he went – to do laundry, to put more wood in the stove, to make more coffee, and it felt good, doing nothing all morning except doing – and Nathaniel, at one point, walked into the bedroom on the pretense of folding a load of laundry, then ran to the other side of the bed and hid. Nathaniel then slowly raised his head over the edge of the bed, feigning looking around to see if anyone knew where he was hiding, caught Jack's eyes, the boy's thumb in his mouth, then ducked back down. When he did it again, Jack smiled at him. Nathaniel got up, ran past Jack out the bedroom door, ran down the hall, and hid behind the sofa in the family room. He heard Jack's feet running clumsily behind him, padding nicely on the wood floor. Nathaniel again popped his head up, scanned, found Jack's eyes, and the boy smiled again, his thumb still in his mouth, and Nathaniel again went running by the boy, hiding in the bathroom, again hearing the boy's feet run after him. Nathaniel did the same scanning, found Jack's eyes in the same way, but this time there was no smile. Nathaniel came out of the bathroom and ruffled the boy's hair, something that felt right and an affectation, or maybe it was practice.

After putting Jack down for his nap, a more normal nap time, Nathaniel waited on the porch and then, after a few minutes of thinking about what he had to do when he got back home – the cat litter, vacuuming, calling in to work – he watched his father's car drive up the dirt road toward the house. Nathaniel looked at his watch and thought that his father of course arrived almost exactly on time, his arrival coordinated to occur, like the phone calls of the previous day, during Jack's nap around two which could last forty-five minutes to an hour or two, depending, and was of course perfectly executed by his father. It was warmer outside, though wet. The rain system had gotten trapped in the mountains on the way to the Atlantic, Nathaniel had read on his cell phone. Nathaniel watched his father shake out his coat on the porch, take off his shoes, and enter the cabin, all without addressing Nathaniel, so that Nathaniel followed behind, saying internally in a sarcastic voice, Hi Dad, how're you? Oh, I'm good. Good to hear. His father sat on the family room sofa, got out a little green notebook and pen, and immediately asked Nathaniel what exactly had been said on the phone, the pen poised in his right hand for note taking. Nathaniel told him he didn't need to take notes and his father replied that if they really wanted his help, this was how he helped, so please tell him what had happened because this woman was going to be here tomorrow. Nathaniel looked at Stefanie, who'd joined them, then began recounting the phone call. He told his father that luckily he and Stefanie had thought to record the call, so his father could listen to it if he wanted. The woman,

Nicholas's mother-in-law, Tammy, had used racist language, and Nathaniel, already sidetracked, said that maybe that was something they could use in court, if it went there, which he hoped it wouldn't, but it seemed like it might, this woman, she's pretty determined, she called Stefanie 'Chiquita Banana,' she told me to have the boy packed and ready, like she's going to show up, pick up the kid, and then disappear into middle America. His father stopped writing and said, Chiquita Banana. Do they still make those? Nathaniel said that that was sort of beside the point, the point was, shit, he'd lost his train of thought here, what was the point he was trying to make about the phone call, he asked Stefanie. She was standing in the kitchen, which was directly next to the family room, and now stepped into the family room and said the point was that this Tammy person was not who April or Nicholas had wanted to be Jack's guardian.

She said to Nathaniel's father that she personally knew from April that April would not want Jack with her mother. Nathaniel's father was now intermittently writing notes and also looking through nearby boxes that Nathaniel had pulled down from Nicholas's attic, presumably looking for the will. He asked how Stefanie knew that April didn't want Jack with this Tammy person. Nathaniel watched his father adjust his reading glasses on his face and poise the pen over the notebook. He observed Stefanie watch him slump back in his chair, and he tried to indicate to her how grateful he was. Stefanie said that April routinely complained about her mother, confiding in Stefanie more than once that her mother was a cynical, bitter person, and it had made April very sad that this was the case, that she couldn't talk to her mother without hearing something negative about the world, something vaguely racist, or something negative about the way she and Nicholas were raising Jack. Like, Stefanie said, when Jack was first born, she remembered April telling her this, it was so clear, she remembered that April told her that her mother came to visit and she didn't hold the baby, didn't change the baby, didn't even interact with him at all because April had told her mother that she and Nicholas were co-sleeping with the child, and her mother said that if that was really the choice they were making here, the mother didn't want to get too close to the kid only to lose him in a month's time when he suffocated in his sleep. She'd be glad to help out around the house, but she wasn't going to form a connection with a death sentence, Stefanie explained April had told her. April's mother had actually left the next day and said when the kid was sleeping in its crib then she'd come back, but until then, April and Nicholas would have to fend for themselves because she wasn't going to have a hand in putting a newborn in such a dangerous situation, basically a death trap, and that if the kid lived, it'd be through luck alone. I mean, that was the first week Jack was here, Stefanie said to Nathaniel's father who was writing notes in his notepad. Nathaniel watched his father, who was nodding his head in a lawyerly manner, such a practiced affectation that Nathaniel could only barely discern the grief beneath his father's poise. When Jack was a toddler and sleeping in his crib, Stefanie said, her mother visited again. This was just the second time since Jack was born, Stefanie explained. *The second time*. Got it, the father said. Second time. Okay, Stefanie said, so I guess what happened was after April's mother put a regular diaper on Jack, from a pack she had brought as a gift, April asked her mother to please use cloth diapers next time – you know Nicholas and April. Ecologically mindful. So April said this, very politely, showed her mother where the cloth diapers were, how to use them, etc, and then she guided her mother through the house, showed her the toys Nicholas had carved out of wood, the quilts she herself had made, the crib Nicholas had built, the cloth diapers, the balms she'd learned to make at her holistic healing class, picture frames she'd made with old pieces of metal and wood, and all kinds of stuff, and her mother stopped at one point, I guess, and just looked at her. Gave her this stare, is what April told me. And then walked out of the house. She came back an hour later with her SUV filled and like five hundred dollars of plastic toys and Pampers and a tub and wipes and plastic spoons and bowls and sippy cups and all kinds of shit, all of this stuff that Nicholas and April were completely against, and the mother said to April: you're teaching him to think he's better than everyone else. Well, he's not, and you're not either. This is the country you live in, and you're teaching him that other kids are doing something wrong and he's doing something right. This woman told April that April was going to mess up Jack in every imaginable way.

Nathaniel watched his father stop writing and, putting his notebook down and pulling a stack of folders from a box, carelessly leaf through the papers inside, and then toss the folders back into the box. He said, That can't have really happened, right? He looked at Nathaniel. Nathaniel shrugged, feeling grateful to not be talking, to be fully listening. He felt pulled out of himself by Stefanie's words, which was what she did for him, over and over, and momentarily, feeling again the presence of Nicholas's absence from the world, he felt a sort of gratitude. He wanted to tell Nicholas thank you, though he didn't know what for, in the same way he wanted to tell Stefanie thank you. He closed his eyes, as though searching for the source of this thank you that had suddenly arisen in him. He opened his eyes and saw out the window that more rain had begun. He heard it sweeping spattery gusts onto the tin roof. Nathaniel, watching his father stand, crossed his legs in the desk chair his brother had made, and though he'd never heard the particular information that Stefanie had related, he told his father that it was definitely true, this Tammy woman was really rooted in her ideas of what being a good American was, and she really thought that meant going to Toys 'R' Us or wherever. Still though, Nathaniel said to both his father and to Stefanie, wanting to sort of aid her, they shouldn't be completely unfair here, and that it might be a helpful tack to attempt some flattery or praise in order to appease her – for instance, Nicholas had told him many times that the mother-in-law also said that the baby was lovely, and posted pictures of him on Facebook where she was definitely a proud grandmother, and, Nathaniel remembered, April said that she did eventually apologize about all the toys, which Nicholas accepted in a way only Nicholas could, thanking her for the gifts and, after she left, donating all of it to charity. But apparently she did apologize for acting the way she did, Nathaniel said. Nicholas told me that she had told April that she just wanted her grandchild to fit in and be liked and not be viewed as some backwoods weirdo and to please keep that in mind and let the kid have some normal toys and normal books and normal everything. Nathaniel said that maybe they could use that when talking to her, like show that he and Stefanie weren't as, you know, far out as Nicholas and April. Maybe we could invite her to our place? Make her feel like she has a hand in this? Nathaniel took a contemplative pause, though he already knew what he was going to say, and then he said he thought it was important that they approached the situation in as even-handed a manner as they could, which was what he imagined Nicholas might say in a similar situation, and then he continued by saying that, on the other hand, maybe he was wrong and such a tack wouldn't work. After all, he did remember when April had first gotten pregnant and all the drama that had attended that event. According to Nicholas, he said, April's mother told her to end the pregnancy, so that's something we could use as well. Nathaniel's father pulled his phone from his pocket, read a text message, sent a text back, and then shook his head, said that he was sorry to cut the trip short, but that was all he could do today, he had to get groceries for Nathaniel's mother. Thank you, he said, he'd call tomorrow, he really had no idea, now, what to do, but he'd think about all this. He closed his notepad, hugged them both, listened at the hallway for Jack, as though saying goodbye through telepathy, then told them good luck with Tammy and stepped out of the house and put on his shoes and coat and went walking down the stone path toward his car.

Nathaniel again began looking through boxes they had packed, searching for the will, thinking that he just needed to search for the will and find it and then everything would be solved. Stefanie helped, going through dressers and shelves and cupboards even. After spending a few minutes looking through boxes that he had already looked through, and knowing that he'd find nothing there, he went to the second bedroom, opened the center drawer in the desk, and pulled out Nicholas's laptop, carried it out to the living area, and put it down on the coffee table and said, We're probably going to have to get into this, right? Feeling, as he said it, that it was a violation, that not only did he not want to search through his brother's computer for some document, he also didn't want to take it into a computer store and ask them to crack the password or whatever they might do, it all felt a little too much, like why couldn't Tammy be reasonable? When he asked Stefanie what they were supposed to do with this, did they take it into a computer store if that's what it came to, she looked at him and said, A computer store isn't going to crack the password. Nathaniel then started trying passwords, typing and re-typing, knowing that there was no chance that he was going to guess one, and when Stefanie said it, You're never going to guess it, and as he turned his head to say he knew, he saw Jack was standing in the hallway, watching both of them, Nathaniel trying to open his father's computer, Stefanie going through his parents' things. For a moment Jack stood there, little jeans on, the socks on his feet loose and worn, dirty-looking, his sweater maybe a bit too tight, his eyes looking not at Nathaniel but at the computer. He began crying. Nathaniel closed the computer, stuffed it behind a pillow, and went over to him and picked him up and told him that it was okay, buddy, everything was okay.

After calming Jack, after telling him it would be okay, after telling him they were here, after Jack had asked again why they were putting all of his mommy and daddy's things in boxes, after Nathaniel tried to put him down for a nap, but couldn't, he'd just napped, after he stopped crying and was staring vacantly and holding Nathaniel's pantleg as they walked around the house, after Nathaniel quietly looked at Stefanie above Jack and shook his head to convey that he didn't know what they were doing, they didn't know what they were doing, after she went to the bedroom and he could hear her own muffled sounds of crying, after taking Jack to another part of the house so he couldn't hear, after thinking again that he didn't know what to do, that this Tammy woman would be here sometime tomorrow and would be wanting to take Jack away with her that afternoon, or the following day, which he couldn't let occur, wouldn't let occur either that afternoon or the following day, but what about the day after, and the day after that, after sitting with Jack and singing with him on Nicholas's guitar and trying, again, to not think about his own loss, his brother gone, and trying to be there for Jack, after spending the afternoon with him, taking a cold walk out on the trails, telling Jack maybe they'd see a turkey or a coyote, after Stefanie prepared lunch, Jack still hovering against his leg, after they ate, after Nathaniel kept thinking of the town, what they thought about all this, what they would know and wouldn't know when it was all done, what people would think about him, if he could do this or not, was he like Nicholas or not, whether his father believed he could do it or not, after all this the early evening still hung in a grey fog of rain, a rain that Nathaniel once thought acted as a sort of cloak, a privacy for them, but which now he felt was obscuring things, like a veil pulled over the world, so that he couldn't see clearly. Later, Tammy called and said she was stopping for the night but would arrive tomorrow morning and would pick up Jack then if that was okay, and when Nathaniel had said to her that he hoped she knew she wasn't going to just take Jack tomorrow, that they were going to talk about this, Tammy had said, Whatever gets you to sleep at night, Nathaniel, he's coming with me. After this phone call occurred at around five in the afternoon, Nathaniel's father called again.

He was calling from the hotel. He asked Nathaniel if maybe he should call Tammy and talk to her. Nathaniel sat up on the sofa and looked at Stefanie, hand over mouthpiece, and said, quietly, the lawyer. He replied to his father by saying that he could do that if he really wanted to, but he didn't have to, that Nathaniel had already been talking with her, and it had ended amicably enough, and she was going to arrive tomorrow, Nathaniel told his father on the phone. Maybe it would be good, his father said, for the mother-in-law to know that there was another group on the same side, that maybe that would discourage her from making a claim of guardianship when she saw an entire side of the family against her. Actually, yes, Nathaniel would be really grateful to his father for that. He didn't want her here in the morning just trying to haul off Jack.

There was a pause on the line then there was the sound of sweeping, gusting rain on the roof of the cabin, the wind suddenly picking up, a very strong gust, seeming to increase the longer it went. Nathaniel told his father to hold on a second. He listened, though he wasn't sure why he was listening. From the upstairs bedroom loft (once Nicholas and April's bedroom), he heard Stefanie and Jack talking.

He climbed the ladder to look into the loft and could see the blue glow of Stefanie's laptop lighting the room. Stefanie was sitting cross-legged on the bed and Jack was sitting in the space between her bent legs. Stefanie was playing him music and singing quietly. Then, from the back of the property, he heard a crack, like the snapping of a giant's bone, then the resultant crash of limbs and leaves. The wind picked up again, spraying rain on the windows below the porch.

Nathaniel backed down off the ladder and said sorry and reiterated that it'd be great if his father let the Tammy woman know that she was outmatched here, thanks for doing that. There was another brief pause on the line then Nathaniel's father said that that wasn't exactly what he had in mind. What he had in mind was to construct a sort of compromise, the compromise being that Jack would stay with him and Katherine, the grandparents. Nathaniel stood up, said hold on to his father, and ran to the bottom of the loft ladder, whispered for Stefanie to get down here, and put his father on speakerphone. She climbed down the loft ladder, leaving Jack listening to music, and Nathaniel said, Is he sleeping? She said yes, he's out, and then Nathaniel mouthed to her, holding the cell phone away from his face, I can't believe this shit. He told his father he was back and his father told Nathaniel, before he got upset, to hear him out, to think about the goal. If the goal here was what was best for Jack, then please consider his position, because look, to be perfectly frank, this woman had a clear argument against Nathaniel and Stefanie becoming the guardians, especially if they didn't find a will, which was looking more and more likely to be the case. Nathaniel had a record, for instance – he'd been arrested and convicted of possession of marijuana and driving while intoxicated, and yes, while all that happened eight or nine years ago, it was still something Tammy was undoubtedly going to bring to court with her. Stefanie wasn't a natural-born citizen. I'm an American citizen, Stefanie said, that's such bullshit. But not a natural-born one, Nathaniel's father said, hi Stefanie. So I'm on speaker, okay. So, yes, you're an American citizen, but a naturalized one, since you were born in Mexico. I have no idea if that might be a factor, but it could be. I'm just asking you both to hear me out here. And look, the important thing that's going to come up is that Stefanie, I don't mean to be insensitive here, but Nathaniel told me that you had an abortion. Dad, Nathaniel said. His father continued, saying, Yeah, okay, that was some time ago, yes, but you still had an abortion, and you two, you both travel for work. You're both gone all the time. Nathaniel, you're gone four days a week. How's that going to look? Nathaniel said that they'd have to think about it, and his father said he wanted him to think about one other thing, before they started thinking about it. Think about it like this: look at them and look at April and Nicholas – so different. Wasn't it true that Nathaniel and Stefanie didn't want children? Hadn't Nathaniel conveyed that he felt himself to be too selfish a person to have kids, and also didn't want to be tied down by kids, wanted to travel and do exciting things and go see the world, which was what they'd been doing for the last few years. Look, Nathaniel's father explained, did Stefanie and Nathaniel consider how April and Nicholas had been raising Jack? Nicky and April didn't even own a television, Nathaniel's father said over the phone. They took those things very seriously – your brother literally thought television and media in general was something that kept people from experiencing real life. They only owned a computer because Nicky had to write his articles, but they didn't even have internet at their house. Nicky drove up to work to email people. Every day he drives to work, even when he isn't teaching, checks his email, and if he doesn't have a class, he drives back home, Nathaniel. Drove, Nathaniel said. He doesn't do any of that anymore, drove. There was another pause on the line and his father continued, saying, they don't have a dryer for god's sake. His father wanted them to consider that Jack had been living this very particular life. What's going to happen when he goes to your house and you watch Netflix every night, or you're home at three in the morning from the country club restaurant, or Stefanie is out of town twice a month? Nathaniel felt a sort of blankness in himself, an inability to respond – his anxieties being presented to him as though through slideshow – but then he said that it wasn't as though his father and mother were some better option. They didn't live like April and Nicholas, they had a dryer and a TV and internet, come on. But we're finished with our careers, his father said. We have time to devote. Plus, your mother, this would mean so much to her. She hasn't spoken for over a week, and I think this silence is okay at first, but at some point it's selfish, and she needs something to pull her out of it. She's writing these little notes, so she's talking, but she's not talking out loud, and she needs something. Nathaniel said that was completely backward thinking, that you couldn't use Jack to help Mom, and his father said that wasn't what he meant, and Nathaniel said that this was of course what his father would do, take a situation that was about something entirely different, and turn it into something he had to solve, his parents' selfishness was so glaringly obvious, he wondered how a person as intelligent as his father couldn't see it. His father said, Nathaniel, this is a conversation, just a discussion, it's not the end, I just wanted to present it to you, it's not set in stone, it's the beginning, and Nathaniel said, No, it definitely wasn't, and hung up the phone by pushing the little red button on the screen. Stefanie said she didn't know what to do now. She said they just had to stick by what they knew, what April and Nicholas really wanted, they had to consider that this was a difficult situation for his parents, too, not just them, and that this was just a bump, they'd come around. Nathaniel thought of the text first, then wrote it, which read, I don't understand why you wouldn't talk to me first, and then sent it to his mother, who, after a moment, wrote back a text that read, I don't know what you're talking about. I'm about to call this Tammy person. Will let you know how it goes. Nathaniel showed the texts to Stefanie and, feeling a brief anger that resolved into confusion, which in turn slipped into a hesitant understanding, said, My dad didn't even talk to her about this.

By the time the cold day ended, Nathaniel observed that there was more rain, so light it almost seemed to rise from the trees on the mountain rather than fall from the sky. An almost full moon slid between quickly moving clouds. He imagined the eastside of the town, his father and mother, where they watched television in the hotel they were staying at, a room on the second floor – his father described it to him, needlessly Nathaniel had thought – which overlooked a small ravine where a river flowed, kudzu curling around trees. He wondered what his mother and Tammy had spoken about, but was tired, and didn't try to conjure it – what was the point, he thought. He pictured the downtown, the mother-in-law maybe arriving late in the afternoon and settling into the Bed and Breakfast he had arranged for her, eating Baby Ruths and reading one of the six *People* magazines she had brought. He saw the town, people exiting their yoga classes, sweaty and red-faced, smiling and open, people eating dinner on the patios of restaurants, students readied in their dormitories and apartments for the coming night, drinking beer and rolling joints, the streets emptying of noise and people going home or leaving home, the surrounding mountains alive with unseen animal life, and the mountains seeming to hold the town, which was how Nathaniel always saw it, like a hand holding a hand, pulling dark toward all beings, the slow erasure of the myriad things in existence.

In his dead brother's house, Nathaniel carried Jack from the loft to the boy's bedroom. Nathaniel read him a book, the bear book again, and when he finished reading to Jack, the boy fell asleep for the night, asleep once more, as though sleep was the boy's response to loss. Nathaniel watched him, and then lay down next to him. Jack was wearing just his blue underwear and a white shirt, his hair was fine and soft, very dark, and his closed eyes, with long lashes, appeared woven shut. Part of Nathaniel wanted Jack to stay peacefully asleep forever and part of him wanted to tell him something, though he didn't know what, and he kept thinking of what he wanted to tell him, thinking of the night he received the phone call, the phone call which had come after several years of Nicholas convincing both the families to visit together, since Jack so rarely got to see his grandparents or aunt and uncle, Nicholas tempting all of them with visions of springtime mountains, hiking on wooded paths, batcaves, hot springs, waterfalls, organic foods, the impressive meals Nathaniel would make, and not only that, but their nephew, Jack, who was really growing up pretty fast. Both sides of the family had waffled about dates and travel until all finally relented and the visit had been scheduled, a weekend in the spring, certain food items bought for April's mother and for Nicholas's parents, other items that Nathaniel asked to have on hand so he could make a couple nice meals, the house was cleaned, cold spring rains swept through, and five days out, Nathaniel received the phone call, which he couldn't keep from visualizing, as if compelled to by some alien source: Nicholas and April were involved in a car accident on a winding mountain road in the rain, late at night, after a beer tasting and dinner party for Nicholas's tenure, a party which, Nathaniel learned from the police, the couple had left very late, and coming down the winding mountain road, it was speculated that his brother had been tranced into a brief sleep – rain on windshield, wind in trees – his eyes closing, and when he woke, the car was heading off the road into the trees and Nicholas had overcorrected and the wheels slipped on the wet asphalt and the car went into a tailspin that caused it to careen directly toward the dividing concrete abutment, which the car hit and then skipped over like a stone, all soundlessly in the quiet rain on the mountain, sending the car airborne until it again landed, flipping three times, literally rolling down the mountain road in the wrong lane, and both the brother and his wife were killed (the wife probably died instantly, the police said, the brother later in the hospital). The police on the scene noted that three deer were eating grass near the car. Nathaniel thought about the accident going unreported for some hours, imagined Nicholas trapped, ensuring his death, and leaving behind a blue-eyed, dark-haired, happy four-year-old boy who could not stop crying in Nathaniel's car on the way back from the hospital, saying repeatedly, Where's Daddy? Where's Mommy? Lying next to Jack now, all Nathaniel wanted to do was go back in time, if not to when his brother was still alive, which his mind couldn't compute, then back to the moment sitting in his car with the boy, back to the moment he had first held Jack again after several months, the boy crying, back to the moment when he had known exactly what he had to do.

KATHERINE

Thought after thought, do not become attached. [. . .]
Whether it's a past thought, a present thought, or a
future thought, let one thought follow another without
becoming attached. [. . .] Once you become attached
to one thought, you become attached to every thought,
which is what we call bondage. But when you go from
one thought to another without becoming attached,
there is no bondage.

—*PLATFORM SUTRA*

Our life is shaped by our mind; we become
what we think.

—*DHAMMAPADA*

Louis Walters had a mole on his cheek, which, if he didn't shave, grew long, curling hairs from it that, Katherine had noticed in the past, were thicker than his facial hair. One of the hairs was white and coarse. Katherine had pulled it out with tweezers once, declaring an experiment. Two weeks later, it was growing back, and in his guest room – Louis Walters' wife was out of town, which she often was – Katherine rolled on top of him and, squinting, had said, Let me see. Jesus, it's an unstoppable hair. Terminator hair. If you just let that thing keep growing, I bet it'd turn into a fingernail.

Katherine could see the hair now – slightly longer than the rest of his facial hair – in the Skype window on her computer screen. Louis Walters wore wire-frame glasses and his head was shaved bald. In his forties, he was in extremely good shape, tall, very fit, and his eyes, dark green, were set in his face in a way that, coupled with his baldness, made him appear somewhat bug-eyed, which the glasses helped, making him appear handsome even if he wasn't exactly handsome. He was wearing a grey checked button-down, his upper body and head on the screen. She'd contacted him – in the space of time David had left to go on a hike, to clean out his mind, he'd said, and to pick up some groceries for the room – because she wanted to discuss their

71

situation with him. This was what they called their affair: their 'situation.' It'd begun as a kind of semantic denial of what they were actually doing, then it became a joke. She often said things like, I'm not sure if the situation we're in is sustainable. I'm not sure we can keep using up our own inner resources on each other. We have to protect some for those we're already with. They talked about the relationship, their situation, in environmentally apocalyptic terms, which seemed apt. She didn't know how it'd happened. You melted the glacier of my heart, she'd once said to him, mocking a woman in a romantic comedy. The problem with that, he'd said, is that it'll make the ocean of your understanding overflow and flood the land of your life. They'd been in his office that time, and she'd looked at him and said, Oh, good one. There was the sense of accident about it all, as though she'd somehow tripped into the situation, like tripping on a sidewalk into an easy and mindless trot. But it had all colored darkly when she learned about Nicholas, when Nathaniel called her and through tears – she could hear them – told her that Nicholas was gone. Now she felt she had to end this thing with Louis Walters. Nicholas being gone somehow clarified how awful she was being. She couldn't take it anymore, that's what she was going to tell him.

Louis Walters was saying something, his face slightly blurred and pixelated on Katherine's laptop's screen, about how he wished he could be there with her, that he was glad she had contacted him, because he wanted to be there for her and this way – meaning through the computer – he got to be there for her. He hadn't called or tried to message her, he said, because obviously she was around David a lot and also he didn't want to complicate an already difficult thing, so he'd been feeling just totally and completely helpless. He was so glad she'd called. He wanted to hug her through the screen, hold her close.

She typed that she felt like shit for contacting him. Real shit. She continued to write, without looking at his face, that she hated that she'd contacted him so much, actually, that she was going to log out of Skype right now, after she said her piece. Which was this. She shouldn't be doing this. They shouldn't be doing this. This was something they shouldn't be doing and they should've both known they shouldn't be doing it, she wrote. Doing what, he said quickly. Doing what, exactly? Because I hope you're not saying what I think you're saying, and if you are saying that, I think you need to just give it a little time. This is a stressful time for you. He cleared his throat, swallowed. A very stressful and difficult time, I understand that, and you shouldn't be making, you know, rash decisions.

She picked up her coffee, which was lukewarm. It had been made in the little Keurig machine supplied by the hotel. She knew that the plastic of these Keurig cup things was somehow dangerous for her health, cancerous or something, as well as being ecologically unsound, but it was just for a few days. Plus, the package, the Keurig cup thing, said hazelnut mocha on it, and the picture of a hazelnut mocha in a ceramic mug on the foil of the little plastic cup had looked so good. Also, she'd thought while staring at the cup, what wasn't cancerous and ecologically unsound? She looked at Louis Walters while drinking her coffee. He was probably cancerous and ecologically unsound, she thought. Then, without immediately noticing, she laughed, and then noticed she had laughed outwardly, when Louis Walters said, What's funny? She shook her head. Since she wasn't speaking, she could take as long as she wanted to reply. She looked at the rest of the room. The laptop was angled in such a way that she could view the entire room, but Louis Walters couldn't. He could see the wall behind her, maybe some of the window. She wrote, Hold on, then she sipped the coffee again and watched him reading her words. Let me help, he said. Let's think about something else. Tell me about the town or something. She wrote that she'd been there for less than a week and she disliked the town more than ever, in the same way she disliked herself right now. She wrote that the problem with the town was the same as her own problem with herself: it was in the middle of nowhere, destitution and rural decay all around, mountains cutting it off from everything else, in the same way that she was alone in her life, the mountains of thoughts in her mind finding no expression or understanding in other people, cutting her off in the same way the mountains isolated the town. Except me, Louis Walters said. You find understanding in me. She just looked at him. I can feel me understanding you, he said. So you must feel it too. Just barely, she wrote. Plus, I shouldn't even be talking to you. We shouldn't be talking at all.

She put the mug down feeling as though she was doing something right, finally. Louis Walters made a pained face and she typed out an apology. You don't have to apologize, he said. And you're not cut off. I want you to know that. And you're understood. I understand you. Her own small face hovered in the corner of the Skype window, the cliché of grief: her hair wild, her face appearing old, no make-up, washed out in the dull light coming through the hotel window, her eyes far off, red. It looked like she'd been in the woods all night on the run from an insane serial murderer, whose chasing and murderous intentions toward her in turn made her insane. That she had this thought, and many others, that she was even talking to Louis Walters, that she was doing anything when Nicholas was dead seemed like a kind of betrayal, like what she should be doing, somehow, was being in constant mourning, in non-stop grief, which she was, sort of. She didn't know anymore. She didn't know where her mourning stopped and her life began, as though the two could be separated. But it felt that way: it felt like, here Katherine, these are moments supplied for grief, and here, these other moments, don't forget, they're your life. She knew this was a falsehood, yet she felt it. She pulled her hair back in a ponytail, which made her look worse, her face even more tired. She rubbed her cheeks for a moment, reddening them, then looked at herself in the Skype window again. She was wearing her Professor Sweater. David called it that. I see we're doing Professor Sweater with jeans, David liked to say. Very professorial of you. Immediate profundity. A presence of ever-refining knowledge. Cute, too. The thought of David out in the world, her in here talking with Louis Walters, made her wince, close her eyes. When she opened them again she couldn't understand why she was talking to Louis Walters when she didn't want to be talking to him, didn't want to be hurting David, didn't want to be doing any of this. Yet she was. It sometimes felt as though the universe had given her her life in the form of a puzzle, and she'd dumped the box, spread the pieces, turned them over, and slowly started fitting the pieces together, but when the picture became too clear – there she was! – she began forcing pieces into her neighbor's puzzle, messing it up purposely. Who wanted to complete a picture they already saw, already knew? And now that Nicholas was gone, it was as though she was again looking at the puzzle she'd started long ago, and then had abandoned. A little layer of dust covered all the pieces, obscuring what had once been clear.

Katherine watched Louis Walters on the screen. His face was larger than it seemed in real life, and somehow more unattractive. Then she thought that this *was* his face in real life. It was just on a screen. She watched him read her message again and then watched his nodding head and him say, Just get out of there. I don't see why you're staying. There's nothing you can do there, really. If I was there, I'd tell David there was no point in the both of you staying there. What's that going to do? Why is it when something terrible happens people believe that proximity to the event matters? We have phones, we have computers, we have automobiles, planes, what the hell. I don't get it.

She looked at his speaking face and wrote, It's not about Nicholas. Or being close to Nicholas. We have to help pack the house and get everything cleaned up. It's also Jack. It's about who will take him. Louis Walters read, nodding, then shaking his head, then was saying, I know, I know, but why can't that be accomplished with a phone call, a text, an email, then a quick drive into rural depression and a quick drive out. Part of the reason you feel so shitty is because you're in a shitty place. She put a finger up, stopping him. The mother-in-law is supposedly coming, she wrote. April's mother, I mean. That's why. She called Nathaniel and told him. Apparently she started Monday night, and was now driving across the entire country. Four full days on the road, staying in motels, and eating junk food. It's, what, Tuesday, so she'll be here by the end of the week. Why else would she be driving out here from South Dakota or wherever she's coming from? Huh, Louis Walters said. I mean, wow. Does she have any legal right? Katherine wrote to him that she didn't think so, and then, after pausing a moment, wrote that David believed that they had to present the seriousness of their concerns through the seriousness of their presence. Also, he wanted to help Nathaniel pack, so we're here, she wrote. That sounds like David, he said. She wrote, David seems to have closed his mind to the fact that we will never see Nicholas again. He's being who he is – focused on the problem at hand, what to do with the material possessions, the house, the distribution of things, and to some degree, what to do with Jack. He's being the distant observer and eventual fixer of all situations, the lawyer, the mediator and moderator of all conflicts and problems and emotions into the simplicity of fact. I can't stand it.

The last line was unnecessarily mean. After all, David was the one who was trying to take care of things, he was the one who was out, first to help Nathaniel pack some boxes at Nicholas and April's house and then to look for the will just in case this Tammy woman was thinking she had some right to guardianship, and then he was going to pick up some essentials for their hotel room's small refrigerator because Katherine couldn't stand meeting any more people from the town. David was doing all this and here she was typing to Louis Walters that she couldn't stand him. David was taking care of her, trying to, and maybe it was all a little overdone: you stay here – I'll get some groceries,

I'll help Nathaniel pack, and when the time comes, if it comes to it, I'll meet with this Tammy person. You don't need to even think about it. Plus, maybe this Tammy person just wants some of her daughter's things – that might be it, too, he'd said. Let's wait until we find out what she's doing, though Katherine had thought that if she was driving over thirty hours, it probably wasn't for some clothes. She'd written to David on her phone, while he stood waiting, that she wasn't going to miss talking with this Tammy woman, if it came to that, but then she'd thanked him and said she felt bad and frustrated at herself that she couldn't do anything, couldn't go out and deal with the people in the town again. It was as though her annoyance at herself translated into annoyance with him. Before leaving for the cabin, he'd asked her if she would be okay alone. Because I don't have to help Nathaniel pack today? he'd said. I can stay here. She'd typed to him, on her phone's screen, that she'd be fine, please, go. He'd gathered his wallet, put on his shoes, and went to the door, only to step back into the room. I shouldn't go, he said. It feels wrong. She typed on her phone, GO. I can't see it, he said, stepping back into the room. Go, he said. Go, then I'll go. Are you sure? She looked at him, raising her eyebrows. Okay, he'd said. The message I'm getting is that you're going to be fine, you could actually use a little time alone, and I can go? She'd looked at him flatly, coolly. I'm going, he said. Then, as soon as he was gone, she'd wished she hadn't sent him away.

She told Louis Walters that she'd be right back, and got up to make another Keurig thing. She stood before the machine, debating about whether to use it again, and thought of how this time in the hotel room was the first time she'd been alone except for maybe the bathroom or the shower, completely alone with the idea that Nicholas was now dead, he had died in a car accident last week, nearly a week ago. She felt confused, as though time was working in some way she no longer understood. Every other moment, there'd been someone there with her. Back in Charlotte, David was in the house with her, Nathaniel and Stefanie had stopped by on their way out of town to go be with the boy and to start packing up Nicholas's house, and the next day her sister came over and stayed a night. Her sister had taken her on a walk through the neighborhood. On the walk, the neighborhood had seemed changed, seemed to lack depth, as though she were on a sound stage, and that if she went into any of the houses all she would find was the wood supports holding up the faces of houses, and behind that, barren land, no lives being lived. She told as much to her sister, Margaret, who told her, It's just because it's so new. It'll stop feeling like that. Walking next to her sister, unreal houses around them and tree branches creaking in the wind, Katherine had said, You don't understand. It's felt like this for years. She felt her sister look at her. Then they'd walked on without any more speaking and Katherine had felt mean, unreceptive. She'd given her sister a hug when they got back to the house, thanked her. She told her sister, Thank you for getting me out of the house, though as she said it, she was aware she was saying it without meaning it, saying it because she knew it was what her sister believed she was doing for her, and so, Katherine had tried to return this consideration to her sister, and said this clichéd thing – thank you for getting me out of the house – in an attempt to be considerate of a clichéd attempt by her sister. Anything you need, her sister had said, as though she were being given the line from a director behind Katherine's head.

In the first few days after Nicholas died, people seemed to huddle around Katherine like she was some delicate, slightly old animal, whose fur wasn't so thick anymore, was a little ratty in fact, and it was cold out. People seemed to believe she was in need of cocooning or deep hibernation, covering her in blankets and bringing her food. Eat, they seemed to suggest, and then sleep for a couple months, and once you wake, you won't have to deal with this at all. It'll all be gone. Hibernation Therapy. Eventually, people left, and she went into her office at school to be alone. She stepped into her office, left the light off, closed the door, and took a breath. She sat at her desk and turned on her computer. She didn't know what else to do. She checked her emails. There were several from colleagues. Condolence emails. A moment later, there was a knock. Colleagues came by with kind, understanding words, withdrawn and pained body language. Some came with flowers. One came with chocolate, which she couldn't understand. Apparently David had alerted them. The younger faculty members didn't come by. They were the ones who sent their condolences as emails, a distancing Katherine almost admired. She also knew they couldn't come by. Young men and women who, while intensely intelligent, had not seen death in their lives. She barely had time to see it herself – Nicholas was dead, a car accident, and all she kept thinking from that first moment was, That's not possible. She was a faculty mentor to one of the lecturers, one of the ones who'd emailed her a note of personal sorrow and sympathy. Kylie

Newman. She wore vests, a grey, a black, a green one over a starched shirt. She'd once said, This is my lesbian uniform. She had dark hair, short on the sides and long on top. Vigilant, semi-aggressive, hip hair. Hair that it seemed you could have a conversation with and might be more interesting than the person beneath it. This hair, coupled with the vests and starched shirts, jeans, and weirdly, cowboy boots, made Kylie Newman look like a dorky version of a gunslinger. Katherine liked her. Thirty or so, intelligent, her work focused on digital media, of course, and yet Katherine saw the child in this woman still. Everything about her was still at play. Katherine thought that Kylie Newman knew sadness only as a romantic reaction to actual suffering. It was a game still. She'd broken up with her girlfriend, she once confided to Katherine. They'd been talking about the election of a conservative governor, how this deeply worried Kylie and the girl's eyes had become far off, glazed, the vest and the entire persona she presented to the world appearing like a costume. She told Katherine that her girlfriend, now ex-girlfriend she corrected herself, had gotten into a graduate school in Illinois and it made more sense to separate than to try to do a long-distance thing. She told Katherine that her girlfriend, now her ex-girlfriend, had said that they were either going to pony up and get married, or it was time to move on. Kylie Newman had said it was something about the phrase 'pony up' that had allowed her to see with clarity that this wasn't the person for her. It was so hard, and she was afraid of being alone, but she'd done it. Jesus, Katherine had said. Luckily, Jesus has nothing to do with it, Kylie Newman had replied, which seemed to Katherine yet another occasion to exclaim 'jesus.' Still,

Katherine envied the ease of this separation, the un-actualized suffering of it. Something as simple as moving to another state, an off-putting phrase, could cause it. Katherine found herself secretly missing, as Kylie Newman relayed her breakup, her more careless days. Friends that came and went, boyfriends, too – time didn't seem to exist then. It was as though she'd once been living in a kind of Bob Dylan-y heartbreak album, where the world had a rhythmically structured sadness that contained a little note of hope or defiance: the sadness of people leaving! But it'd be okay, there were always more people to get to know/to meet, bars to drink in, mountains to hike, countries to see, and people she didn't, couldn't know! When Katherine was young, everything had been enriched by the uncertainty of her future: would this person merge with her, become part of her, or would he leave her? Who was this man, what was his existence like, would he really see her? What about this friend, was she a real friend, an authentic person? Anxiety and worry about the future now seemed like a gift, and whatever difficulties Kylie Newman had, Katherine knew that there was a deeper suffering there that she hadn't even touched, and she knew this was true because she longed for Kylie Newman's type of pain. If she could have that anxiety and worry again, that uncertainty about life. That uncertainty seemed to be endless, until it wasn't.

Katherine lifted a corner of the tinfoil lid of the Keurig cup. The coffee inside emitted almost no odor. She tried to smell it like a Folgers commercial, the one where the robbed mother around Christmastime seems physically warmed by the act of smelling. Yet now she smelled very little, a scratch-and-sniff of actual coffee smell. She held the plastic cup containing ground coffee. How long had the coffee been in this plastic entrapment? She placed it in the machine, turned it on. Water gurgled and began to move. She considered why the world had changed for her. There had been a kind of subtle shift in her understanding and perception – so subtle it might not be there, like tremors you believe you're imagining – that had permanently altered the ground upon which she viewed the world. It wasn't marrying David that had done it, it wasn't having children, it was some time after that, some time she could not precisely discern. A slow transformation, like a jagged rock rounded after years in a stream, and after that, ever more eroding away, until that rock was a small, smooth pebble, and then that pebble a grain of sand, washed away. Driving on a freeway out of town no longer meant experiencing the open country, an easy freedom. The summer no longer meant the feeling of endlessness, time seeming to stop, of everything bloomed and alive as though it would never change. Drinking too much didn't mean the loss of inhibition, it meant an escape from her anxieties and worries, often about Nathaniel and Nicholas and their respective families. Her children were no longer the incredible beings who, as babies, pooped their diapers and giggled about it, who as toddlers fumbled hilarious nonsense into the world, who as children found awe in everything: a tree, a cat, a cloud, a bottle cap. They were now men whose lives seemed to be made much like hers: repetitive days of certain frustrations, certain anxieties, their own worries, their worlds reduced in the same way she felt hers was reducing every year, year after year. She looked back at Nathaniel with a kind of surprise: she'd found him such a troublemaker when he was in his teens, rebellious and unkind, drinking, smoking, getting frequent speeding tickets, almost in trouble for stealing the Nelsons' car, but luckily Janey Nelson had been in the car with him, pleaded with her father that it was her idea. While maybe he got a little nicer after high school, he continued doing stupid things in college: arrested for drug possession, failing out of classes, not even going to classes according to his dorm mate. Katherine had been so scared for him for so long, but then he'd found cooking and things had changed. Music, sports, books, he'd always liked these things, but he was never any good at them. She told him to become a teacher, but he laughed at her and told her he had no interest in going back into what he'd hated for so long.

The coffee mug was halfway full, the coffee smell now stronger, as though water had brought the grounds to life. She looked back at her computer on the desk, near the window. The computer was facing away from her. She felt a strange aloneness – a person was just on the other side of a piece of metal, in the room with her and not – an odd separation. She wondered vaguely what Louis Walters was doing while he was waiting for her. She thought of how so much of what she was thinking she would not communicate with him, how she was alone with her thoughts, as she was so frequently. She remembered how culinary school came next for Nathaniel, and they paid for it in the same way that they paid for college, part of his grad school, and there was a fear that he would just drop out of culinary school as well, turn into a drifter, a drug dealer, a homeless person, maybe a mental patient, but he didn't drop out. He flourished. He was a good cook, a chef, really, he was a chef. The first meal he cooked for her was one she would not forget: a simple grilled turbot with white wine emulsion, cabbage and carrot puree. Later, he moved exclusively, and she thought, riskily, to vegetarian food. He wanted simple, elegant, and also affordable, and also, humane. She couldn't believe she still bragged about her children: well, Nathaniel's a chef now if you can believe it. He's been written about in two magazines. Oh Jesus, she had spoken the words of a television mother. In the years after this, though, she found that, strangely, he was her last tic to the world of youth. At the time, Nathaniel's 'existential crisis,' as David had put it, had been an inconvenience in her life, a deep worry. Yet he had also enlivened her life. There had always been Nathaniel to think and worry about, and now that he was doing fine, she saw that both her worry was overdone and at the same time her worry had given the world an uncertain quality that allowed her access to kindness and care and, eventually, awe at the fact that Nathaniel was succeeding. For some time she couldn't see an outcome for Nathaniel, now she could. For some time she couldn't see his life, now she could. Her worry and anxiety, which still arose in her mind like a practiced emotion, was no longer connected to anything, to Nathaniel, and certainly not to Nicholas, who'd shunned what she deemed ordinary social life in order to take his family off the grid. She missed both of them, but didn't worry about them in the same way. And couldn't be awed by them in the same way. In the same way she couldn't be awed by David. By herself. She understood it all too much, understood her life too easily. It was as though she'd figured out the math equation of her life and the answer was unbelievably banal: C equals twelve. She had been a girl, she had been a young woman, she became a woman, a mother, a professor, and now she was whatever she was, it didn't seem to matter anymore. She had fulfilled her evolutionary duty. The universe seemed to have sensed Nathaniel was going to figure it out, watched with close attention, then had patted Katherine on the head, gave her a little certificate, checked off her duties for existence, and was finished with her. We're ready for you to die, the universe seemed to say. Thank you for your service.

The coffee finished. The last drips fell into her mug. She didn't want to go back to the computer, to the glowing Apple logo. She didn't want to continue talking to Louis Walters, continue distracting herself from this situation with Nicholas's son, from Nicholas himself, from Jack. She looked out the window: the mountain in blue morning mist. She considered how she and David used to hike almost every weekend. She remembered a time, years ago now, they were walking, and she'd said, We're on a planet in the universe. Yes, he'd said. Be aware of that. Let's be with that idea this whole hike, no talking. Yes, she agreed. No talking. Or, a little talking. Yeah, a little talking's fine, David had said. They'd hiked some, their feet crunching leaves, mist moving between the autumn trees, leaves coming down in the wind, hanging in the air, deep oranges and browns and reds, the burned colors of the season, a shedding of life, the smell of dirt, fungus, crisp, colder wind, rush of the breeze through trees, swirling, the cries of hawks, their bodies warming to the walk, breath visible in the morning air, she felt her own being emptied out, cloud-like, as if being dispersed. It was beautiful, really beautiful, then she sort of started thinking about Nicholas, Nathaniel, wondering how they were doing, her once-young boys out in the world, then her job. I'm good with just general talking now, David had said after a little while, breathing harder. It's been like fifteen minutes, she'd said. I feel we've done our duty. We got it pretty clearly, David said. We're on a planet in the universe. Duly noted. There was a playfulness, a kind of easy letting go into the world, or an easy receiving of the world, occasionally complicated with anxiety and worry. Now though, walking in the woods was walking in the woods. She could not pull up any of the prior transcendence, if that's what it had been. She wondered if David felt it too. They were just on a walk. The trees were trees, the leaves had fallen.

In the hotel room, her coffee ready, she went back to the computer and Louis Walters' waiting face. She sat and blew on her cup of coffee then put the mug down. She wrote that she'd just been thinking of Kylie Newman who'd written her an email, one of those condolence emails. She wrote that she'd been recalling the time she'd been envious of Kylie's breakup with her girlfriend. I remember feeling the world must have opened up to her again in her sadness. I thought, Katherine wrote, that soon it wouldn't open like that anymore. Things would be what they were. A girlfriend leaving was just a person exiting your life. Your son's death was not mysterious or strange. It was what the world did. There was nothing else to it. Louis Walters said that he wasn't sure it was that simple and that they were sort of getting off point here. So what if we're getting off point, she wrote. Maybe that's the point, to get off point. Good point, he said. Not funny, she wrote.

She wrote to Louis Walters, who was both in the room with her and not, present with her and somehow not, how she remembered being in her office and getting the email from Kylie Newman that read, *I'm so sorry for your loss. I don't know what else to say beyond that, so I'll just end with this quote, from Tolstoy, which I've found comforting in my own difficult times: 'The meaning of life is life itself.'* In my office, I'd almost guffawed, both at the quote itself and the idea that it came from Tolstoy, in front of the computer, Katherine wrote. Then, inexplicably, I cried. I remember it with startling clarity because it was the first time I really cried hard since learning he was gone. I had my phone on the desk, my face in front of my computer, the light of it almost palpable on my face, that heat, you know, Kylie Newman's weird email staring at me, a bunch of colleagues had been by and had given me little half hugs, shoulder hugs, and full hugs, dropped off flowers, and I cried. What was I doing in my office? I remember thinking. I couldn't stop. It was all suddenly there: Nicholas was gone. Along with his goneness, I sensed that part of the reason I was crying, beyond my own sadness for myself and what and who I had lost, was for this Kylie Newman person. She hadn't felt real suffering yet, the banality of it, the confusion of that banality. Of course, she knew it to be a fact of existence, certainly, knew, most likely, it was coming for her, but she had never touched it, and thus, it had never touched her. Her girlfriend had left her, she was heartbroken. But there was a certain sort of sense, a logic to a leaving girlfriend, the separating. There was no logic with Nicholas. He was here then he was not. I cried because I was in my office. Because of this email from Kylie Newman. Because of everyone who stopped by. Because Nicholas was gone. Because I couldn't convey to anyone what this meant to me. Because I don't understand what it means. I want to understand. That's why I'm not talking, and also because I can't take talking with people.

Katherine stopped typing. She remembered that she had been in her office to be alone and was crying in front of her computer, her door still open because colleagues had been visiting, and she couldn't get up to close it, she was crying, just crying, and feeling as though she was falling a little. The shadow of a person, Mark Feltzer, had walked by, then he had slowly backtracked, stuck his head inside her door, and asked if she needed anything. There were flowers on her desk, a box of chocolates, her computer glowing in the dark room, a room in which she hadn't turned the lights on, and now her phone was also glowing with a call from David. No, she'd said. Just close the door please. He did, with a contemplative little nod and lips pursed in understanding. She thought of this Kylie Newman person and felt sick knowing that this playful person would be slipped out of herself when certain realities arose. She felt a deep sympathy for her: she hoped it wouldn't happen. Then thinking of Kylie Newman transmuted into thoughts about Nicholas, which she could barely stand. She remembered how Nicholas had seemingly slipped from the world, years before, too young, she often thought, his alienation present from a young age, distant from people, even as a boy watching people, thinking about them, much like herself, she thought now. She cried for this and for Kylie Newman and for the fact that Nicholas was gone. She cried for his past self and his gone self, for herself and for Kylie Newman, for the people who had brought her gifts, had mumbled only partially felt sympathies, no less sincere for it. In the hotel, sitting before the computer, waiting for Louis Walters to say something, she remembered crying for herself, for her son, for this other person she barely knew.

Before Louis Walters could say anything else, she wrote to him that she remembered feeling and thinking all of these things in front of her computer, crying, when he arrived at her office. You opened the door and immediately shut the door behind you, pulled a chair next to mine, and held my shaking shoulders. I remember, Louis Walters said. She looked at Louis Walters, and wrote, Why don't I feel any different? He read the message and seemed to think, opened his mouth, and then said he didn't know. Concerning what? Concerning us? She shook her head and wrote that that was maybe the most selfish thing she'd heard in a long time. He said, Okay, so concerning Nicholas. Well, I didn't know you didn't feel any different. You hadn't told me that until now, and I actually can't understand how that could be true. So that's why I asked concerning us. But, to answer your question, Louis Walters said, I think you're probably still too close to it. You're trying to look at yourself and figure out who you are now, now that, you know, he's passed away. She put a finger up, stopping him, and wrote, Say 'died.' I don't like passed away. It implies he went somewhere. He didn't go anywhere. He didn't pass. He isn't away. He's dead. Just gone. Not away. Away feels like he was once in this way, and now is in this other way. Away. He's not. He's dead. Louis Walters read and said, See, just that there, just you talking about it like that. I think you haven't had any time alone to digest this. Why the food metaphor? she

wrote. Why, when we're talking about understanding something, do we say we need to 'digest' it, or let it 'marinate,'
or say that we're 'stewing in our juices'? You're right though,
I need to roast on this a bit. Haha, Louis Walters said. She
sat back in her chair. I need to sign off, she wrote. I don't
like this. This, talking with you, this is me trying to bring a
normal something from my life in order to feel normal and
not feel the change of things. I'm distracting myself. Louis
Walters said he wouldn't characterize it like that at all. She
wasn't distracting herself, she was afraid of being alone and
right now, she shouldn't be, he said.

She looked away from the laptop and saw a text message
lighting her phone's screen. David. Doing okay? it said. She
looked at the computer screen and wrote to Louis Walters,
One second. She picked up her phone, hesitated, then
replied, All is well. After a moment, another text arrived,
which read, Artisan wheat or Tuscan bole? She could barely
comprehend the question and wanted, for a brief moment,
to write back, Sunbeam White. You choose, she wrote. She
put the phone back down and thought that Louis Walters
was wrong in the same way her husband was wrong. She
knew she needed to be alone. She could feel the information being conveyed to her as though in alien code, through
telekinesis or something. Be alone and know, this intuited
information seemed to say, repeatedly. But know what? The
hotel was the first time that she'd had the chance to be really
by herself in over a week. With David gone, before she'd
contacted Louis Walters, she had tried to just sit in the hotel
room, to just sit there with the fact of it, feeling only the
fact of Nicholas not being there, as though calling up the
experience in her office, to feel authentically devastated, but

sitting alone in the hotel room – two plastic cups from the night before on the dresser, one about half-filled with water, the other empty, smudgy fingerprints on the plastic, orange peels next to the cups, David's overnight bag on his side of the bed, opened, a shirt hanging out, her bag zipped closed in a corner, the small refrigerator clicking on, the heater clicking off – she couldn't understand it, couldn't recall any sadness, felt only a sort of blankness. She had gone to the window, which she was staring out now, not looking at Louis Walters.

The mountain loomed out the window, mist gently rising from it, dispersing, and below, the town's main street was empty in the early morning. If the mist wasn't moving she could've been looking at a postcard of a rural American town. She thought of when she had still been speaking, maybe three days after, still in her own house, and she'd told David that she didn't understand. She knew Nicholas was dead, but the world seemed no different. The world isn't different, he'd said. *Your* world is. She hadn't been able to withhold her frustration at the comment. How thoughtful of you, she'd said. How intelligent. Philosophical even. David sat next to her in the breakfast nook and said he was sorry, this was just how he thought about these things. Sunlight came through the window and fell against the wall in the elongated shape of the window. He pulled his chair close to hers. He'd put his arms around her, hugging from behind and the side, very much like how Louis Walters had the previous day in her office. And because of this, she hadn't wanted David touching her anymore. She felt as though he'd be able to sense this other man on her, some psychic connection would flash in his mind, and he'd know she'd already been comforted in this same way. And he'd know it at the worst possible time. This same hugging, she irrationally thought, could lead to David feeling this man's presence in other ways. Moments like this had occurred before. If she watched television after being with Louis Walters, she couldn't do that with David at home. If she ate food with Louis Walters at work, she took her dinner into the family room, claiming that her back hurt. If she drank a glass of wine with Louis Walters, she didn't have one in the evening with David. And in the moment David comforted her by holding both of her shoulders, almost like picking up a child from behind, she withdrew from him. As she did it, she also wanted David's tenderness, his warmth, his body next to hers, and his words, whatever they might be. She wanted his comfort *and* she didn't want him to touch her. In the space between these wants, she felt frustration and annoyance at herself, which immediately she had directed at David with her sarcastic reply. After a moment of composing herself, she had told him as gently as she could that she understood what he meant, her world was probably diffcrent. She just didn't feel it yet. She apologized. She was just easily frustrated, that was all. He got up to make coffee, she remembered now as she watched the clouds drift up the mountain. Her annoyance at him, at herself, had also been a dispersing cloud in the sky: there and then gone. And after the annoyance was gone, she had considered this thing David said, turning the phrase over in her mind like turning over a moon rock: *Your* world is different.

She considered it again now. *Your* world is different. Before Nicholas was gone, she woke in her house, or she had before coming to this town, and she still did that. She woke in a room. Before, she had opened her computer. She had read the news, emails. She had drunk coffee. She had urinated, defecated, showered. After he died, she did all of these things, still. Everything was exactly as it had been except now she noticed that fact: everything was exactly as it always was. It was not monotony she was noticing. Long ago she knew some perspective on the world had been lost, some vital seeing of it. This was worse than monotony, that growing banality of her life, the clear understanding of it. This was worse and it was nothing she could pin down. Before Nicholas was gone, she did certain things. After he was gone, she continued doing them. Yet now she saw that she was doing things with the accompanying thought of why do this thing: there was, suddenly, an awareness of the arbitrariness of what she was doing. Whereas over the past however many years, starting in her early forties and progressing to now, when her boys were no longer boys, her husband was more of a roommate than a husband or lover, the world had slowly drained of both meaning and mystery, this was something utterly more stark: Nicholas was dead, yet she had to have a bowel movement. Things will become more different, David had said the evening before they drove to the small town where Nicholas lived, had once lived. She had said to him that she hadn't been able to exercise. That was something different. He'd nodded his head. He said, I know that's sarcastic, but things will feel more different and then they'll feel more the same. Or more normal, he said. You'll get used to it, I mean.

Louis Walters asked her if she wanted to talk about Nicholas. She'd nearly forgotten he was there on her screen. She looked at the computer and shook her head, not bothering to write. She took a sip of coffee and then typed to Louis Walters, asking what he would do if his daughter died, how did he think he would feel? She honestly wanted to know, and she was sorry it was such a morbid question. Louis Walters immediately said that it was nearly impossible to imagine, he would, he would feel, devastated, thoroughly devastated. That probably doesn't help. She wrote that it didn't. I would, he said. I don't know. He paused, picking at a napkin on his desk with both hands, tearing little shreds off it. Katherine thought that he had no idea. He had no idea, for instance, that he wouldn't be interested in eating. She hadn't been interested in eating and still wasn't interested in eating, though she ate. She thought of how two days after she sent and responded to several emails, informing other faculty members at the university that she would be gone for some indefinite amount of time, and could anyone take her classes for a short while, she had then written an email in which she explained that her son had died in a car accident, that he'd been driving on an isolated, rural mountain road, late at night, in the rain, and had somehow lost control of the vehicle. He and his wife had died. She wrote that she wanted to write this email so that people wouldn't be gossiping and spreading false information, that this was the true information. Writing the email she could barely understand why she was writing it. She had felt both oddly comforted by writing the facts in the email, as though she had some clear handle on the situation, and completely distant, as though the woman typing was not her, that this was not even close to the action she should be taking. She had signed off by saying that she was thankful for the department and her friends there and their support, though she didn't particularly feel that at all. After writing that email, she had responded to one student, who asked for an extension on a paper. One week, she'd written, slowly typing out each letter, as if watching her mind form the thought, the reply. Then she had gone into her office, stupidly, to be alone, and her colleagues visited one by one, except the younger ones, and she'd cried, they'd witnessed her crying, she was inconsolable, of course. She'd even forgotten that she'd written the strange email about her son. She thought that maybe David had alerted her colleagues. No, it'd been her, and she'd gone in and cried, ridiculously. Louis Walters had pulled up his chair and hugged her from behind, awkwardly, as her husband did a day later. Louis Walters had told her to take the semester off. She had been, and still was, having an affair with him. She was doing things though she didn't care to do them. Looking at his face now, the cliché of their situation, the fact that he was a male in a position of power and she was his inferior, was almost beyond belief. Yet, at sixty-two years old, she had been talking with him, sleeping with him, meeting him in his office, locking the door. It had been a little antidote to the poisoned monotony of her life. It was a terrible, definitely a mean, selfish thing, yet she had done it. What Nicholas's death brought into stark relief was this: she was doing it still. She couldn't believe how completely foolish she was.

She sat forward and wrote to Louis Walters that it felt as though behind each action were both the space Nicholas had left behind and Nicholas himself, as though pointing at her life: her memories of him as a baby, as a toddler and child, an adolescent, a young man – all memories which were so much like dreams they barely seemed to have an

existence, barely there in her mind, but which she often
tried to sharpen and make clearer, like digitally enhancing
surveillance footage – and then as a father himself, then as
nothing, a person suddenly ended. In this endingness, a
revealing of herself. Louis Walters read the message and
said that she was proceeding through the stages of grief
from what he could tell, and from what he could tell, this
was depression she was experiencing. She wrote to him that
if he said another thing about the stages of grief she wasn't
going to talk to him anymore. He put his hands up, nodded,
and said, I don't know what to say then. I shouldn't be talking to you anyway, she wrote. You've said that enough, he
said. I can sign off if that's what you want. I'll disconnect.
She looked at him, his sad, hurt face, and she wrote, Don't,
if only to not create any more hurt.

Katherine thought that it was impossible to explain to
someone who hadn't experienced it, which was why Louis
Walters had just been so dismissive: how in each of her
actions – putting on shoes, tying the laces, standing from a
chair – she felt the unfairness of this double Nicholas, the
one who was there and the one who was not. There was an
anger at his being gone, and underneath that anger, a sadness that sometimes overtook the anger, like a wave over-
taking another wave. Both anger and sadness could flare up,
matchlike, into heated intensity, a feeling in her body, and
then wisp out. Reality itself seemed both clearer and more
remote: like nothing much at all, like she was experiencing
her life as though it were a book, a thing she was reading
and interpreting, but barely experiencing, except in brief
moments. There seemed to be a veneer of thought over
everything. The walls in this room were walls, they were

called walls, there were four corners, no, more than four, she counted, six, six corners, called corners, in this room, which was called a room. The window was a window, a word. The pane of glass, the air outside, inside, the mountain looming, the streets below, all first thought of, then there. Even now the only thing that felt real was this thought. She was first a character in the book that was her life in her mind before she was a real person. She knew that her life before this moment was like this, too, that everything she experienced was her experience of experiencing it. It was as though she was narrating her life while living it – this was the narration of her life, she was doing it now, again and again, moment after moment, and couldn't stop. The thing she was attempting to do with this thinking, she thought, was find a way to access Nicholas again, and through him, herself. But with Nicholas gone, could one really have a thought about him, who was an absence? It was like trying to paint on the air. When considering Nicholas's absence, her thinking and feeling couldn't locate the object of that very thinking and feeling – there was no ground, nothing to grab on to, nothing upon which to contemplate or judge or perceive, and maybe this was the falling feeling she had felt in her office, some groundlessness.

A car pulled into the hotel parking lot, which at first she thought was David's, but upon closer inspection was a Jetta and not a Passat. She watched it move ghostlike in the foggy morning air, soundless and smooth. It pulled into a spot and an Indian man and child emerged. Not a child, she thought, an adolescent. Visiting the college, she thought. What's wrong? Louis Walters said. Talk to me Katherine. Just talk. No writing. She looked back at the screen, rubbed her eyes and cracked her neck, and then wrote that she thought David's car had pulled into the parking lot. Has it? Louis Walters said. I can go. She typed that it wasn't his car, she was mistaken. Like I am about so many things, she wrote. Now that's being dramatic, Louis Walters said. Look, if you really feel guilty, then let's talk when you get home. But pretending you don't want to see me anymore because you feel lonely, because you're with Mr. Distant, who won't even openly talk about Nicholas's passing, I mean, it's hard to blame you. You need someone to talk with. Please stop, she wrote. Let her think. And don't use the word 'passing.' She needed to think about what she needed to do. Once again, she wrote, what I really need to do has gotten lost. It's not lost, Louis Walters said. There's nothing you *need* to do. There's only things you can do, and you can speak, and that's what will help you, talking this out.

Another text arrived from David, which said that he'd be home soon, but he wanted to stop at the patisserie. Did she want a croissant or something? She needed to eat. She held her phone up, showing Louis Walters her typing to her husband, no longer hiding it from him, a thing she had done initially, as though she had to hide Louis Walters from David, and David from Louis Walters. No, she wrote to David. Then, Thank you. She didn't like that Louis Walters had used the phrase 'Mr. Distant' to describe David. Not that it was inaccurate, but she was the one who called David that, Mr. Distant. She hated that she'd told this to Louis Walters, because now he used it, like it was his, or theirs together, when it wasn't. Louis Walters would ask about Mr. Distant, ask if she and Mr. Distant were ever, you know, intimate anymore, a slight jealousy that crept into their situation. He'd ask if Mr. Distant was still talking to College Sweetheart. This was another thing, regrettably, that Katherine had told him: one afternoon, David had inexplicably left his iPad open to his personal email, and she couldn't help but pick it up and swipe through. Startlingly, she'd found that he'd been conversing with a Laura Moser. Frequently. This was not another teacher in the law school, she didn't think, no name that she knew, yet she did know the name, somehow, though she wasn't sure how. She couldn't help but click on one of the emails to find out who this person was. She wished she hadn't. Laura Moser wrote, in the particular email that Katherine had opened, that she couldn't imagine being married for so long, that she'd divorced twice, would never get married again, though she wanted a partner, a companion, and a lover. But more than anything, Laura Moser wanted the freedom to be herself, something that'd been kept from her by her previous husbands, who were controlling traditionalists with the thoughts of liberals and the actions of nuanced, complicated, subtle misogynists. What Laura Moser really wanted was an open relationship, the freedom to take lovers and friends without jealousy or pain, and that was exactly what she was doing. She was living out her life exactly as she wanted, doing what she wanted, and you know what she'd found? Getting what you wanted did make you happy. Katherine had to quit reading, closing out the email, though she had then gone back and read through all of them, little pieces of nostalgia from both David and Laura Moser, sentimental, about how much they were in love in college, and trying to figure out exactly what happened, why they'd parted, David, in one email, writing that he often thought about their lovemaking – he actually used that word – and said it'd been something that'd never left him, that no one had ever been as good as her, as uninhibited and free, and that, he was embarrassed to admit, he still used these memories. He used her thighs, her breasts, her hands, her hair and eyes, even her feet. The word 'used' had made Katherine want to vomit. This Laura Moser woman, in a subsequent email, confessed the same thing, and had been so embarrassed about it for so long, she didn't know people in their fifties, no, she thought, sixties, still fantasized about sex with old lovers, but she did, and now she could openly share her fantasies with her current lover. Sure, occasionally there were issues, but mostly things were completely smooth sailing. In one email, Laura Moser claimed that she often thought of the time when she and David found a house being built and used it as a place to escape the dorms, how easy it was in those days to sneak into places: cemeteries at night, houses still under construction, the restaurant she worked in, after hours. No thought of consequence. Then came a string of emails in which they detailed their favorite sexual memories, which nearly caused Katherine to destroy the iPad, but she'd composed herself, read on, and then even worse, a string of emails that detailed their most tender memories, and after that, comical emails about their past arguments. David shaking Laura Moser out of her sadness on the campus green one night, telling her a guinea pig's just a guinea pig, dammit, I'm a person! In an act of what she viewed as complete composure, Katherine had sent all the emails to herself, forwarding them, then sent them to David, who was at work, teaching a class, one by one. Eighty or ninety emails filling his inbox. He'd had no explanation when he got home, and merely said, Yes, I've been talking with her, but that's it. Just talking. Nothing more meaningful. And anyway, we're just reminiscing. About fucking, Katherine had said. Oh come on, David had said. Aren't we over all the jealousy by now? No, Katherine had said. We're not. Then, several months later, she'd met Louis Walters. The emails were not the cause of her affair, but they opened things up for her, allowed her some space that might not have been open otherwise, allowed her to view herself as capable of being someone else, as capable of being with David and not. She eventually told Louis Walters about the emails, about David – who he'd met in person at department parties – and about how he was Mr. Distant. When Louis Walters used them in conversation, it felt as though he was accessing some part of her life that she felt should've been closed off, easily red-taped, though she knew it was her fault, since she brought them up. And she'd probably brought them up to make herself feel better, to let Louis Walters know that she wasn't the type of person who would just cheat on a person, there had to be some pain there first, so she portrayed David as a remote man, Mr. Distant, which she called David to his face as a little joke, a playful thing – they did a kind of comic superhero joke, like when they were eating dinner and he'd suddenly completely tune out of the conversation, then suddenly return, and say something like, I just thought of the moment my mother, when I was a young boy, hit me with a switch. It only occurred one time, and I had a scar for years, and Katherine had said, Mr. Distant, with the powers of staying visible but being completely gone. It was a passive-aggressive joke, with an element of truth, she knew, added in, and which she knew David knew. But then that was why it was funny. In addition to the Mr. Distant thing, she also portrayed David to Louis Walters as having emotionally cheated on her, a phrase she actually used – I know David didn't cheat on me cheat on me, but he sought out emotional connection with another woman, and that would be bad enough, but he sought, and found, it should be noted, this emotional connection with another woman who was once a lover or girlfriend or whatever – and she had told this to Louis Walters, she knew, so that she wouldn't feel so bad doing what she did with him, but also as a way to present to Louis Walters that her cheating with him was not something she did casually: she had to have a reason for it, some kind of inner damage that she and Louis Walters were treating, like a course of antibiotics for some infection in her existence.

Louis Walters asked her if she knew she'd just been holding her coffee cup and staring for the last couple of minutes. It looks like it's getting cold, he said. There's no more steam. She put the mug down, then picked it back up, sipped it, and then put it down again, and wrote, Yes, I knew that. I did it on purpose, to see if you thought it matched your image of what a person in mourning should look like. He smiled a little. Does it? she wrote. I suppose so, he said. She wrote that if she wanted to hold a cup of coffee without drinking it, letting it get cold, that's what she was going to do, and if she wanted to stare at nothing and feel nothing, that's also what she was going to do, and if he didn't want to do that, he didn't have to and could sign out. I understand, he said. I just thought you should know you don't have to hold a coffee cup for all eternity. There are tables available. Surfaces upon which to place items we don't always want to be holding. She nodded without giving any recognition to his little joke and thought that the worst part about telling Louis Walters these things was that she had liked, for years, that David was a remote man. She liked his distance from the world, as though he were an alien sent to observe and watch. It was a fascinating trait, one which served to relocate Katherine's own perspective on the world, served to show her the advantages of watching, of distancing in order to understand, a distancing from oneself as much as from the world. What was even more fascinating was that David could be pulled from his distance like a tethered astronaut slowly pulled back to the ship. She could do it with a hand on his thigh, a cool look, playing with the curls of his hair. She liked being able to turn him from mind to body with the ease of flicking a light switch, and additionally she liked his mind, which scrutinized everything, but which was also fair, generally kind, just poetic enough. Bringing him back to his body had become more difficult, though. He taught two grad school law courses at the state university, reticently moving toward retirement, and in this transition, which she felt might bring him back to the world, and to her, he'd simply found (beside the email situation, she thought) another solitary activity: gardening. He said it reminded him of being a boy, of growing up on a farm, before his father had sold it. He liked working with dirt. I like digging up the back corner of the yard, he said. My hands. Jesus, I forgot they were here, he said. Look, he waved his hands, put them on her body, look, my hands, he'd said. Arms and hands and head. He'd gently headbutted her, and she'd laughed and slapped him away – all this before she knew about the emails, before Louis Walters. She'd liked to watch him in the garden. Pulling out the rocks, digging, tilling the ground, bringing manure from the hardware store, constructing a small fence around the vegetable garden, a garden that was already quite large – neighbors commented that it took up most of their backyard – and got larger every year. He made and remade the fence each spring, citing wear and tear from rain and animals. The fence was a small wooden thing, which allowed him to anchor chicken wire, covering over the small plants, and then some kind of veil-like covering for the herbs. He wore work boots and jeans when gardening, a loose flannel. He was in decent shape and looked so much like Nicholas. When he came inside for water, there were patches of sweat around his neck and armpits. Sweat on his face and arms. He smelled like a mixture of his sweat and deodorant. He didn't wear aftershave. He watered the garden, weeded, cut the plants back, sprayed organic sprays to rid the garden of pests. He brought in leaves from the plants with small holes in them: beetles. He looked up photos, compared. He brought in roma tomatoes with blackened ends: end rot. He brought in leaves with their ends gnawed off: slugs. He inspected the leaves of plants and soil in the same way he inspected the vegetables themselves, with care and concern for what he was growing. He sometimes brought in a jalapeno chili and would hold it up, like holding a tiny baby kitten, turn it around in the sunlight, then take a bite, eating the whole thing raw. She'd never seen him do such a thing. She understood two things then: he'd found something else to pull him out of his distance from the world, to pull him into some connection with his body. The other thing was that

David cared about what he was doing. She'd almost forgotten what that felt like. When she commented one afternoon on the fact that David looked like Nicholas out there, she almost, for a moment, hadn't been able to tell the difference. There was Nicholas, she'd said to him. Then there was Nicholas and you at once, and then just you. Hmm, he'd said. Then, You mean he looks like me? She'd been surprised by the question and the force of its actuality and logic. Yes, she said. That is what I mean, I guess. It makes me feel closer to him, doing the work, David had said. He was referring to how Nicholas had built his own house, had his own, much larger garden, an acre. A greenhouse. To both the boys, really, he'd added. They talked with Nicholas infrequently on the phone, a landline, which she couldn't believe still existed, in his cabin-like house. He reported on the land he was clearing, then burning, for a garden, a little farm. He reported on the barn he was turning into a workspace, in order to build a greenhouse and additions to the house, to be able to take the house completely off the grid, using solar panels on the roof. It'd be a lot of work, he told them on the phone, but he liked the work, which was so different from his job teaching anthropology classes. It was more like his fieldwork in the Amazon, he said, where he both examined the culture and role of drugs in the indigenous experience and also, tangential to the project, had helped build houses in the nearby village with a missionary group, just randomly joining up with them, he hadn't cared they were religious. They listened to him on speakerphone, his voice both his and not, somehow different, though she didn't know how, exactly. He called with reports, not to talk. Not to share, as he once did, his internal world. She never knew how he was feeling anymore. If he felt April was right for him, if he genuinely liked the small town he was living in, if he was happy. Nathaniel, Nathaniel would talk to her for hours about his troubles, his anxieties, his new vegetarian dishes, his idea for a restaurant that he couldn't get a good enough loan for, his care for and grievances concerning Stefanie, occasionally apologizing for what a shit he'd been in high school and college, and she loved Nathaniel for this, but she missed Nicholas. He'd gone and never returned, even when he did return physically. When he was building the cabin on the mountain, April, pregnant, had stayed with Katherine and David, and Katherine had occasionally overheard April talking with Nicholas, Nicholas saying something about how he was starting now, and she'd heard April say that he still had to text her even if they didn't speak for a week. Katherine hadn't known what to make of this, but April was in the kitchen, so she had to ask, she couldn't not ask, couldn't pretend she hadn't heard. I'm sorry for overhearing, Katherine had said. But why aren't you talking for a week? Are you having a disagreement? April had been holding her belly, which was not large yet, only about four months pregnant, and she'd said that they weren't fighting or anything, but that Nicholas spent a week in silence each year. Since when? Katherine had said. The last three years at least, April said. To what end? Katherine had asked. April said just to be quiet, just to shut up, at least that's what Nicholas had said. It has something to do with the idea he got from a shaman, though I don't know what exactly, that it's language that can open things, and language that can close things, and too much language is a prison. That's what he said. You should ask him, April had said, and then poured herself some tea. When Katherine told this to David in bed that evening, he'd said, Hmm, sounds like Nicholas. She'd wanted to talk about it more, but didn't. David had picked up his book, as he always did at night. Sitting in front of the computer, not talking with Louis Walters, she didn't even know if David knew that part of the reason she wasn't speaking now was to feel something about Nicholas, though she didn't know what. She didn't know how to be quiet. Of course she was tired of speaking to other people, but what did Nicholas see in this quiet? she wondered. She sometimes felt as though he'd located some secret, in the space of his silent weeks, she imagined he'd discovered something unfathomable, the truth of existence or at least his own, but now that she wasn't speaking, all she really felt was that she was still speaking internally. She had no idea how to be quiet.

Her phone buzzed, which caused Louis Walters to seemingly glance at the area of his screen from which he heard the buzzing sound. She felt the strangeness of the effect: she felt that everything in her room was unavailable to him somehow, that they were in separate realities, that the screen defined this separation, and yet now she remembered that wasn't true. He was there with her and not at the same time. She picked up her phone, read the text from Nathaniel, that said, Mom, the lawyer is acting strange. Can I talk with you in private? She read the text and when Louis Walters asked what was it, she wrote, My son. Give me a moment. The lawyer is acting strange, Nathaniel had written. It was their little joke about David: the lawyer. She almost wrote, when isn't he? But didn't. After all, she wasn't even speaking. She thought of how this week of silence that Nicholas did once a year had seemed so out of the ordinary to her, but to David it was just another Nicholas thing. He'd easily dismissed it, or not dismissed, not accepted either, but just assumed normalcy. Didn't look at it too long. This was the routine they followed, too: she taught at the university, she met with students, she wrote a paper or two each year, which were accepted and published in journals that no one read except her colleagues, who greeted her small success with pleasure undercut by an obvious jealousy, and this was what she did, while David did his thing. They spoke to their sons, mainly Nathaniel, met with Nathaniel a couple times a month, and maybe saw Nicholas twice a year, not looking at anything too much, certainly not the idea that they were aging, that their children were gone from them, into the world, that they didn't really know Jack, their lone grandchild, that well, and death was closer. She and David discussed their separate lives over dinner, occasionally meeting in the middle of the relationship, shedding their singular selves, but not looking too closely. They went to a movie twice a month, they drank coffee in coffee shops, they watched television, sometimes many hours of it, they walked their dogs, they talked about how Nathaniel and Nicholas were doing, Jack, too, occasionally April. David told her he wanted to try growing a rare heirloom tomato next year, it grew very small, very red, didn't require much water, was intensely flavorful. Very hard to grow. She had told him something like Nathaniel would love to have some of those, that she would too. He told her that was exactly what he was thinking, wouldn't it be neat if Nathaniel could visit for a weekend and just choose things to make from the garden, like his own personal farm-to-table thing. Again and again

David surprised Katherine with his thoughtfulness – it was surprising because he could be so distant, and so cruel, as with the Laura Moser emails. She told him that sounded like a good idea. If I can grow them, he'd said. Katherine thought now that there'd be these small occasions of coming together that barely even counted, separated by larger spaces in which it seemed almost no real communication occurred, then a fight. David occasionally claimed that she didn't do any laundry, didn't help with meals, didn't help with the house, and she, in turn, claimed that she never saw him, he was always in his office or in the garden, he seemed to take no interest in her or her life. Though as they had these fights, she wondered if she wanted anything to change. She liked that she could leave for a weekend, attend a conference with a co-worker, she liked that she could go to her feminist book club alone, and talk with the other women there, that she could go on a hike alone, walk the dogs alone. At night, in front of the television, streaming some detective show, there was still David on the sofa with her. Nothing had been lost really. He'd rub her feet while watching the show. He'd absently comment on the contrivance of an episode. They'd laugh. She felt no passion from him, no desire from him for her, certainly, but there was some comfort she didn't want to disrupt. There was comfort, and directly below that comfort, a danger in the comfort itself. She didn't know why exactly. Maybe it was that while she seemed to feel things emptying in the monotony of their lives, David was able to find one or two things that supplied meaning. He was able to find some meaning within the monotony that she could not. Gardening every day. She wondered if Louis Walters was in her life simply because she wanted something new. Loneliness was the accusation she often directed at David. She sat inside while he worked in the garden, she watched television while he researched old cases to present to his classes, she called Margaret, her sister, and they complained about their jobs, she called colleagues to see if they wanted to meet for coffee. She was free in her aloneness and didn't want to be alone but still wanted to be free. This felt irreconcilable, some cage of language and wants she couldn't see out of. She enjoyed her freedom, and she did feel alone, but she also knew that she was using the accusation of feeling lonely almost as a preemptive measure. There was something other than aloneness there, but it felt unreachable, unknowable. If he ever found out about Louis Walters, of course, she could use it, her loneliness and David's distance, in conjunction with his little email affair with College Sweetheart. It was an accusation she cultivated in the same way he tended to the plants in his garden, so that if she was ever found out, she could point clearly: I told you I felt alone. But in her most shameful moments, she was afraid she was only bored, bored with David, bored with herself, bored with her life.

She typed to Nathaniel, Is he looking for the will? If that's what it is, don't worry about it. We're just not sure why this Tammy person is driving across the country and want to make sure our ducks are in a row. She had no idea why she typed that phrase. She couldn't imagine what else David could've said or was doing that would've offended Nathaniel or been strange in a way that was beyond David's usual strangeness. Maybe he was worrying Nathaniel by making up some battle that was going to happen with this Tammy person, but even though the police had bungled that, even though no one had contacted this Tammy person until four days after the accident, even though she'd been in, in David's words, a serious rage when he finally contacted her and told her, Katherine knew that even if this woman put up a fight, she had no legal rights. Jack was Nathaniel's charge now, everyone in the family had to know it, and she was glad for it. He was the right person, despite the troubled years of his youth that, in retrospect, felt almost banal. She put the phone down, and looked back to the computer screen, where Louis Walters said that they hadn't really been talking anyway, but that he'd be right back. He was going to leave his computer on, he wasn't leaving her alone, but he had to take the dog out very quickly. He now held up a Shih Tzu, and said that Morten had been circling his feet, just give him like ten minutes and he'd be back. She began writing that this was probably a good time to sign off, but he said, I'm not saying goodbye. Right back, he said, and left the room. She saw him carry the dog out of the room, his back to her momentarily, then there was only the room where Louis Walters had been sitting. His desk chair swiveled slightly to the right, turning around with the motion of him getting up and leaving, the remnant of the act. The chair soon stopped moving. The Skype window showed bookshelves behind him, a side table covered with what appeared to be papers he was grading for his classes. Several stacks in different manila folders. A coffee mug on top acting as a paperweight. Another coffee mug on top of the bookshelf. Morning sunlight came slanting into the room, cut neatly by the blinds, then jaggedly lying across the uneven surface of the shelves and books. There were two framed photographs on the bookshelf, in which she could see both his wife and daughter. In the photograph of the daughter, she was holding Morten. In the photograph of the wife, there was Louis Walters. His bald head, smiling face, slight bug eyes hidden by glasses. He was moderately good looking, intelligent, and successful, though who among her and her husband's friends weren't? Hovering behind these thoughts, like a haunting of them, was Nicholas, Nicholas's life, his absence, that she would never see him again. There were sketches of further thoughts and feelings at the remote corners of her consciousness, which her thoughts of Louis Walters, and other things, covered, repeatedly, over and over, the thought, for instance, that there would never now be a new photo of Nicholas like there could be a new photo of her, or David, or Louis Walters, just as the photo of Louis Walters with his wife that she was looking at now through her laptop screen was a picture of a Louis Walters that had been and was no longer, and there would never be a photo of Nicholas now that was a photo of him that could possibly contradict his presence. She looked at the photo of Louis Walters and his wife and wondered who he was to that woman.

She thought that what Louis Walters was to her, mainly, was younger. A younger person, a man, a romantic interest who'd taken an interest in her when that had not occurred in so long, had seemed like it maybe couldn't occur again. So long, in fact, that at first, she hadn't even noticed his advances, like she'd deprogrammed herself, years ago, from noticing romantic advances. Oh, she could still flirt, but if someone else did, she couldn't see it, couldn't believe it. She had spilled her coffee one morning in the sociology department's parking lot. She had pulled in, set the coffee on top of her car, and then pulled out her bag with her laptop, the day's lectures, papers that needed to be handed back. When she shut the door, she did it hard, unthinkingly, and the mug had sort of flipped off the car, hit the ground, the lid cracking, the mug rolling away and spilling all the coffee. Fuck, she'd said. Louis Walters happened to be walking by, and he'd waved at her. He'd given her a kind of weird look, an unhappy or confused smile, and kept walking. Later that day, he'd left a coffee on her desk in her office, and then she thought, Okay, maybe I wasn't giving the guy enough credit. That was nice. She sent a thank you email. After that, he walked with her each morning into the building, having learned they both arrived for teaching at the same time. She caught him sitting, waiting for her in his car one morning when she was late. He pretended to be shuffling papers into his briefcase, also just arrived, so that they could walk in together. He bought her lunch, on the department. He left occasional lattes, banana bread. She began to get it. It'd been so long. Is this real? she thought. Or is my sex software failing? Then he called her into his office for her annual review and not only found no faults with her teaching, but said something about the fact that she was the most elegant person in the department by far. He made comments on the two papers she'd published that semester: 'The Bechdel Test and Social Networking' and 'Voting Against Oneself: Why Rural America Is Blind to Itself.' He said that he loved that she brought the Bechdel test into everyday life as a way to challenge its descriptive nature and association with mere pop culture, and that in doing so, she basically questioned its usefulness, and she'd replied with the idea that she wasn't questioning the test's authenticity, she was

merely attempting to figure out if it had any practical appli-
cations beyond being used in film and other narratives, and
that, somewhat lamely, of course it didn't, it couldn't. I said
hello to a woman today when buying my coffee – does that
mean I interact with enough women? Is the narrative, the
film of my life, complete, full? That's really the difficulty I
discovered with the Bechdel test, she'd said. That if two
women can say 'Hey, how's the weather,' the movie somehow passes the test. This is meant to show, Hey, look how
patriarchal and misogynist movies are. Two women can't
even talk about the weather, but I can't help but feel that
the test is actually granting too much space, and confusing
some people about a film's or story's overall openness by
leaving out the idea of 'meaningful' conversation. So its
mere descriptiveness acts as a confusing factor in a way.
Yes, yes, he'd said. That's exactly it. He'd continued the
meeting, commenting on her body of work, and then said
that on a personal note he liked watching how she moved
in front of a class, her presence in the classroom. There was
a quiet power, a certain elegance to her movements, as
though she were dancing through the lecture. She almost
couldn't reply, until she said, That's more than slightly
exaggerated. He'd then said, See, it's that directness that I
never see anymore. It's so refreshing. I know you're not
bullshitting me. I have no idea if you're bullshitting me,
she'd said. There it is again, he'd said. Who says that to
someone? Especially their boss. Later that week, the end of
the semester, she went to his office – she'd scheduled a
meeting – sat in the chair across from him and asked him
if he was making advances toward her. Yes, he'd said. I am.
Good, she said. I want you to be. That began it. They made

love in his office, she gave him a blowjob like a naughty secretary, they met at his house when his wife was away. His youth served as a doorway to her past, her own youth, her own passion, her carelessness – some thrill of living. It was difficult to even think of how clichéd this was, that because she was dissatisfied and bored in her own life, with herself, with the fact that she was aging, was, in fact, old, or deemed by society as old, at sixty-two, that she had accepted the advances of a man younger than her, as though this could really do anything, change anything. She hoped this wasn't true. She hoped that she was, in actuality, lonely, but she was afraid that she wanted to be young again, didn't want to be growing old. As a young woman, she'd been terrified of not being pretty enough, smart enough, interesting enough, but in this anxiety the world presented itself forcefully, fearfully. This feeling had returned with Louis Walters: how could this younger man find her so attractive, she wondered, while sitting in front of her computer. He desired her with a certain hunger. He went down on her in his office, propping her in his office chair, her feet on his desk. She walked out of his office with a buzzing feeling of secrecy. Passing her colleagues in the hallway, her students, she felt as though the world had transformed into a mysterious place again: no one knew what she'd just done, no one knew who she was, no one knew, including her, what would come next. Maybe he'd come into her office, tell a student that he would have to meet with her another day, send the student away, then bend her over a desk like a scene out of a noir film. She was free to be desired again. So maybe that was why Louis Walters. It wasn't that David made her feel alone, it was that he made her feel ignored. Though when she thought this, which she had thought before in the same way she was thinking of it now, as though it was the narrative of her life, the recursive theme of her thinking, which she constantly ignored and then re-approached: did it actually matter what the motivation was if the act itself was a hurtful one? Was she simply distracting herself from what she was actually doing by thinking that there was some way that what she was doing could be justified?

Louis Walters arrived back in his office. He was wearing a jacket now. He unzipped it, hung it on the back of his chair, and then still standing, said, Shit, be right back. Forgot my tea. He ran back out of the room, returning a moment later, with a steaming cup of tea in his left hand. He sat at the desk, the glow of the screen paling his face some, and then blew on the tea and said, Thanks for waiting. I have one thing I want to say, then I'll let you go. I'm guessing David will be back soon. She wrote to Louis Walters that she knew she'd said it, but she felt bad for communicating with him when she was supposed to be here with her family. This is, she wrote, an admittedly small amount of what I'm actually experiencing right now, but I can't do it anymore. Not now and not ever again. Look, can you just speak out loud? he said. I feel weird sitting here reading your messages waiting for you to write something while I talk. It feels odd. I'm okay with silence, but I'm not okay just hearing my own voice. It feels like I'm having a conversation with no one, with myself. It makes me feel a little nuts. So, here's what I'm going to do. I'm just going to sit here. I'm going to just be here with you. There was a pause. And as a last note, he said, I really can't believe David left you alone.

She looked away from the screen, out the window, to see if she could see her husband's car. He would come back soon with a few things to put in the mini-fridge: bread, salami, cheese, fruit. Also wine. She'd told him she couldn't go out into the town again, couldn't bear going to dinner, being seen, or seeing anyone who might have known Nicholas. When David arrived back in the hotel room, Katherine knew she wouldn't tell him about Louis Walters, and she further knew that she wouldn't end things with Louis Walters. She looked into the parking lot, which she could view out the window, over her laptop. If she were to see David's car pull up, she would tell Louis Walters goodbye, close out the Skype window on the computer, open up a web page, something from the *Washington Post* about climate change, the protesting of the Kodiak pipeline, the indigenous people who were protesting there. Maybe an article about the raid on an Iraqi city to free it from terrorists. Perhaps a video about posture, about how proper posture can correct bowel problems, though David might take that as a passive-aggressive comment about his own posture. Maybe something completely ignorable, some new recipe, a quiche, which she baked every Saturday morning – to show that she was being normal, she was getting back to normal. Or maybe something more to the point: How This Mother Dealt with Her Son's Death. Or, maybe something that would make David think of things: How My Son's Death Made Me Realize I'm Afraid of My Own. He'd say something about the fact that they had plenty of good years left, almost half a lifetime. She hated that it would be something, that she would choose something to cover over what she was doing, that she couldn't just stop talking to Louis Walters right now.

She looked at Louis Walters' face, which was supposedly just sitting there for her, just being with her, but which she really knew was waiting for her to type something. She saw herself in the small corner of the Skype window: tired, her face washed out by the cold light coming in the window, make-up-less, her hair a little out of control even though she had pulled it back into a ponytail. When had she done that? It had been all down and wild around her face, and sometime in the conversation with Louis Walters she'd tied it up, yet she couldn't remember doing this at all. How long had it been? How long has it taken, all of this, sitting here? What other parts of reality were excised, deemed unimportant?

She watched herself seeing herself, the twoness of her: there she was, in the same hotel they'd always stayed in when they visited Nicholas and April, and eventually Jack. I don't want to be talking to you anymore, she wrote. I'm going to sign off now. Katherine, Katherine, Louis Walters said in the Skype window, look, this is the last thing. I don't think this silence is healthy. I think it's good for you to talk. For you to get out what you're really feeling. You need to express it. Get it out. You'll feel lighter, better. She felt an anger rising in her, the same anger that had been present, along with the sadness, since learning of Nicholas's car accident, an anger and sadness that arose in her mind like a wave, then settled into a still, glassy surface. I won't feel lighter, she wrote. You can't reduce everything down to a psychological concept, as though pain's something we can shed like skin. You can't talk me into feeling better. Do you want to know what I'm doing right now? What I'm doing right now is this: my husband left to get some groceries, and for the half-hour or so that he's been gone, I decided to text you, Skype you, and talk with you because I didn't feel like being alone. I felt like distracting myself, and I did this knowing that I'd feel worse doing it, because we're doing this thing that is both hurtful to my husband, and by extension the rest of my family, and I know your wife would be devastated too. So, I knew that I'd feel worse by contacting you, but I didn't know in what way, so I did it because since I didn't know in what way I'd feel bad, maybe there was a chance it could make me feel good. There was some safety there, in not knowing exactly how I would feel bad, like the feeling bad couldn't happen if I couldn't locate the specific of it, like it would remain in abstraction, but now I do feel bad, specifically because now I feel alone, whereas before I didn't. I wanted to see you to make myself feel less alone and now I feel more alone because all this shows about me is that I don't want to actually deal with whatever's going on. I know I was the one who contacted you, but I can't talk to you right now, she wrote, and probably never again.

She watched Louis Walters' pinched and hurt face. She'd hurt him, she'd wanted to hurt him, and she was viewing it now. After a moment, she wrote, I'm sorry, writing it more because it was what she was supposed to do than because she really felt it. Or, maybe, she did feel sorry, but she also didn't – part of her wanted him to be complicit in her shame, to be shameful together, another kind of intimacy, another kind of deceit. I shouldn't have written that, she wrote. No, you're right, he said. You're right. I know you're supposed to feel bad. To feel, you know, terrible. I mean, I guess I don't know. My kids are both alive. That sounds really insensitive. This is hard. Me talking, you not talking, this is bad. I feel it's revealing bad things about me. There's an imbalance to this that I don't like – your not talking, it allows me to say too much. It's like you can see more of me and I don't like it.

She looked at him without acknowledging him. She felt it, what he was talking about, this imbalance. He was right. She'd felt it with others. With strangers in the coffee shop, with colleagues at the college. With David, all the time. She sensed people were uncertain how to react to her silence. Of course, first there had to be the realization that she was the mother of the man who died. But that almost always occurred quickly. This town, everyone knowing each other, it was a reason she hated it, but not the sole reason.

The first night in town – away from her house, her job and colleagues, away from Louis Walters, away from her life except for David – they'd eaten at a local place, and she had felt a grateful anonymity through the meal. A space in which to be genuinely sad, genuinely lost. She didn't have to be the grieving mother, as she had to be at her school, in her neighborhood, with her family. She could just sit and eat food and feel whatever she felt. And she did that. She ate her locally sourced trout and grits. She drank a glass of house chardonnay. She ate some bread. David sat across from her, not talking, occasionally glancing at his phone, then at her, as if to say, What's wrong, but knowing that, finally, for once, he couldn't say that, couldn't ask it. He knew what was wrong. Yet in the space of that dinner – the hanging lamps above each table lighting the place only dimly, the dark of the outside streets, old-style streetlamps, an imitation of gas lamps coming on – she'd felt she could just eat, not be noticed, not be anyone, not be the mourning mother momentarily. Then the owner had paid for the meal. It's taken care of, their waitress, a middle-aged woman said. David had looked around. Katherine kept her own eyes on the table, on her wine. She took a sip. Then the manager came over. He had a beard, was a big man, had been speaking earlier to some other customer of the numerous handcrafted beers on draft, and when he came up to the table, he put a big fist there, gently pounding the table, like a mime might, and said, I can't understand what you're going through, but I want you to know that we're all here for you. Your son and his family meant a lot to this community. He'd been looking down when he said it, then he looked up, giving Katherine a deeply pained look, his lips pursed hard into a frown, and his head nodding with profound understanding. She'd done her best to close her eyes and not glare at him. He was only trying to be kind, she'd thought. When she opened her eyes, he'd still been standing there, looking around awkwardly, as though he should be congratulated for his empathy. She couldn't believe he was still there. Thank you, she'd said after a moment. David had put a hand on her hand, which was holding the stem of her wine glass. She wanted to ask them, David and this manager, to please, could they just stop and watch what they were doing, because, none of it, nothing, it seemed, felt anything other than rehearsed, scripted, the outward gestures of grief, a performance, an attempt at mimicking some inner feeling. Then she'd thought, maybe that was grief: that one could come to view oneself from such a distance that one was no longer in one's life, but was watching it, completely separate from others and one's self. Then he'd gone.

Afterward, she and David had walked the few blocks to their hotel. David stopped in the old-timey drugstore to get bottled water and mixed nuts for the evening. She'd waited at the front of the store, felt herself staring vacantly at a stand of Corn-Nuts, thinking of what this man had expected from her. Had he wanted her to reach out, take him by the shoulder, and thank him for finally acknowledging her suffering? She knew this was an awful way to think, and that she should push it from her mind – the man was only trying to be kind, she repeated to herself, an echo of the thought she'd had in the restaurant, only fainter, less compelling. David had come back to the front of the store with the bottled waters and mixed nuts and they went to check out with the clerk, a young woman, homely, probably from a local farm, Katherine remembered thinking now, and in the middle of scanning the nuts, the clerk had looked up and said that she'd lost her sister when she was little, so she knew exactly how they felt. God bless.

Katherine looked at Louis Walters' waiting face and typed to him that what caused her to stop speaking was this: after eating dinner in the town, and hearing all these sympathies that felt empty, that night, she wasn't able to sleep. I thought, she wrote, did Nicholas really know these people? He never spoke of them. The only people he spoke of were April, Jack, and two people from the college, sometimes his students. The next morning, we, David and I, went to breakfast at a diner, where the waitress, a girl named Amanda, after taking our orders and getting us coffees and waters, finally recognized us, or realized who we were, or was told who we were. She said, Oh my god, you're the grandparents. During her speech, I watched this girl, wondering if she'd come to the realization on her own, if our grief was that apparent, or if someone had told her. I'm so sorry for your loss, she said to us. Nicholas and April and Jack sometimes came in here. We all loved them so much. It's such a tragedy. Poor Jack. Poor little thing, I can't imagine. I have a boy who's four and a little girl, just one a few weeks ago. I can't imagine it at all. They're my heart. Katherine wrote to Louis Walters that she remembered the way the waitress had stood there holding their plates of food, an early bird special and a vegetable omelet. I decided right then I wasn't doing this, she wrote. I wouldn't suffer the inanities of an entire town's superficial sympathy. I looked coldly at the girl, feeling my anger like a kind of force field around me. I wanted to project it out, to touch this Amanda woman with it. David saw this I think and to interrupt me he said, Thank you for that, Amanda. Now, I think our breakfast is getting cold. And the woman, startled, had said, Oh my god, I'm so sorry, and set our plates down. Whenever she returned, to fill up water, or coffee, she did that same sort of sad, pursed lip understanding face the manager at the restaurant had made the night before, the same one that all people had been making in order to convey their sadness and understanding. Eventually I stopped drinking the coffee and water, stopped eating. I just wanted to leave. When we finished the breakfast and went to our hotel, David asked why I hadn't said a word through breakfast. He asked if I was all right. I pulled a pad of paper from the desk, wrote on it that I was now in a period of silence, I didn't know for how long. That's what started it. Even writing this now feels like a cop-out.

Katherine stopped writing. She remembered how David had looked at her, his mouth open, then he nodded, swallowed, and said, I understand. He'd walked over to her, held her, fully pulling her into him, and she'd cried. She wanted Nicholas back so bad was what she wanted to say to David, but she only cried into his shoulder, resolved to her task. Then she remembered Nicholas spending a week a year in silence, and she realized that that was what she was doing. She hadn't done it consciously, but she was going to now. Not to find out anything about Nicholas, not to honor his memory, but just to do something that he'd done, to feel close to him and to one of his actions. She didn't feel any closer. David had released her and begun unpacking, and for some amount of time, she'd felt that her original intention, which was to avoid the stupidity of the townspeople, could be transformed into something more meaningful if she allowed herself to do it: it would force her to confront the actuality that her son was gone, she thought. That she would, also, one day be gone. That was better, she thought. She didn't dislike the town in its entirety, but the sort of detached, hippie view of things, the hip-Appalachia façade, coupled with the Cracker Barrel aesthetic of the surrounding rural areas, was more annoying to her than anything she encountered in the medium-sized city she lived in. Everyone here was so 'authentic': musicians, artists, outdoorsmen, hunters, academics. A weird little mix of a community. She didn't want anyone in the way of her grief, she wrote to Louis Walters, and yet they were already all over it, representing it to her. She wanted to meet it alone, without distraction. So I choose silence.

Yet even now, in the room waiting for David to return, not talking to Louis Walters, only writing to him, she knew she was finding distractions from this confrontation, and every time she came back to the realization that Nicholas was gone, she felt the pain as though newly beginning again. Every time her mind reconstructed her reality for her, and that reality first began with Nicholas and then the negation of Nicholas, and the same in turn for April, it was like experiencing the news all over again. She looked at Louis Walters, who was now smoking a cigarette on the screen – it was something she didn't like about him, but he was free to do what he wanted. He sat there, waiting for her, and she sat in front of her computer, alternately looking out the window at the view of Church Street, the farm-to-table restaurant she'd eaten at twice, a bookstore, some small boutique, and then, above the street, as if floating above it almost – the clouds and fog were so thick – there was the mountain, some indiscernible distance away.

Do you want to know the other reason I'm not talking? she wrote. He nodded his head. I'm not talking because I keep finding ways not to look at what is happening, because there are so many distractions from what is happening. You know my other son is with Jack right now, she wrote. When Nicholas made him Jack's godfather, I thought: What a nice gesture. It felt like the right thing, but I never thought it'd have consequences. It has consequences. It's Nathaniel. This is the chef? Louis Walters said. Yes, she wrote, the chef. It's not that I don't think he's the right person, or that he and Stefanie aren't right for Jack. I think they are. But I'm worried for Jack's way of life. It'll be so different with Nathaniel. The same if he comes with David and I. I think the real reason I'm not talking, she wrote, is because of Jack. It's obvious to me now. I learned a while ago that Nicholas spent a week in silence every year. Which was what he wanted Jack to be able to do when he was old enough too. I think that's actually where this is coming from, she wrote, though I didn't realize it right away.

Almost simultaneously, David's car pulled into the parking lot and her phone buzzed with a text message. She looked at the text, a number she didn't recognize, and then read the text, which said, We need to talk, and not understanding who this text was from, she quickly typed to Louis Walters that she had to go. As she typed it, she looked up the area code of the phone number, saw that the number came from an area code she didn't recognize, and realized this was April's mother contacting her. We need to talk, the text read. Louis Walters was saying something, but Katherine wrote, Please don't try to contact me. She'd contact him if she felt she could. She thought about saying that she missed him – if only because she might want to see him again – but she didn't. Suddenly this was clear. She missed his hands on her, his mouth on her, his body making her body feel like a young body again, but these were all things she also had come to hate, and in this way, she did not miss him at all. She missed the pleasure he provided, a momentary pleasure, and everything else, she felt, which was beneath the pleasure, was her sickness. Some brief pleasure was what she got from Louis Walters, and the rest, none of which she really liked and almost all of which made her feel bad, she did to herself, and so she wrote, Bye,

Louis, and closed out the Skype window, and searched for an article about how to make quiche with goat cheese, and texted April's mother back: Let's all meet when you get in on Friday so we can discuss exactly what is going to happen.

TAMMY

Flowers fall even though we love them; weeds grow
even though we dislike them. Conveying oneself toward
all things to carry out enlightenment is delusion. All
things coming and carrying out enlightenment through
the self is realization.

—DOGEN, *GENJOKOAN*

Your mind is [. . .] always attempting to leave here and
now, to look for purpose or meaning beyond itself.

—DAININ KATAGIRI

There were accidents along the way, stupid people, Tammy thought, driving recklessly, making it harder for everyone else, but most annoyingly, there was one not two hours from her house, right at the beginning of her drive across the country. Good omen, she thought, sitting in the traffic. She felt some generalized anger at everything in her perception – at the flashing lights of police cars passing her on the shoulder, at an ambulance, a fire truck, the red tail-lights of other cars and trucks and semis, the steady rain, the people inside the cars, even the buildings and restaurants off the side of the highway, the night sky polluted by city light, a sickly grey-orange, the leafless trees – and this anger shifted to an annoyed boredom, a sort of wispy feeling of wishing stupid people out of existence. The world might be better then. If there was something some mad scientist could slip into the water that only affected stupid people, causing them to Facebook themselves to death or something, uploading pictures of themselves and their pets for days on end without eating or drinking, growing sickly and tired, eventually falling asleep in front of their webcam, dying a selfish and peaceful death, feeling loved by themselves and their pit bulls. Tammy thought the headline in the paper the next day would be, FB Users Die in Front of FB, Immediately Improving the World.

For a moment, she thought of April, whose house she was driving to, who she kept thinking she'd be seeing, but wouldn't be seeing. There'd only be Jack, and she knew this was her one opportunity, a chance not only to correct mistakes she'd made as a parent to April, but also to give Jack the kind of life he deserved and to show everyone that she was capable of doing this. And she was driving to the boy to do this despite the fact that she hadn't been told that her daughter had been in a car accident, had actually died in the car accident, until four days after the crash and she was driving there now, four days later, despite the fact that the other side of the family barely registered her existence, that they didn't like her, and despite Steve's disapproval. Yesterday, when they had first learned about the accident, Steve had been his usual caring, considerate self. Like her, he also couldn't believe it'd taken her four days to learn about the accident. It had occurred early Wednesday morning, and the wreck wasn't discovered until Wednesday at daybreak. And yet she didn't find out until fucking Sunday. The story was the authorities contacted Nathaniel and that side of the family, but hadn't contacted her because April didn't have the same last name, had no will, no contact information for her mother, then some mix-up occurred where supposedly someone from the other side of the family was supposed to contact her, but never did. She got a bunch of apologies and we're so sorries from David after (somehow, who knows fucking how, Tammy told Steve) he finally realized she hadn't been contacted. She heard David's explanations that the other side of the family had forgotten, they'd all forgotten, in their grief it had all gotten mixed up, and the police or whoever hadn't done their damn jobs, and he was so sorry, this father of Nathaniel and Nicholas had said, apologizing over and over to her. But his apologies counted for nothing, she'd thought. Steve had said that it was bullshit was what it was, and after doing some bitching together about how small-town police cut corners, but really that it was this other side of the family that was worse, she'd then said she didn't even want to think of any of it anymore. And she didn't want to. She wanted to think of April, of Jack.

She told this to Steve, and he agreed that that was what she should be thinking about. He had said that he too had lost someone close, a thing she already knew, but so he knew what she was going through. She'd watched him speaking, watched him talking about himself, not with surprise, but with curiosity. Was he really talking about himself at this moment? They'd only been seeing each other seven months, but he had already moved in, they had already shared whatever they typically hid of their pasts, they were too old to do any testing of the relationship, and so moved in together easefully if only half-enthusiastically. It felt to Tammy like a kind of maturity. Steve had told her many times about the old girlfriend, and he did it again after news of the accident. How he'd been driving on a country road after being at a bar. Back when he was still drinking too much. He'd seen a green light turn yellow too late, the car skidded through and they were hit by a truck. His old girl-friend, who was in the passenger seat, she was the one hit by a truck. She died instantly. While telling her this, Tammy was always amazed at how easily he could take a situation and make it about himself while at the same time forgetting that he'd told her all this several times, once right when they began seeing each other, and then a few months later when her cousin died. He even told her some version of the story when her mother got sick and had to have her gallbladder removed. There were always slight changes to his story: one time, they were drinking beer, one time, whisky, one time, it was raining, one time, it was only misting. The one thing that didn't change was the way the story ended. With the notion of the guilt he carried around and that the accident was his rock bottom, that made him quit drinking, that made him take responsibility for himself and his life. At first, Tammy had admired this, had admired him. She still did. But in the last month or so, she'd begun to pity him. He seemed a man consumed by his past. An event that happened over twenty years ago shading the rest of his life. She felt she could never replace the dead woman who she only recently realized he was sort of romanticizing. When Steve learned April was gone, he'd said, I know what you're going through. It's like, you know, they tell you they're dead, but you can't help but think you'll see them tomorrow, or in a few hours. It's almost like you want to say, Yes, I know she's dead, but then you wait for her to show up at your door. And I bet your daughter was just like Sloane for me. You're afraid of forgetting the perfect things this person did. The way she'd cut off her split ends while sitting on the sofa and then there'd be hair everywhere. Or how every Thursday was fresh gulf shrimp. She just had to have it. Stuff you didn't even notice before, but that you now saw were the perfect things about these people. Tammy'd listened to him, feeling both the loss of April and the loss of Steve, finally realizing just how much he hadn't moved on, how much he felt, but almost never said aloud, that he killed the girl, and that made her feel like he was pathetic, made her hate him some, and made her want to take care of him too. But mostly it made her pity him and wonder what he would've been like had he never met this woman, or at least if their relationship had ended in a normal way. Though what was normal? she'd wondered. At least you can see it as just one of life's things though, Steve had added. You have no guilt in this. You didn't cause it. It was as close as he'd come to it, saying it this way. Partly in order to make him stop talking, to stop him thinking about himself, she'd looked at him and said, Jack's coming to stay with us. Steve had sat back from her on the sofa then stood up. He went to the kitchen, got a cup of coffee for himself, for her. His typical measured movements. Careful. Considerate. He wanted to appear considerate, she knew. She hated that she'd said Jack was going to live with them as a way to take him a down a notch. You want to make this about you? she'd thought. Let's see what this looks like when you're actually involved. When you're forced to stop thinking about yourself. At the same time, she knew the boy needed to be with her, that she alone among both sides of the family knew what the boy needed. She'd been an overworked, overstressed young mother, who hadn't paid enough attention to April, and she knew this, this alone – attention and care, really being there – was something she could give Jack. She knew it because she'd failed at it. And she didn't trust Nathaniel or Stefanie, she didn't trust Jack's grandparents on the other side, simply because things had come too easily for them. Jack would be there, but would they really be there for Jack? In addition to this, she was afraid, she could acknowledge that, that these other people would push her out, or at the very least would neglect her, ignore her, and she wouldn't know her grandchild, and that wasn't happening. Steve brought her the coffee and told her that he understood what she was going through, he knew that pain, that loss, but getting the boy wasn't going to make that loss go away. Trust me, he told her. I tried so many things to make that pain and loss go away. You can't. Plus, look at our lives. We can't look after a four-year-old. That wouldn't be fair to him. You have to think about him, Steve had said. Tammy had taken the coffee, drunk it and tried to appear satisfied. Tried to appear pleased with his point of view. She was careful not to say anything though. Just drink your coffee, she remembered thinking. Then do what you know is right, which was what she was doing now, in the car, on the way to Jack, the only real option there was. She hadn't even told him she was going. The last thing he'd said to her was something like, Let's think about it and then we can talk about it in a couple days when you're more clear-headed. He had also said, Maybe I was wrong earlier, maybe this is something we could pull off, but let's sit on it first. Tammy had agreed, gone to work, and left around five in the evening, well before her shift was over, asking Dolores to cover for her, and then, only a couple hours into the drive, hit the accident she was sitting in now.

She tried to sit up and look down the highway, but could see only the taillights of cars reddening the road and her windshield. There was a soft humming from the car's heater, so different from her own car, an old Jeep Cherokee from the nineties. The heater in the Cherokee rattled, like there was a squirrel working a tiny unicycle that fanned the air toward her. Tammy had even told this once to April. She liked picturing it, the little squirrel in there, but then April tore off two of the vent things one day trying to find him while he was napping. Tammy told her he'd nap or go grocery shopping when the car was stopped, but six-year-old April had broken the vents and so Tammy had to tell her the truth, which ruined the thing for her, too. The game was gone not just for April but for Tammy too. She turned up the heat in the car now. She sometimes forgot new cars were like this one, which was a Jetta, with a lighted, digital display, the phone connected to the speakers through Bluetooth. Her own Jeep no longer had a glove box door, a headrest was lost long ago when April was still young, just a teenager – a fight they'd had in which April calmly pulled the headrest off Tammy's seat and dropped it out her window. The brakes had started to grind, again, too, and the wheel pulled hard to the right if Tammy let go. She sometimes felt like she was fighting the Jeep, that what it really wanted to do was turn around and go home, like an old dog on a walk. But this rental, this car, felt like if she were to let go of the wheel, it would convey her to where she needed to go. She'd been going, moving easily and smoothly in the car, barely driving it seemed, like a capsule through the night in a futuristic movie, conveying her toward the kid. Then she hit the traffic.

She called her sister Jeannie for something to do and told her that she was stuck in a traffic jam and needed some advice about Steve. Jeannie asked what she meant and Tammy told her that Steve didn't want Jack to stay with them. Not only that, but she was driving now to North Carolina and hadn't even told him. He thought she was at work. He would not be happy when he found out what was actually happening. There was a quiet moment on the line before Jeannie said that she hadn't realized Tammy was the guardian. Tammy said that she wasn't necessarily the guardian, that no one was necessarily the guardian, that April and Nicholas had never stated who the guardian would be, but she had to be. It couldn't be the other side of the family. She'd never see Jack then. She told Jeannie that she didn't necessarily want to be doing this, she just had to. For Jack. That was how it was for her: part of her didn't want to do a thing and another part had to. A constant fighting in herself. Did her sister ever have that? It felt like that was her entire life, fighting with herself and the world. Not only was she fighting Steve, not only was she going to have to fight the other side of the family just to get Jack in the place he should be, she was also fighting the damn traffic. It was how her life always was. Same as always. Just turn around, her sister had said. What's the point of driving? How long is that drive anyway? Fly out or something. Her sister said that this was a hard enough time for Tammy without having to drive across the country. Do herself a favor, turn around, go home, talk to Steve, tell him whatever you need to tell him, and then buy a plane ticket. Tammy told her sister that she knew she didn't have money for a ticket, even with the bereavement rate. Plus, she had no choice. She'd gotten off a few days from the hospital now, this week, and that was all they were going to give her. She couldn't drive back now and walk in and say, Hey, I'm going to take my shift after all, Dolores, thanks for coming in though. But hey, I'm flying out tomorrow night, so could you cover these new hours instead? Please. That wasn't happening. Plus, if she wanted to be part of Jack's life, she had no choice but to go now. The other side of the family was already there. They were already making plans. Without her. So, she had no choice. She was going. Also, Jack was the one chance she had, she said, to make things better. To correct some wrongs, and to finally feel right about her life. Just like Steve, these people didn't care about that though, she explained to her sister. They were all probably figuring out the nicest way to tell her she wasn't going to get to see Jack ever again, she told Jeannie. They're probably debating how much money to give her that would equate to a grandmother's relationship to a four-year-old boy. That's not necessarily true, Jeannie said. Don't think like that. I don't understand how that's helping anything right now. You're not there. You don't know. Maybe just try to be open to whatever happens.

Tammy paused, watching another police car pass by on the shoulder, the siren off but the blue lights flashing momentarily in her car, then lighting, strobe-like, the windows of the cars in front of her. Each of the thousand drops of rain on the windshield of her car flashed with the reflected blue light then were wiped away. She explained to Jeannie that she didn't know these people, she only knew what April had told her, and sure, they appeared all nice on the surface, but underneath that surface they wanted what they wanted and they got it. It's how the world was for them, she told her sister. It was the only way they knew the world. It gave them what they wanted. Plus, they had money to get what they wanted, and if you were both lucky and had money, you didn't need anything else. Really, Tammy said. Maybe money was luck. I'm not talking about these people I've never met anymore, Jeannie said. I'll talk about something else, but I won't do this gossip thing with you about people you barely know. Like you wouldn't be thinking the same shit, Tammy said. What Tammy wanted to say was that she had called Jeannie for some support, for someone to be on her side, but now that she saw Jeannie wasn't, she said that Jeannie couldn't understand. She'd never been in this position before. And because Jeannie didn't have kids, she never would be in this position. But thanks for the help, Tammy said. Jeannie said she was sorry, but she understood, this was a difficult time – stop saying that, Tammy said, you don't understand. Jeannie said she didn't know what else to say. After a moment, Jeannie said that, look, dinner was just finishing and Randall was hungry. It'd been a long day. I gotcha, Tammy said, feeling self-pitying and frustrated with herself. Say hello to Randy, Tammy said, in an obvious mocking of bright and happy. Jeannie said she'd call back after dinner to see how Tammy was doing and hung up.

Sitting in the unmoving traffic, now without Jeannie's voice coming from the speakers in the car, surrounding her, almost blanketing her, she felt the force of her aloneness. She equally felt the force of her not moving, of not having anything to do, of being confronted with just sitting there for who knew how long. Her car moved slowly forward and for a moment she thought the traffic was going to open up, but it didn't. She pushed hard on the brake pedal before nearly rear-ending the Nissan in front of her. She thought of Jeannie in her house in Florida and wished she was there with her. Jeannie said that what she liked to do when life presented her with a dilemma was to consult her cards. Tammy knew that Jeannie would prepare a joint, light the candles, and then get out the tarot deck. Tammy pictured

Jeannie, on her sofa, legs curled up to her, in her little apartment, with this new black boyfriend, Randall, maybe in the kitchen. He was apparently a good cook, and Jeannie'd be there in the darkness of that apartment, the wood slatted shades always drawn, the sound of the ocean waves out the window, the oil paintings on the wall all painted by Jeannie, her dreams, she said, not very good paintings, but strange enough that Tammy was always surprised by them: a cracked moon reflected in a puddle, which itself, you came to realize, was reflected in an eye. She felt a momentary longing for Jeannie's life even though she knew she judged it. She saw her sister as a faux-mystic, a pretend-gypsy, and underneath all the tarot and palm reading and scarves and dark dresses and long hair, Jeannie was just a pothead. Still, to live on the beach, to feel some easefulness in life, to not have to work every day, to be as carefree as Jeannie presented herself to be. And yet when she and Steve learned about the fact that Jeannie was dating a black guy, they told each other it'd last six months, was a novelty, that they were too different. At that point they'd only seen pictures of the guy through Steve's FB (I thought you hated this shit, Steve had said when she was looking, to which Tammy remembered replying, Not now I don't). He was not a big guy, not a small guy, just an average black guy. Average black guy, Tammy had said to Steve. He's definitely no football player, Steve had replied. She couldn't get one of those? Help this family out. She sometimes felt a snap in her mind when Steve referred to the family as his, as though he was fully a part of the family in the time they'd been together, as though she hadn't plucked him from complete anonymity, but then, who was she? Just a person with a sister, parents, and a daughter, and now, potentially anyway, a black brother-in-law. Still, she had people. Steve didn't have anyone. She knew it must be hard, so she let Steve have this, she granted it to him: it's your family too, she told him once, and he'd looked at her, not understanding why she said it. She didn't explain. She wondered if Jeannie had granted this to Randall as well. He was newer though, so maybe not yet. Her parents, who were now great-grandparents, certainly hadn't. She even suspected news of Randall was a contributing factor in one of her father's recent strokes, that left his face droopy and his words muttery. You're kidding? Steve had said. Oh no, Tammy told him. I can just see my dad seeing a picture of this guy, asking Mom, is this Randall, and her nodding and then a part of my dad's sphincter squeezing so tight and hard that it scrunched shut a pathway in his brain. Knocked him out cold. Jesus, Steve had said. Hey, he survived it, Tammy had told him. She knew her parents wouldn't even consider the thought that Randall might be part of the family, but Tammy got it, if this black guy did it for Jeannie, if jazz and Tyler Perry and smoked pork butt or whatever did it for Jeannie – all of which she knew were clichés and stereotypes, but whatever – then good, she deserved something decent. Someone in the family did. Plus, maybe he was an understanding, thoughtful person. Maybe Randall was the type of person that would be okay with having a boy unexpectedly have to come live with Jeannie and him, unlike Steve, who was a different type of person.

Her phone buzzed with a call. It was Steve. She didn't want to answer it. She wondered if he knew she wasn't at work, but decided it was just his normal phone call during her nightshift at the hospital's front desk. Yet, if he somehow had found out, she didn't want to hear him attempt to convince her that her heart was in the right place, but logically speaking, practically speaking, this was not her place. There were other family members better suited to this than them, which had seemed to be his primary argument, along with the idea that she was reacting in a selfish way, and that what she should really be doing is grieving her dead daughter. Her phone continued its buzzing and instead of answering it, she ignored the call, let it go to voicemail, and put the car in park and got out. A light rain fell. She pulled up the hood of her windbreaker and walked toward the accident, stretching her legs and observing the line of cars, some angled off toward the concrete barrier separating their side of the highway from the other side, the cars on the other side moving freely and easily. The angled cars were people trying to get a look, to see how far ahead. It doesn't matter how far, a trucker yelled down at her. Every lane is closed. She smiled at him and he told her to climb up, that it'd be awhile. She ignored the comment and kept walking. A gust of wind made her pull her windbreaker around her and tighten her hood over her head. She glanced to her left, where a man in some kind of Nissan was staring at his phone. Behind her, a woman was in a Ford, staring at her phone. She noticed that around her, almost every person in their car was looking at their phone, their faces framed in a strange glow of blue light, making them all appear ghostly and unreal. But they were real, with real lives, different from hers, some better, some worse, there was no way of knowing which. She imagined Jack, and his being with her making her own life better. No, not better, she thought, more real.

So often she felt like a ghost in her own life. She went to work, she filled out insurance forms, people treated her as though she herself was a form, she watched television with Steve, she occasionally went for a drive through the cornfields, everything the same, every day repeating itself, just like every row of corn, every block of field. She imagined Jack eating breakfast with Nathaniel and Stefanie. She imagined how lost those two probably were, how when she arrived, it might take Jack a minute, but then he'd remember her, the toys she'd brought him, maybe some subconscious memories of the times she'd fed him a bottle when he was little, and he'd eventually sit next to her on the sofa, like he did the night April had been reading to him and he'd just stood up with the book, walked over to her, and sat on her lap. No words. No asking. He just came over to her and wanted her to read like he'd felt that she was family, not that he'd been told it. And she'd read to him with April watching. She remembered wanting April to see it. To see her. She'd wanted April to see that Jack could feel they were related and that she knew what she was doing, despite the fact that April, and Nicholas, thought she didn't because she hadn't been the perfect mother to April. But they didn't take into consideration how difficult things were for her then. An eighteen-year-old girl, trying to do it all alone, April's father not there to help. She imagined that Jack would do the same thing now. She would arrive, pull up in her rental, walk up to the cabin, and when Jack saw her, he might hesitate at first – he only saw her once a year, after all – but then he'd remember the times she'd read to him, the times she'd swung him in the swing, the times she'd sung to him, the times she'd made him French toast, and most importantly the feeling of family he'd gotten from her, and he'd come to her, take her hand, and it would all be clear. If only April could see that, that Jack chose her, not the rich kids. It was a disgusting thought to have. Her daughter was gone and she was thinking of how she'd show April, and everyone else, that she was the right one for Jack. Not only that, but that it would be his choice. She shouldn't be thinking it. Out of respect for the dead. But she couldn't help the glimmer of a thought that said that maybe April hadn't done a good job of reminding Jack that she was family too, that she mattered, that she was part of Jack's life, that April was wrong. It wasn't only Jack's choice though that mattered. She would have to come up with an argument, something to convince Nathaniel and Stefanie, the other side of the family, that Jack belonged with her.

The cars started moving again, and she jogged back to her rental, shook off the rain, got in, and she was driving. Another phone call from Steve. She again ignored the call and after a few minutes of moving slowly, maneuvering to the far left lane, she passed the SUV, motorcycle, and F-150, which looked destroyed, as though a boulder had been dropped on its hood. She noticed herself register that there were people standing on the side of the road, heads down, soaked by the rain. Two women, a younger and older woman, sisters, or a mother and daughter. Their hair lank and wet. Then another body, a man, on a stretcher being put into the back of the ambulance. She watched, her head turning as she drove by. A movement in her, like a hand inside her chest trying to unclench and pry apart another hand that was in a fist. She closed her eyes and breathed, then remembered she was driving here. The highway began to move by her. She saw these people momentarily in her rearview, growing smaller, their bodies against the enormity of the highway, the rushing cars, the world around them. Then she couldn't see them anymore and she was driving, watching the rushing freeway. The visual illusion was still something that she enjoyed – that when in a car one could feel like the entire world was moving by, the rush of pavement, the buildings and trees, the concrete abutments, the moon and clouds, a grey nighttime moving outside, while remaining still. While thinking this, driving, her headlights made almost tangible by the mist and rain, solid beams of light into the night, she thought of April, how she'd heard about her daughter's death, how it was so different from the accident she'd just passed. Everyone had survived the accident she'd just passed. Even the man on the stretcher, or gurney, or whatever it was called, he was moving, he was looking around, she could see him. He'd be okay. The lives around him, he'd join again, like a fish pulled from the stream and then tossed back. That man on the stretcher didn't have to be envious of the faces that were watching him, didn't have to feel that they'd go on without him. But April had been alone on a mountain road. No other cars. They weren't even found till the morning. It'd be worse to die on a highway, Tammy thought, hitting another vehicle, seeing other faces, all these other faces that were going to outlive you, lying on the pavement or stuck in an ambulance and knowing that everything was going to outlive you. That other worlds would remain complete, intact. These other people, the world was going to stay there for them, they were going to stay in it, however good or bad it was, but you were not. Not only were you dying but you also had to try not to feel envy that other people were not dying. But you would, she thought. You definitely would. You'd feel envious that everything was going to keep going without you. That you were the most insignificant part of the world in that moment. Your death was the proof of that. Your own death was so small that the world took no notice, and the pain of it, whatever pain April'd experienced, whatever fear, the fear that you would never be in the world again, that the world was gone for you, was also completely insignificant: there and then gone. Dying on a highway, you'd see passing cars, people looking in at you, the lights of buildings, restaurants maybe, a gas station, and you'd know that you were soon to be nothing, while the something that was everything else went on like the stupidity it was. She thought of how maybe April got to see Nicholas, though he was supposedly unconscious, so that didn't really count. That was better anyway, being alone. Being alone when you died was the best way to die because it was how everything was: you were alone. Maybe you had friends when you were a kid or a teenager, maybe you had a family, maybe you had everything you wanted, but when you were dying you realized you were utterly alone. That you always had been, Tammy thought. People didn't know that. People thought you went to some perfect place or that you went back to the universe or that you were reborn, but that wasn't it. It was just finished. You were done. You would never see, feel, think, be anything again. It was why Tammy was fine with however hard her life was, because it showed her that loneliness was banal, boring even, nothing to be that afraid of. When she died, she hoped it could be like April, completely alone. Being completely alone in that moment was even better than being with maybe one person who wouldn't make you feel like they were just going to go on without you. There were so few of those people in anyone's life, Tammy knew. She had once thought that maybe Steve was her person, but he wasn't. He was just another unmoored soul. The person, she knew, was Jack. When she was older, after she'd sent him to school, or maybe even after she homeschooled him, anything but the Montessori school that April and Nicholas sent him to, after she'd helped him learn a trade, maybe something with cars, after she helped him get into a decent little state school, maybe a partial scholarship, after she'd got him set up in the world, he'd be the one that would come to her when she was going to disappear into nothingness. He'd hold her hand, tell her he loved her, would thank her. Before April's death, she'd thought that person would be April, but now she knew her witness would be Jack. If you were lucky, you got a witness, you got one person to watch you die and say, This person was here. This person affected something in this world, and that something is me. She felt almost nauseated that April hadn't had this from her, but as Tammy well knew, you did not get what you wanted. You got lucky or you didn't, that was all, though it helped to arrange your luck. And with Jack she got a new start: both to be there for someone and for someone to be there for her. Some disconnection had occurred between her and April. Something was missing. Something had been missing for a long time. Or maybe was always missing, she didn't know. Like those model airplanes and cars April used to get, which had infuriated Tammy some. She had wished April was doing something a little more feminine by ten. Though still, Tammy had helped. They'd build the plane or whatever it was, and inevitably, it seemed, as the thing took shape, it never looked quite as real as on the box, never looked like an actual plane or battleship. That was their relationship: it was only the semblance of the thing itself. Some incomplete mother–daughter model, missing some key piece, from the beginning of April's life, as though Tammy, in not wanting the child initially, despite doing what she thought most mothers did when their baby finally arrived, which was feel a complete and utter love, had somehow created the lack, as though she was the model maker and had willfully misplaced some key component of the model. This only intensified throughout April's life, falling into the background in certain moments, when she was a young girl, then becoming more obvious again as a preteen in her hatred of her mother's boyfriends (who were, admittedly, often idiots, just as Tammy was often an idiot), then turning into April's identification not with other young teenage girls, but the sports boy crowd, so that she dressed and acted like an afflicted teenage boy, which was infuriating to Tammy and which April seemed to delight in infuriating Tammy with, only for April to change again, in college, into an intellectual, taking philosophy and psychology classes and treating Tammy herself with a sort of openness that felt ironic in its sincerity. And then the final change, Tammy thought, was the most obvious move in explaining the distance between them and what was missing between them: after Nicholas and April met in grad school, after they married a year later, they moved far away from the Midwest, into the mountains, isolated and alone, and lived a life that Tammy knew April felt was a sort of rejection of everything that Tammy had taught April: to fight for oneself, to try to move up in the world, to live with family even if you disliked them, which was what Tammy had tried to do herself when she was a young mother. She wouldn't let any of this happen with Jack, and that was exactly what Steve didn't understand.

A car came up behind her, in the middle lane, and tailed her closely. Tammy signaled to change lanes and then did, the BMW speeding past. She watched it weave between a truck and an SUV, moving into the left-hand lane. She observed, with mild annoyance and the vague thought that the driver was probably on a cell phone, the BMW moving fast and swervingly. The rain was falling harder, she now noticed, and she increased the speed of the wipers by bumping the wand next to the steering wheel upward. She called Steve back and before she could say anything, he said, I've been calling and calling you, Tam. I called your work. Dolores said she's filling in for you. He was surprisingly calm. She had a hard time understanding if his calm and concern were real or not, if he was using it, as she'd begun to learn he used calm and concern, as a way to manipulate her, in the same way he'd seemingly tried to manipulate her in their earlier conversation when she told him she wanted Jack to live with them, by telling her that she was still in the grieving process and could not possibly make that decision and to give it a few days. On the phone now, she told him she was driving to North Carolina. He said that that was what he was afraid of, and he wanted her to know that more than anything that was disappointing to him because obviously she felt she couldn't tell him. Oh, that's disappointing, she said. No, no, that's not what I meant, he said. It's disappointing, I mean, I'm disappointed in myself. What he meant was, the fact that she didn't tell him made him feel bad because he didn't want to be the type of person who she had to hide things from, he didn't want to be the type of guy who told her she shouldn't go get her grandchild or something like that, or that she shouldn't be the guardian, and he was sorry if he put that in her head, or if what he'd said came off that way. That was not the way he wanted it to come off. He was disappointed in himself because obviously he'd put that in her head and he didn't want to do that. If she wanted Jack to live with them, he would definitely, fully support that. But Tam, he was just sharing a concern, and that concern was based on his own experience. When he lost Sloane, that was one of the most confusing moments of his life. He didn't know up from down. He quit his job working construction because it reminded him of her, how she'd bring him lunch at work and they'd eat on a picnic table or under a tree near whatever building he was working on. She'd bring a thermos with coffee and whisky in it and share it, and he'd go back to work with the warm feeling of her inside him. What he should've done was take the two weeks his boss wanted to give him, but he'd quit, and gone on a bender instead and nearly killed himself in *another* car accident. He realized her situation wasn't the same, but. Stop, Tammy said. Stop talking. For one fucking minute stop. There was quiet on the phone. Then she told him she didn't want to hear about Sloane. In fact, one month, she didn't want to hear a Sloane story for one month. Or maybe they should just start with a week. How about that? One week without Sloane coming up. She felt an anger that she'd been suppressing become centrally focused, like a glowing coal in her throat, that allowed her to say what she needed to say to him. In fact, it seems like I know everything about you and Sloane, I know your past, I know your lowest point, I know your recovery, but you know almost nothing about me and my past. And that's because you never ask. I mean, sure, I shared things, but you don't really know. You don't know me and April. You don't know why I'm doing this. Why I'd want to. Because it's always Steve and Sloane. As though no one else has had hard times. As though Steve and Sloane were the real Bonnie and Clyde, but in this version, only Bonnie dies, and Clyde goes on to live a guilt-ridden and self-pitying life with a boring woman named Tammy. There was silence on the line and Tammy felt the heat in her throat cooling, as though expressing these words was like cold air settling gently over the burning coal. After a moment, she said she was sorry, and Steve said that no, she was right, she was definitely right, he knew he made things about himself and he knew he had a problem, his past was his problem, and he was the one who was sorry, he should've done a better job just listening to her or whatever it was she needed, but see, instead, part of him gave advice, probably because he'd been in AA for so long and he was a sponsor, as she knew, and people were always asking him for advice. So, he had that habit of making things about himself and giving advice, but he really didn't mean to try to convince her one way or the other. Tammy said that he was doing it again, was he aware he was doing it again? Fuck, Steve said. Yes, I see it, he said. I'm done now. I'm stopping.

The highway was becoming hillier, and the bunched trees, set back from the road, seemed like black malignant growths along what had once been a flat, clean skin of land.

The rain was slowly thickening on the windshield, changing to sleet, and the cars around her, she noticed, had decreased speed. She was in the right-hand lane, but was passing all the other cars, and she touched the brake gently, slowing the Jetta from eighty, to seventy-five, to seventy. She was surprised at how easily the outside world could disappear. In talking to Steve, she'd barely even seen it, she'd barely even remembered she was driving. Now though, with the sleet, she felt a danger that made her pay attention. She saw a sign showing upcoming cities, Salt Lake City in forty miles, and she knew the mountains were coming, leaving Idaho and entering Utah and Wyoming before moving on to the flatter plains of Nebraska and Iowa. Billboards along the highway, lit up in the sleeting rain, advertised for McDonald's, Shell, BBQ, Fireworks, Adult SuperStores, the Bible, the miscellaneous array of stupid American rural life that she knew she was a part of, that was her heritage.

Steve said that he wanted to know what she was going through and to please talk to him, he was ready to listen. That was his problem, he knew, that he was always wanting to fix things, and he said he would try not to do that, a thing he knew he sometimes did, and would just listen, if that's what she wanted. He said he knew that he could be a selfish asshole and he was sorry, but please explain to him so that he could understand why she wanted Jack to live with them. Not that she shouldn't want that, or that she should have to have some explanation, but just so, so that, he said, hesitating, confused now, stammering. I get it, Tammy said. Just hold on a minute. After thinking for a moment, she told Steve she thought it started from the very beginning: when she had April at eighteen, her parents insisted they live with them. The arrangement had slipped Tammy out of needing to be a mother. She became a worker, not a mother. Her father demanded it. There had been, Tammy said now, a strange relief: she'd been frightened of being a mother, and while she felt a joy she had never experienced when April was delivered safely into the world, the fact that she wouldn't be doing this alone and would, in fact, have to be a worker, could leave the house, would have help, even though it was her parents helping, was a sad relief. She felt guilty for feeling it, she said.

In the car, the sleet-rain increased its ticking onto her windshield. She thought of when her father told her that what was going to happen here was he and her mother were going to take care of April until Tammy saved enough to get a place of her own. She was the one who'd fucked up. He wasn't going to pay Tammy's way, she wasn't going to leech off him, but he'd help. Along with feeling secretly relieved, then ashamed at this relief, she'd also been surprised even at that offer of help. Her father wasn't a man who did such things. Suddenly the trees dropped away on her right and there was open farmland, fields broken apart by barbed-wire fencing, and in the distance, set in rolling hills, farm houses, barns, with hazy lights seeming to struggle against the sleet and rain. She told Steve that when she had April, her father had changed. She remembered seeing him in the kitchen, she said – making bacon, flipping bacon, his beard greying and long, lumberjack-like she'd thought – and holding April at the same time he was making breakfast, singing to her, and she remembered clearly seeing that the baby had aged him, caused him to grow older, and also softer. This helpless thing, smiling and happy, had opened him up. She witnessed less drinking and smoking from her father. There was a new No Smoking rule in the house. He'd implemented it one night over dinner, maybe two weeks into April being there with them, sleeping, or often not sleeping, in her crib, and Tammy's father, while passing a bowl of potatoes or something, said that there'd be no more smoking in the house, and that when it was cold, if you needed to smoke, then people could smoke in the garage, but no more in the house, and though Tammy'd wanted him to state the reason, wanted to ask him why he was saying this now, even though she basically knew the reason, she hadn't had to ask because he then said, It's not fair to the kid to smoke in here. She told Steve that she and her mother had sat quietly, a little stunned, and then finished their meals. She told Steve that maybe Jack could do something like that for them. She said that when she was with Jack, she also felt again the possibilities of what she herself could be. Like her father years ago, she wanted a change, was ready for a change, was tired of being in an ugly world that was only against her, that didn't allow her to care for anything, and here was a chance to care again. Just like when she witnessed her father hold April, sing to April, make faces at April, give April a bottle and let her sleep on his chest, she wanted that again with Jack. She knew part of it was selfish. But part of it was for Jack. She knew the right way to take care of him because she'd done it the wrong way for so long. Just like her father seemed like another person with the new baby, like he'd been taken aboard an alien craft, her father's self removed, and then the aliens had implanted some other being inside his skin, she wanted to feel new again, and she wanted the world to also feel new again.

Steve told her that he understood that, understood wanting all that. He said that there was nothing wrong with wanting that, but the problem was, it seemed to Steve, that that was just Tammy wanting Jack so that, you know, her life would be better. I feel like that's not taking into account certain practicalities, Steve said. Like clothing, shoes. Diarrhea. Sickness. Also, this isn't a baby. This is a four-year-old kid. He's not going to want to be sung to every night. Tammy said that she understood that, that she was just using an example – she didn't think Jack was going to magically change everything. What she was trying to say was that maybe a change in her life would be a good thing. Maybe having to care for someone else would do her good, in the same way it did her father good. That was all she was saying.

Driving in the sleeting rain and not actually seeing the rain, or hardly seeing it, only some mechanical part of her driving the car, she remembered how she drove to work, at nineteen, leaving April at home, and cried in the car, thinking of her father holding her baby. The image of her father holding her baby didn't move her because of its beauty. She remembered crying because she was witnessing a kindness that was never afforded her. A kindness that she didn't even know existed in him and was now easily available, as though he'd been saving it up for someone more worthy, and that more worthy person was her daughter, who Tammy had not even wanted. She spoke toward the phone in the stand near the digital display and told Steve that for the first two years of April's life, she worked two jobs, two shifts – one at UPS, and another bagging groceries. She eventually became a clerk at the grocery, then assistant manager. She saved money. She found the apartment. She didn't want to leave completely, but she didn't want to be in the house with her parents anymore. She couldn't deal with this new father anymore. A father who was finally a father, she told Steve. Something he had never really been to me. Her parents, her father, took care of April during the day, feeding her and clothing her and changing her diapers and wiping her spit up. Her mother knitted and read the Bible. Her father walked the baby through town in a stroller. When Tammy came home, exhausted in the evening, or in the morning, if she worked a nightshift at UPS, she'd hold April and the baby would cry and cry. She didn't feel like a mother, or a caregiver. She had loved April, of course, but she didn't feel the love was the right love. There was something in the way of it. She knew now it was her father, and she also knew, she explained, that the reason she was driving across the country was because if she didn't do something, there would be something even bigger in the way of her and Jack, that there already was something in the way, and she had to do her best to knock it down.

Steve said that he remembered some of this. Hadn't she told him at some point that her parents would not help with April when Tammy was in the house? That's right, Tammy said. Steve said that, see, he really did listen, and that she had told him some of these things. She rolled her eyes at the boy-like comment, but was also pleased. She didn't remember telling him and yet he was saying that he remembered her telling him that when she came home from a late shift, maybe it was one of the first times she'd come home late, after a shift at UPS, he thought, he wasn't sure, and the baby crying, spit-up on the baby's shirt, a wet or pooped diaper, and she tried to eat some dinner and hold the baby at the same time. Her mother had come up to her to take the child, possibly to change her, and soothe her while Tammy had a meal, and her father came into the room, standing in the kitchen. You told me, Steve said, that your father said something like, Not if she's in the house. We don't help if she's in the house. This is her responsibility. Your mother tried to argue against your father but he took the baby and handed her to you. I mean, I remember you telling me that and thinking that that was just awful. Tammy said that wasn't all. That there was more to it than that, that she had withheld this from Steve because she was afraid of what he'd think of her. Her father, while not helping when she was in the house, still corrected Tammy as he'd always done. No, he'd say about the way Tammy held April. Like this. Your forearm under her butt, that's how she likes it. Stable base. And if you bounce her, well, don't. Don't bounce her. She doesn't like being bounced. And he'd hold her and April would be soothed, contented, and this man, who had been no real father to her, was being, suddenly and unexpectedly, a good father. So many moments of turning away, gritting her teeth, wanting to scream, Tammy told Steve. She told him that she knew now, and probably knew years before, realized it years before, but felt it more now that April was gone, the shame of what she felt: that her father had made her envious of her daughter. Her father had made her resentful of her own baby because her baby got from her father the exact thing she knew she wanted. In this way, she told Steve, she'd come to understand that her father had made her fight herself, fight these feelings in herself, and she worked hard to keep herself aware that none of this was April's fault, and she worked hard as a worker, to keep her mind on the goal of getting out, which had become at the time a bigger goal than Tammy had ever had, maybe, she told Steve now, the only goal she had ever had, really, and filled with a sort of cosmic significance: leaving home meant being a mother, and she felt that same significance now: getting Jack meant correcting the mistakes she'd made with April. She said into the phone held neatly in the little stand near the Jetta's digital display screen, I want to be able to sit in the family room with Jack, to teach him things, now that I have time. We can do flashcards. We can learn to make models together. I know what Jack likes. I've been with him, taken him to movies, to playgrounds, on bike rides, I know how he likes to play during the afternoon and then sit and read in the evening. Nathaniel and Stefanie don't know these things. And I know what I failed to do with April, and what I failed to feel. Or what I felt that was wrong. That won't be there with Jack. I was hoping you'd want to do that, that you'd want to be a part of that for Jack. Steve said that that made sense, he didn't realize any of that, and he wanted to answer her, but let him think for a moment because this was not something he'd considered, how could he have. As he was saying it, as her car was ascending, moving steadily upward toward the mountains, the call dropped.

In the distance, through the rain, Tammy saw the lights of a police car and thought there'd been another accident, but as her car approached the flashing lights, she saw that it was the BMW that had passed her fifteen minutes ago, pulled over. Rain like a thin veil over the car and two men. The driver was being given a sobriety test, the cop shining a flashlight at the man. The beam of the flashlight made clear by the rain. The driver, in a long raincoat and dark clothes, had his hands extended, like a man walking a tightrope. The cop wore a bulky jacket over his uniform and a little plastic covering over his hat. All passed in a moment, gone, the blue lights behind her. Sleeting rain ticking on the car and windshield with more intensity that, along with the rushing sound of her car over the highway, created a white noise of weather and road. In the space of time in which she passed by the sobriety test Tammy unwillingly recalled the time her father forced her to drink a bottle of whisky. She'd come home late from a party when she was a sophomore, drunk, driving the car drunk, and when she arrived at her house, every light was on. She knew her father did it. So she'd know. So when she pulled the car into the driveway, she'd know. So she'd feel his anger before she even saw him. She turned off the car and got out and walked up the path to the front door and went in, quiet and head down, not wanting to meet his eyes. She didn't have to look up to know he was there in his recliner, sitting up in it. He had a beer belly then (which he lost a good deal of after April arrived), and always smelled of cigarettes. He told her to sit. When she didn't move, he'd said, Is there something about the word sit that you don't understand? She'd moved then, into a chair he had out, right in front of the coffee table. The bottle of whisky was on the coffee table, and he told her to pick it up. She didn't move. If you want to drink, he'd said. Pick it up and drink. She'd looked at the bottle and heard him say, Now. She picked it up and drank. Then put it down. He reached across the table, took a swig, and put the bottle back down. There were small beads of liquid in his beard, like there often were when he drank anything, something that bothered Tammy, like why couldn't he drink in the way everyone drank and not get it on his face. Now you, he said. They finished the bottle like that and when she was vomiting in the backyard, on her hands and knees she was so drunk, the frozen ground and grass hard and cold beneath her knees and hands, she heard his calm lecture: If this is what you want, that's fine with me. But I want you to know what this really is. This is what it is. You will turn into this person, on hands and knees. Or you'll turn into what I am – I drank half that bottle and feel nothing. I don't feel a thing. And that I don't feel a thing is disgusting, but what you're doing is even more disgusting, and you should feel disgusted by it. It was a discipline beyond discipline, conveying her toward her own eventual meanness, she thought. And yet, even at the time, very drunk and vomiting what she'd had for dinner that night, a cheesesteak and French fries – she could see undigested chunks of bread and fries, thinking she'd never eat a cheesesteak again – even at that moment, repulsed at her father and herself, she detected a message of love in what he was doing: he didn't want her to be like him. It worked, she thought, driving through the sleeting rain. She never drank again. She could still very clearly remember the cold ground of the backyard, frozen and hurting her knees, and the smell of alcohol and vomit and also of cold, clean air. It was so strange, that deeply unpleasant, repulsive smell mixed with that crispness of cold pine and snow, as though even the gross things in life – one's body and garbage and the smell of skunk or a dead dog on the road – had their own pristine quality, something beyond good and bad, all just what it was. She experienced that basic banality years later when April was in the world, pooping ridiculous green slime or runny peanut butter-looking liquid, and while unpleasant, Tammy didn't care, wasn't repulsed, could see such things only as another example of something she should be grateful for, which was weird. Of course then when she saw a disgusting or ugly person, she'd forget all this and feel repulsed, but she tried to remember April as a baby, pooping everywhere, out the top of diapers, onto shirts, onto Tammy, and when older, vomiting on Tammy when she ate too quickly, and when out in the world, feeling repulsed at some ugly person, she'd check herself momentarily, and try not to be like her father, try not to see things, supposedly ugly things, as ugly, to know that there was a person there. Uglier were the pretty ones, the Facebook perfect ones, the ones who didn't acknowledge their animalness, Tammy thought now. The supposed disgusting things were not what was unpleasant, what was unpleasant was other people, their selves, what they thought, their self-righteousness and stupidity, not their bodies. Her father never saw that, but she did. She remembered feeling years later – when her parents were taking care of April while she worked, then not taking care of April when she entered the house again – that April would never know these things about her father, never know his cruelties. Part of her was grateful for that. Part of her was grateful to her father, she thought driving now in the rain, but another part of her was envious and resentful and that part of herself she hated. She hated that she was resentful that her father hadn't thought to treat her, his own daughter, any better, which in turn translated into Tammy being envious of April, her daughter, whose life, she had immediately seen at the time – like the world had stamped its approval on it and forlornly handed the certificate to Tammy for safekeeping – would be easier than her own. She wanted her own life to be easy, she remembered thinking, to be like this car through the rain, effortlessly passing through the unpleasantness of other people and the world, but it was not like that, so she worked hard those two years while living with her parents, not really being a mother to April, in order to get out and get to some easier place in her life. She might not get to be young again, but she could at least be a mother to April. She worked hard and was proud of that, she thought in the car without feeling as though she was in a car, or anywhere at all, and after two years, she'd made enough and left. She remembered thinking that she wouldn't be indebted to them, to her father, and she most especially wouldn't watch this man give to her daughter what he never gave to her.

A car cut her off even though she was in the right-hand lane, and she felt a heat in her chest. Fucker, she said. The highway suddenly materialized again, her car moving swiftly, and she felt a sort of danger: she hadn't even been seeing the road and in its place she'd been freely thinking about April, of her father, though she hadn't wanted to be, as though something in her was preparing her for motherhood again. As though something in her was reminding her of mistakes so that she wouldn't make them with Jack. Like she had a shock collar on and each time she wanted to venture into the world freely, the thing went off, reminding her that she wasn't free. And yet, she knew, there was no shock collar: it was just her. It was just herself reminding herself, which made Tammy want to shout at this other Tammy, this annoying double of her: shut the fuck up. She knew that nothing she did could undo what she'd done. Her life was saturated with what she'd done. Jack was the only way to correct any of it. She saw images of him in bed, reading or singing him to sleep, images of him at the dinner table with Steve, Steve cutting his food into small bites, images of the boy on a rope swing once they found a little house, some place with a yard for the boy, images of him when she had to discipline him, but not in the way she did with April, not the shouting and arguing she did with April, a more con- trolled, motherly version of herself, and then, when the boy got older, images of him looking through her records, lis- tening to old music, classic rock and Motown and jazz and her telling him the meaning of these songs to her, images of Jack growing into a young man, maybe he'd forgo college and join the Navy, maybe he'd become a pilot, images of him holding her hand as they walked across the street to the grocery store, images of her younger self once again a mother, but this time focused and patient and understand- ing and wise, and then these images reduced themselves to a single image, as though the images of Jack growing into a man were suddenly rewound into just Jack as she knew him now. A four-year-old boy, alone in his bedroom. His aunt and uncle with him, but April and Nicholas gone, his mother and father gone. She suddenly recalled that the only infor- mation she knew had come from a very brief phone call from Nathaniel when he'd said that Jack was okay, just sleeping a lot, and thinking of this, she began to cry. A moment after this, her phone buzzed with a call from Steve, and she saw that again she had service. She took several deep breaths, composed herself, though she didn't exactly know why, why she'd want to hide the fact of her crying from Steve, but she did, and she hit the green glowing button to answer her phone.

Before he could say anything Tammy told him that he was right, that she shouldn't be driving there, that she shouldn't be doing this. She told Steve that he was right. She was making this about herself. Instead of thinking about Jack, she was thinking about her past, she was thinking about how things had been hard for her, about the fact that she didn't want to be pregnant at eighteen and had missed out on so many things, and she thought that wanting to correct the mistakes she made wasn't a bad thing to want, and she thought that wanting to be a better version of herself wasn't bad either, but wanting to use Jack to do it was. It was no reason for the boy to live with her, no reason for her to be the guardian, she said. Streetlamps lit the highway in cones of light. Highway signs were beginning to crust over in sleet. Tammy saw more billboards for an upcoming exit and told Steve that there were gas stations and fast food places coming up and she was going to stop rather than keep driving because the sleet was getting intense. Steve told her to hold on a minute, don't do that yet, just slow down, drive safely, because he wanted to tell her that she had been right earlier. He hadn't been just trying to make her focus on the grieving process, focus on April, or whatever he'd said before. *She* had been right. He hadn't wanted her to go get Jack. All he'd really been doing this whole time was waiting to convince her that her wanting to take care of Jack was all caused by Tammy's grief-stricken state, and then once he'd done that, he was going to try to convince her that he really did want Jack to come live with them, it was just that he didn't think they'd be able to do it. He said he was going to say that they were too busy, that they didn't live in a good area, that Jack would think they were too old, he was going to say that he himself thought they were both too old, he was going to say that neither of them had savings or anything to put into a college fund for Jack, he was going to point out that he was diabetic, and while generally healthy, this wasn't ideal, and Tammy too had had her own health problems. Steve said that he actually had more than this, though he couldn't remember it all right now, and he was planning on subtly bringing each of these things up, but what had changed his mind was how Tammy'd spoken about her own father and April, and he got it. He really did get it. And while Tammy was now saying she felt she was selfish, he wanted to tell her that he didn't think that. Tammy hung up the phone. She wanted to pick it up and throw it out the window, but knew that such a childish act would be counter-productive. She saw the exit approaching, the glowing lights of gas stations and fast food places, the signs on enormous poles like canes for giants, towering above the mountainous land, the trees, her car, making her feel small. A blinking cell phone tower beaconed her toward the exit and she took it. She took the off-ramp to the right, not caring which place she went to, and finally pulling into a place called Dina's Country Diner rather than one of the fast food places.

She parked and got out, jogged to the front and inside. There was a sign next to the hostess stand asking her to seat herself and she took a booth that overlooked the road, and in the distance, the highway, the mountains, the sleet and rain. On the ground in the grass, the sleet gathered, a speckled whiteness on the grass, but nothing was accumulating on the roads. Her phone buzzed in her pocket with a call she knew was from Steve, and she pushed the button on top of the phone to stop its buzzing. She was no longer angry. Well, she was, she thought, but she wasn't. What else could she expect from him? Of course he wanted what he wanted, just as she wanted what she wanted, and of course both of them were going to try to get it despite the other. That was how things were. The problem now was that she didn't even know what she wanted. She didn't know now if Steve had manipulated her into somehow believing that she shouldn't go get Jack or if she had come to that on her own, and now, in trying to decide if she'd decided to not get Jack, in trying to decide if she was acting selfishly in wanting to bring him to live with her, in wanting to raise him, in trying to decide if she was somehow using Jack as a replacement for April and was not, as Steve had mentioned, properly mourning April, she couldn't see clearly where she had been manipulated and what she really felt. This felt like a new suffering, a sicker kind: her own confusion at what to feel and how to feel it, her own confusion at what was real and what wasn't, and yet, she wasn't mad at Steve so much as disappointed by him, and she wasn't mad at him because she herself had felt herself manipulating him, maybe not consciously, but she wanted him to feel guilty and ashamed by his initial response to her, and she knew she'd formed her responses to him in a way that she hoped would make him feel that way, and that itself, she knew, was a shameful thing.

A waitress, Tammy's age, overweight, with almost grey skin and what appeared to be no demeanor, as though life had failed to give her a personality, came and asked what she wanted. Tammy said she didn't have a menu. The woman didn't sigh or complain at this. She just walked to the hostess stand, grabbed a menu, handed it to Tammy, and said she'd be back in a minute. Tammy looked at the menu, not really hungry, and quickly decided on a bowl of soup and coffee. She glanced around the restaurant, which also had a lunch counter. A man, who Tammy believed must be a truck driver, sat there reading a newspaper. For a moment she felt she was living twenty years in the past. He had reading glasses on and was alternately peering over them or reading through them. When the waitress returned, Tammy ordered and the waitress said, Don't order the soup. Tammy almost asked why not, and then figured it wasn't worth it, and then said, What should I order on a night like this then? The woman looked out the windows, her eyes widening, as though seeing for the first time, in surprise, that there was a world beyond the diner. Brisket sandwich, she said. She took the menu back and said she'd be back with Tammy's coffee presently. The word presently surprised Tammy, like it was some kind of joke, some word this woman had heard in a Bond movie and was trying out in her own life. It was also evidence, just barely, of some kind of personality behind the tired, grey, dope-eyed face. Tammy felt again the phone in her pocket and this time she pulled it out and turned it off entirely. She tossed it on the table, where for a moment, the sound of the phone hitting the tabletop seemed the only sound in the restaurant. It made Tammy glance up, to see who was looking at her, and three booths away, a young man, eating soup and grilled cheese, was looking at her, then away. Then he looked up again, put his spoon down, and said, Did she tell you not to get the soup? The man had a soft, boyish face, freckled, and red hair that was cropped very short. He wore a flannel shirt. Tammy told him the waitress did say that. I wonder why I didn't get that advice, he said. Tammy shook her head and after a moment, the man said, It doesn't taste bad. I just hope they haven't done anything to it. The person, she realized, was the sort of person who wanted to talk, who could not, when around other people, observe silence. I'm Caleb, he said. Do you mind if I just. He got up, picked up his plate of soup and sandwich, put it in the booth next to hers, then went back, and grabbed his Coke, and sat down. Tammy looked at him and his face, which three booths away looked like a man's face, but, closer now, actually appeared to be a boy's. He was twenty, she thought, couldn't be more. He said, If I'm intruding, I can go back, and she shook her head. You shouldn't throw your phone like that, he said. That's a good way to crack the screen. Even the back of it. I know it's in one of those safety cases, but it could crack the back of it too. Tammy thanked him and said she'd be more careful and he said that sometimes old people didn't know exactly how to treat the new phones. His own mother had once thrown one across the room when she was in an argument with his father and she had to drop nearly two hundred bucks to get another and have all her data transferred. I get how phones work, Tammy said, though thank you for noting how old I am. The boy-like man held his hands up and said he was sorry, he didn't mean it like that. He ate, dipping the grilled cheese in the soup, just as Tammy imagined Jack doing in her kitchen. For a moment, she saw the young man as Jack, a grown-up Jack, and wondered what this boy's life had possibly been like. After a moment, Caleb asked where she was headed and Tammy hesitated, considered saying, To bury my daughter, or just, To a funeral, though there wasn't going to be a funeral, but those things sounded too dramatic, and so she said that she was going to see her daughter and grandchild. The man-boy said that it wasn't a great night to be driving alone and then asked if maybe her husband was out in the car and rather than take it as an offensive, overly intrusive question, Tammy said she was divorced and liked driving at night. I like that, the boy said, who seemed more like a boy every passing moment. You don't need a big man to do your work. That's how it ought to be. He told her that that wasn't the way his father saw things for sure, and that actually, he came from a broken home, too, just like Tammy and her daughter. He said that his father, whenever they went on a trip, insisted on doing all the driving, and when there was work to be done around the house, his father did it. Fixed the toilet, the roof, built an addition when his brother came along, never made his mom lift a finger, except for the cooking and laundry. He was glad things were changing, he told her, because the other thing his father didn't let his mother do was talk. He remembered plenty of nights she got a lick to the face for even expressing an opinion. She eventually was done with it all, he said. I haven't seen her for nearly two years, and I'm happy for it, he said. It must mean she found something better. He told her that there was no way he could change anything between his parents and he didn't want to, and there was no way to change his view growing up that his father was like a kind of god, because to him and his brothers, and to his mother, he was, but he could see now that that was all basically bullshit and that his mother figured it out. He told her that he still had to check himself on certain things and that sometimes he got confused, like for instance once he was on a date with a girl and he'd not held the door open for her, he did it on purpose, he thought that she'd probably want to do that herself, in fact, his friends at the community college told him as much, that girls now didn't want to be herded around like cows was the exact words they used, and so he didn't order her drinks at the bar, and he didn't make any suggestions about food and especially didn't order for her, and then later in the night, when they were finishing the date, and he was, he admitted, a little bit drunk, not drunk, buzzed, you know, a lot of beers over several hours, a couple shots, well then we went to my car and I just wasn't thinking and I opened the passenger door for her. Right when I did it, I remembered, and thought, damn, messed that one up, but that's when she said, Looks like it takes you getting drunk to become a gentleman. The boy laughed to himself and glanced up to see if Tammy was smiling and she was, a little, and she nodded at him to indicate she understood. She wondered where this boy grew up – his voice had a rural, almost Southern quality, though they were nowhere near the South, and she pictured his friends at the community college as being first-generation college kids, coming from farm families, blue-collar families, and the boy himself looked like he wasn't a stranger to hard work. He was endearing. Here he was, trying to be some kind of modern man in a world that wasn't sure if that was what it wanted, and he was getting it confused. Tammy herself got it confused.

The waitress brought her food. Tammy looked at the sandwich, a dry roll between which were slabs of meat, French fries on the side. She pushed it away and took the coffee, put cream and sugar in, stirred with a fork. She told the boy that she had a difficult father as well, but she told him the difference between her and him was that she was now a difficult mother. The boy asked if she and her daughter didn't get along, and Tammy said that was one version of the story. She told him that she sometimes got caught up in telling herself this story about her and April – your daughter, he said, and Tammy nodded – and about how there was something dividing them. Stop telling yourself this story, she said she tried to tell herself, but it was difficult, when she'd been telling it to herself for so long. She'd been driving to visit her daughter and she'd been doing it again, she said, telling herself the story, about how they were going to argue, not see eye to eye, not feel like mother and daughter, not agree about what was best for Jack. The boy nodded knowingly and then finished his grilled cheese in three successive dip-bites and said, I think that's what my mom figured out. That she was in this other person's story and she wasn't going to do it anymore, she had her own to make up.

Tammy thought that while she was lying, there was a way what she was saying was true somehow, that there was a story she was telling herself and it was one she couldn't escape: the fact that she hadn't been a mother to her daughter for those first two years was a story, was the beginning of the story about a battle between her and April that lasted for as long as April was alive, that was still going on, even though April was gone, and the fact that they'd grown closer when April'd finally left home, sort of became friends, she thought, and then weren't anymore, was also a story. It was not the full truth, somehow, and was not something she could ever figure out. So why think about it, why try to figure it out? It was like people talking about movies or television shows incessantly online. In two weeks none of these people would remember the shows or their neat little theories and they'd be on to the next thing. That was the best way to be. Move on. Next thing, and try to make it better than the last thing. That's a thing she'd tried to teach April. Move on. Next thing, better thing. That's what she had imagined she was going to do with Jack now, though even that might be wrong. Just like leaving her parents' house with April, to get to something better, you had to make the next thing better. The world didn't help you. The world was something you had to try to wrestle into place like wrestling a sibling into submission. So that you could impose your story. The story you wanted. Just like this boy's mother did. Some people couldn't do it. She, for instance, for most of her life, hadn't been able to. It was exactly what her own life lacked, knowing what to wrestle and when. But now, this thing with Jack, this was the thing she knew she had to fight for. Still, her conviction that this was the right thing, both for her and Jack, she was now doubting.

The boy in the booth seemed to follow her eyes, through the windows and out to the parking lot. He asked which one was hers, nodding at the cars. It was a question asked in order to go on talking and she didn't necessarily want to do that, but she answered him anyway.

Tammy told him that she was driving that Jetta out there in the parking lot. The boy looked out at the car, now covered in a layer of sleet. She didn't tell him she usually drove an old Jeep Cherokee, a car that April had called the White Trash Mobile when she was in high school, but she'd say it in a way that showed she liked the car. Recently though, whenever Tammy picked her up at the airport in the last few years April'd say that Tammy needed to get a new car. Tammy would ask if she didn't like the White Trash Mobile anymore, and April'd shake her head – once their joke, now something she could tell April was ashamed of. Tammy had called April after she'd first married Nicholas and said, So what does the husband think of marrying into a white trash family? April had asked her not to say that, that that's not what she was, not what their family was, and not what Nicholas thought. Tammy told April that she knew what April thought of her, she knew what April thought of where she came from. I know why he's taking you to some isolated place in the mountains, away from our side of the family, Tammy had said. April'd say to Tammy that Tammy was one of the smartest people she knew, she just hadn't refined that intelligence, and she should take some classes, and they'd argue and argue on the phone, and hang up angry and hating each other. Tammy thought that part of the problem between her and April was that both of them forgot the good times. There were years in the small apartment they first lived in, after leaving her parents' house, that she often wanted to go back to. That small place, almost no decorations, a few pots and pans and plates and bowls in the cupboards. Dinner was chili mac or sloppy joes or just popcorn. They didn't have much money, but they were together. Tammy was the mother and April was her daughter. And Tammy was finally on her own, away from her family. Her family was only twenty minutes away, but she was still gone from them. She had her own family. April and her were now a family, and she could make what she wanted of it. She could construct a new story. They could. They did. There was a kind of effortlessness to their days, an easy freedom. Tammy drove April to daycare. They sang songs on the way. She picked her up in the evening and they practiced rhymes. She made them dinner, and they played games – Memory and I Spy, and then when she was a little older, six, seven, eight, they sang Creedence Clearwater songs, Neil Young, Carole King, Stevie Wonder. Tammy was educating April, in her own way, her own unique way. Rhyming games turned into Tammy giving April a verse to remember every day at preschool or kindergarten. Then they'd practice the verse on the way home. When they got home, April put the record on in the family room and they sang together while Tammy made a taco kit dinner or warmed up half a rotisserie chicken and potatoes. They did math, flash cards, adding and subtraction. Tammy felt some desire to go back to school, to become a teacher. She felt she was doing well. She felt like a mother and a teacher. She checked her annoyance in those years with the control of a good Samaritan checking on the flaws of the citizenry, governing herself through herself. When April broke something or spilled something, and Tammy felt annoyance, she recalled her father, and in this way, she didn't let him in their apartment. Her parents, her father in particular, they saw on holidays, and Tammy met her parents on the holidays with the same carefreeness she and April met the world with:

they didn't need anyone else, they didn't need the world, it was just them, and this was a nice stop, thank you for the meal, but soon they'd be gone, gone, gone, and no rules about how to behave in the house, where to eat, when to turn on the TV, how loud, no shoes inside, the heater not above sixty-seven degrees, coats hung here, that was her father's chair, that her mother's, none of these little rules had anything to do with her and April. They observed them and then left them behind, free. Tammy felt that she conveyed to her father by her very actions and living: I am finally out, away from you, who for so long kept me from some happiness. April was hers. She was April's. They were for each other, like the song. She tried to convey this to her father, indirectly, but it didn't touch him. Or she couldn't tell if it touched him. These holiday visits allowed her to keep her parents, and her father in particular, at a safe distance, and yet, eventually, as if sensing Tammy's plan, her father began just dropping by to see April. And when her father was around April, he was this happy and kind man that Tammy didn't recognize. Tammy couldn't believe her father's way around April. Holding her hand, taking her on walks, kicking the soccer ball with her. On her father's visits to her apartment, he'd come into the place as though he owned it, as though there had never been any problems between him and Tammy, as though he didn't know, didn't realize, that Tammy was purposefully keeping herself and April away from him, and he'd say she needed pictures or paintings up or more lamps and that he could buy some of these things if she wanted, which she always declined. He'd also ask how Tammy was, how her job as a dental assistant was going, if she thought she'd go back to school, which he thought might be a good idea, which he thought might be good for April, for getting April a better life, and when Tammy told him it wasn't on her mind at all, she didn't want to be in school ever again, she liked the job, she made good money, she was even saving a little money, he told her he was glad she was doing well and knew she would be. But see, she just had to fuck up first. He had to make her see that she was fucking up, so that she could know how to avoid it. Still, she could always be doing better. Things could be better if she tried harder, but this was good for now, pretty good. In these moments, she would recall images of him shaking his head at her, yanking her dog out of the house once when the dog had peed on a rug, putting a stake in the yard, tying the dog to it, never letting him inside again, and telling a seven-year-old Tammy that she'd lost the privilege of a dog. Now he was giving her backhanded compliments about her work and her parenting. But compliments nonetheless. She was pulled toward and away from him, and this very pulling she felt encroach on her life, cause some hidden tension. She'd wanted to tell him that there was no need to come by, but she didn't want to fight with him either, or she didn't want April to see her fighting him, since April had completely endeared herself to him: she saw the good grandpa! The fun grandpa! The funny and loving grandpa! So Tammy had no choice, like she had no choice in so many things: she let him in, let him be this person she didn't know. She sometimes imagined subtle ways of pulling out his anger, to show April, so that she'd also see the meanness, the calm and almost effortless cruelty, the distance, his man's mind. But she didn't let herself do that, she told the boy. That would've been unfair to

April. If this was what he was now, then she'd accept it. April wouldn't know, her father wouldn't know, but Tammy knew: she accepted, forgave. In those moments, she'd look at April and know that April wouldn't know the hardship that Tammy knew, wouldn't know the cruelty, wouldn't really know this man, and in her acceptance and forgiveness of her father, she was both happy for her daughter and envious. Jealous, really. Jealous again that she saw in her father now the father she'd never had. She'd hated the return of this feeling she thought she'd escaped. Her father conjured it in her so easily, and she worked hard to hide it from April, from her father, and from herself. From herself, too, she said. She didn't want to look at it and she sometimes thought that in not looking, she made it worse. It was the one thorn in those good years with April, the one thing she wanted to wipe from her experience but couldn't. She imagined that if she could let it – her father, her jealousy, her anger – sink from her mind, like a ship sinking on the horizon, she could feel that everything was right, that her life with April in the apartment was complete, but she felt it always there, like the annoying hangnail of her well-being.

Tammy watched the boy finish his soda and seem to accept that she didn't want to talk with him. In case he made another attempt, she picked up her phone and turned it back on and saw several texts from Steve. Each text was a version of an apology, with one text asking her to call him back, and another saying that he'd wait up until she called him back and that she should call him back, or not, whenever she felt like it, if she felt like it at all, and he'd understand either way, and was sorry for not being more up front with her. When she looked up, the boy was standing over his booth, laying down money on top of the tab. He told her good luck and then said that he had a feeling that things would work out in the best way possible for her and her daughter and then he smiled at her and went out to the parking lot. Through the windows of the diner, she watched him get into a pickup truck, reverse the truck, and then drive out onto the road. She imagined it was Jack's truck, that Jack had bought it cheap and basically broken down at a local used-car dealership, and then had fixed it up himself and got it running again, and that Tammy had taught him the lesson of working for the things you wanted and needed because no one else was going to help you out.

After finishing her coffee and eating a few French fries, she paid her bill, left a large tip, and then went out to her car without knowing what to do. The sleet had turned back to rain and was lessening, and before she got in the rental, she surveyed the diner, the parking lot, the road leading to the highway, and in the distance, cutting between what Tammy now could see was a forest, the sweep of cars on the highway, taillights going one way, headlights moving another. Something about the stillness of the forest against the constant motion of the cars momentarily disoriented her. The forest seemed to emphasize the futility of the travelers in the cars, as though wherever any of them were going was not a final destination, but just another place that they wouldn't find home. She got in the car and pulled out, got on the road that connected to the highway, and continued driving toward Jack. Her car, among other cars and trucks and SUVs and semis, was soon up on the mountain road, on a flat, elevated stretch of highway, which widened to three lanes. She felt that being in her car on this cold night was the proper expression of how things were. If she looked to her right or left, as she passed a car or as a car passed her, she might see the face of the driver, might see a young man, an old woman like her, or she might see a husband and wife, children in the back of an SUV watching some cartoon. She liked that, even in separate cars, when she looked, people could feel it, and they'd look, they'd see her in her car, alone, separate, being conveyed to wherever. All were going to different destinations, all alone, like the boy she'd met in the diner. That was why trains were a lie, why the car, that American invention, was the proper expression of how things really were: separate and alone, and cars drew the division. I see you, but I'm not with you. We're, none of us, going to the same place – that was what the car represented. Isolation and separateness, in the same way the trees were separate from the grass, the highway was separate from the mountains, the mountains were separate from the sea, and human life, cities, separate from nature, and you had to either fight your way through all these things that had nothing to do with you or let people pass. A car merged into her lane like some kind of symbolic action she couldn't quite decode, though she gestured at the car as evidence of what she was thinking. For a moment, the rain and sleet seemed to stop, then a gust of wind brought down more. She hadn't noticed it until now, but there were pine trees now along the road, rather than the deciduous trees she'd been seeing. The icy rain gave the pines a white sheen. Her phone lit up, and she saw another call from Steve. She decided to answer and told him she was in mountains. She glanced to her left – toward where? the west? she didn't know – and saw the drop-off of a cliff, the valley below populated with the tiny lights of so many separate lives, lives that would never really know one another, lives distant as galaxies, separated by light years. Steve asked how she was doing. In front of her car, in the right-hand lane, was a semi, and on the left another semi came up beside her and boxed her in. She told him that she was fine, though there was too much time to be thinking, and she'd just gotten boxed in by a couple of semis so she had that to deal with. He asked what she was thinking about and she said, What I'm thinking is what are you going to say now. What are you going to say to try to convince me to not get Jack. Are you going to say that now you're on my side and you think that I should do this, and hope, some-how, by saying that, that I'll become reasonable and think that he shouldn't live with us? Steve said that he wasn't going to say anything like that, and that yes, maybe he hadn't been fully honest with her at first, though he'd been at least partially honest. He did think, for instance, that she needed to be dealing with her sadness about April, he thought that was important, but he was wrong in using that to keep her from the idea of wanting to get Jack. If she thought Jack should live with them, then he shouldn't stop that, and not only that, he wanted to say that he didn't think she was being selfish, that wasn't fair of him, and he was sorry for saying that, but she did really need to think about how their life would change, and while he had planned to say certain things about how time would change for them and how their jobs would make raising Jack difficult and that their age would make it difficult, and while he was going to say these things to sway her, to try to make her see that maybe they weren't the right guardians for Jack, now he didn't want to sway her, but he did want her to think about these things because these things were worth thinking about, worth considering, he said. Tammy asked him if he thought that she'd not thought about these things. He was quiet, and she continued by saying that if he didn't think she'd thought about these things, then he must also think she was stupid. Did he think she was stupid? He mumbled a quiet no and she said that was good because while they hadn't been together very long, she was beginning to think, based on the last few days, that he thought she was stupid, and she'd have to kick his ass out if that was the case. She explained that she didn't like treating him like a child right now, but she sort of figured that's what he deserved because he'd thrown everything she was doing into doubt and he had, she realized now, from the beginning, for completely selfish reasons. It made her wonder if he was only with her because he could maintain the lifestyle he wanted, he could basically be single, he could go out to bars, he could go to his job, he could hang out with his friends, and he got to come home to a roommate, sometimes a date-mate, sometimes a sex mate, someone who occasionally made dinner and did his laundry, she was beginning to wonder if everything he did wasn't for some selfish reason. Hold on, hold on, he said, that wasn't fair. It wasn't fair to take this one example and to then turn it into something bigger. He knew he was selfish, he was well aware, and sometimes he was selfish and he wasn't even aware he was doing it, and he was sorry for both things, for when he knew it and for when he didn't, but he wanted her to know, right now, that he was done, he wanted her to do what she thought she should do concerning Jack, and if that meant the boy living with them, then that was okay with him, no, it was more than okay, he'd support her and he'd help raise the kid to the best of his abilities, though she knew he'd never had children and never really had any intention of having children, but still, he'd do the best he could.

Behind her, another car's headlights appeared, so that she was nearly completely boxed in. When the semi to her left didn't change lanes for some time, she pushed the gas and tried to make the semi in front of her change lanes faster, but it stayed steady, in the same way the semi on her left held his speed. She felt a tightness in her chest, a clenching of her shoulders. The semi in the left-hand lane, which seemed to have been ready to pass the truck in front of her, now was riding right along next to her, and she looked in her rearview and saw headlights were still only in the distance, so she slowed, let the semi to her left pass by, and then got behind him, signaled into the far left lane, and went around both, feeling herself breathing again. She had a brief image of cutting back into the center lane, but not moving ahead of the semi far enough, changing lanes without looking in her rearview, and the back of her car clipping the front of the semi, sending them both into a near-fatal slide toward the guardrail, where they would both crash, the semi flipping and crushing her car. While he was talking, Tammy thought of Steve at home, Steve on the road for days at a time for UPS, how she was often alone in their apartment, how when he was home they sat together and watched television, ate in front of the television. She tried to insert Jack into this picture, like a hologram of the boy superimposed over images of their life. Trying to think of Jack with them made her aware that her own life was barely even there. She was a ghost in the house, looking for something to eat, staring in the fridge, the cupboards, wanting to be somewhere else. When Steve fell asleep early, which he often did after a long couple days on the road, or if he was gone, she sometimes drove through the nice neighborhood nearby late at night, not able to sleep. So many nights she didn't sleep, her mind going and going, though thinking about nothing in particular: work the next day, something April said on the phone, her father's failing health. She'd get up on those nights and drive, and she wondered, Would she take Jack with her on one of these drives if the boy couldn't sleep in the new house? She'd drive into the neighborhoods with two-story houses, three and four bedrooms. Garages. Lawns and trees. Pools in the backyards. The houses lit by landscape lights. A second-story window with a light on. She saw herself driving slowly so she could see the people inside, who were almost always white. She sometimes saw glimpses of bodies. A man, a woman, a child. She hated them a little. For getting what they wanted. For the world giving it to them. Maybe Jack would be in her passenger seat and when he was older, she'd tell him that these people didn't have to work for what they had, and that it was better to have nothing than to have things you didn't deserve and hadn't earned. What had these people done, she sometimes wondered? What weird portal opened in their existence, like an alien door presented to them by some sorcerer, that led them to easeful lives? Of course, they were also the worst consumers and materialistic people in existence, but still, they had something she had lacked, and they'd found a way to it: ease and comfort.

She told Steve that he didn't even understand what this was all about. What this really was about was that Jack needed someone who could devote their life to him, and the other family members, they had full lives. She didn't. She and Steve didn't. Their life was barely there, so unreal compared to these other lives, as though it existed in black and white: an apartment, an old car, an unsalaried job, the scarcest of healthcare, no retirement. She told Steve that they talked a little over dinner, a television show, and there wasn't a lack of communication, there wasn't miscommunication, there wasn't wondering what was going on with Steve, there wasn't the unknowability of this other person. There was just another person there. Just Steve. Just Tammy. She knew what he was, he knew what she was. There was nothing to talk about, there was no communication that needed to occur, their life was barely there. At some point, there was barely even loneliness, she told him. There was the empty space – like a clearly missing book on the shelf of life – where their life should have gone, and with Jack, there'd be a purpose again.

Ahead, brake lights lit up and dimmed in the night, lit up again. Traffic slowing as the flat elevated highway gave way to another downward slope. Tammy thought that the last time there'd been a clear purpose in her life was at another point in her life, when she had felt the need to save April. Now she felt the need to save Jack, but years ago she'd done something similar. Except then it had been her fault. She remembered that in the apartment with April, when April was finally older, eight or nine, Tammy had begun to feel some unease. She felt like a mother, but she also felt a little starved for adult communication. It'd been years since she'd even thought of dating, but there was another dental assistant at work, a man. She'd thought it was time. She told the male dental assistant (which was what she called him since she'd known him) to take her for drinks, a burger. He did, but he also didn't last long: when she brought him home the first time to meet April, he'd almost been shocked the kid was real. At work, she'd told him she had April, and he seemed fine with it. Then he was presented with the reality, an actual child. The reality of this child put him off, and she had seen, suddenly, how hard getting what she wanted was going to be. In addition to this, whenever Tammy went out, April moped a little. When Tammy began seeing other men from the restaurant-slash-bar she went to after work, April gave the guys a hard time. She quizzed them on US history, multiplication, their intentions, and, most pryingly, their families: How many girlfriends have you had in the last year? Do you have parents who are still together? How old are your siblings and what do they do now? The guys took it as good fun, but April also thwarted their efforts. She was a force. Tammy knew the men thought she was a handful. So when things seemed to consistently not work out (almost every man claiming that they'd had a lot of fun with Tammy, but hey, they just weren't in the dad business), Tammy then resented April for it. She found one guy who delivered Fedex to their neighborhood and house, when April was about to be in high school. He had a beard and long, brown hair. He wore flannels. He worked every day, and April'd finally sort of given up on interrogations. She actually seemed to like him. They dated for several months. He spent the night. He watched movies with them, popped popcorn, made meals. But it didn't work out, as so many things in her life didn't, and it was no one's fault, really, if she honestly considered it, no one's fault at all, just a thing that occurred in the circumstances of her life, which were, as they had always been, not exactly right. Just not right enough. Not wrong, entirely, but not right, either. One night, after Tammy went to bed but he and April stayed up to finish some horror movie, Tammy woke and went to the kitchen for water and she found the Fedex man massaging April. That ended that and when Tammy discussed this with April, asking why she'd let him do that, April told her that it wasn't the first time, that he did it at least once a week and that he had told April that if she told Tammy that she wouldn't understand. Tammy had called the guy then, told him that she was filing a report and he would be arrested tomorrow, so be ready, but she never did it. Instead, she moved them away, to a different part of the city, changed phone numbers, gave them a new start, she'd finally had the means to do it, though all April'd said was that she'd moved her away from her school and friends, beginning the divide between them that would eventually carry April away to North Carolina. April hadn't appreciated Tammy, and neither would Jack, Tammy knew, but in time he might, and anyway, she thought, Jack's appreciation or gratitude wasn't necessary. He was too little for it. He just needed a safe space, and that was what Tammy was going to provide.

Steve was saying that he hadn't realized Tammy believed their life was so boring, and that he was glad to be at a steady and settled place in his life. He liked eating dinner and watching television together. What was wrong with that? He told Tammy he sometimes wondered if she felt this way because she didn't get to have a proper youth. He sometimes wondered if she wouldn't resent so much, or take so much for granted, if she'd been granted some wildness. Then maybe she could appreciate quiet things, simple things, like he did. Her car slowed to a stop, a winding trail of cars down the mountain. She said she didn't think it was that. She wasn't resentful. She just wanted something that was hers, and she'd messed that up with April. She told Steve that if Nathaniel and Stefanie took Jack into their lives, she'd never see him, and she'd never get the opportunity to correct some of the mistakes she'd made, along with April's own mistakes with Jack. I don't know, Steve said. I understand, but I don't know.

Her car was coming out of the mountains, and she could see the city she was approaching, which appeared to be huddled around a river. She told Steve that he didn't know because he never had a kid. He never had a girl who at seventeen had stolen his car. He'd never had a son say, I can't wait to get away from you. He'd never had a child, maybe fifteen, try to get out of his grasp after an argument about his boyfriend, a guy some seven years older than her, and how a pair of scissors one of them was holding slipped, and cut him deep through the forearm. He'd never sat with a daughter, both of them sitting on the sofa, not talking, eating Subway, not knowing at all what was going through his kid's head, but he'd also never watched his kid in the kitchen making grilled cheese sandwiches for dinner for the first time. He'd never played Risk on the dinner table for hours, drinking tea and eating pretzels. He'd never shared colds. He'd never had a son slip into his room after watching a horror movie to sleep with him. He'd never watched his kid begin lessons on the piano, an old one a friend had given them, and then finally, after years, watch that same child actually start getting good, singing and playing songs they'd sung when April was a girl. He'd never seen the little feeling of pride in that kid when they knew they were playing well, and how that feeling radiated outward, like a warm light, over himself. Maybe Steve was right, she told him, though not in the way he thought. It wasn't that she needed some wildness or missed her youth, but maybe it was that the bad moments in her life were so much larger than the good ones, that she'd taken so much from those moments, that she applied what she felt in those moments, the jealousy and resentment and anger, and applied those same feelings to the normal things, and in doing so, she'd lost what made things good. She wasn't going to do that with Jack, and knowing this, this made her the right person for the boy, she was certain of it, and there was nothing Steve or anyone else could say to change her mind on that. She'd doubted it, but she knew it again. And tomorrow or maybe the next day, she was going to call Nathaniel and tell him that she was coming to get Jack. She wasn't going to give him a chance to say no, so she was going to wait until she was closer, until the trip was almost over.

Ahead on the sloping road, Tammy saw the old city growing larger, with more and more distinct buildings and lights. It was far down the mountain and appeared to be spread across both sides of the highway. She could see a car, flipped on the other side of the highway, two police cars surrounding it, and a long line of headlights stretching down the mountain road. On her side of the highway, two cars cutting off two lanes, police cars and an ambulance near them. Who were these people? Sitting in traffic, she began crying, thinking of people down there driving somewhere. Thinking of herself driving somewhere. Thinking of April alone on the road at night. She'd be thrown from the car. Her body in the woods. She thought of April and Nicholas and Jack, and she thought of her thinking of them, which equaled her treatment of them, and felt like wanting to admit something to someone, though she didn't know what. The cars in front of her advanced against the rainy night. The black of the pavement ahead of her was mirror-like and shining in the rain. The headlights of the on-coming cars were reflected right below those same cars, as though there was another world just below and opposite this one.

She told Steve that she was going to tell Nathaniel that this was what April wanted and he said that if that's what she wanted to do, okay, and after saying goodbye and telling him she'd call him when she decided to stop for the night, she hung up. She continued through the town. She passed a plant of some kind, lighted and blinking in the night, near a river, probably polluting it, Tammy thought. Then neighborhoods of old houses set on a hill near the river, the houses close together, small yards, working class. On the other side of the river, as she went over a bridge, she could see the old city, town hall. The river was covered in fog, which moved eerily, giving the city a ghostly unreality, as though it could evaporate with the fog. The rain had stopped, she noticed. Her shoulders hurt and she loosened her neck, rolling it around, and in this recognition, she felt the tension in herself, and wanted to loosen it, but couldn't. The city was behind her and again the car was going into the mountains. She thought she'd find a smaller town, one where the hotels would be cheaper, and stay there the night. Welcome to the Wasatch Range a sign said, flashing green in her headlights off the side of the highway. She didn't know how many mountains, rivers, towns, cities, long and boring stretches of farmland she'd have to pass through, but she remembered the mountain range near the end of the journey, the Blue Ridge. Even when April and Nicholas had bought her plane tickets and flown her in, they still had to drive through the Blue Ridge. She wondered why the word blue? The mountains weren't blue at all. They were green or brown or grey, depending, but they weren't blue. Another lie, she thought. Another way the world was trying to convince you it was one way, it was some dream, some beautiful place, when really it was against you, or at the very least it was just there. And you were just where you were, isolated from it. Driving alone in a car through the night to a place full of people who were going to be against you, going to fight you, who didn't know you and didn't want to know you and never would know you, and whose lives were, in all their stupidity and selfishness and privilege, completely separate and unknowable to you, too, and which you didn't want to know, and yet you kept driving through the night toward these people who didn't want anything to do with you at all.

NICHOLAS

Yunmen said to the assembly, 'All people are in the midst of illumination. When you look at it, you don't see it; everything seems dark and dim. How is it being in the midst of illumination?'

—*THE TRUE DHARMA EYE*, CASE 81

There was the ticking of the car's engine and the sensation of falling awake in the dark. The grey outlines of the interior of the car slowly materialized in the darkness – steering wheel and dash and airbag and frame that once held the windshield. Then he felt himself, felt his head pressed against a flat, almost carpeted surface, which he knew, after something in him made an adjustment, was the roof of the car, and that he was upside down in it, still in his seat, held by the seatbelt. In and through the grainy dark, the splintered windshield lay flat on the ground, grass flattened beneath the cracked glass. The ticking of the car's engine slowed. A humming of pain from some distant source, like a tuning fork struck gently, grew louder and more intense. He felt himself falling into himself to the sound of the ticking engine. His vision darkened and he closed his eyes, and after a moment, opened them. The darkness undimmed again, and there was the steering wheel, the deployed airbag, a pulsing pain behind his eyes that sent brief flashes of white into his vision, which slowly faded. Beyond the flattened and splintered windshield was the muddy ground, grass, leaves and brush outside the frame of the car, and further out, the forest. It was dark, but he could see, and suddenly he knew that the forest was lighted by moonlight, almost held by it – that silvery light. That humming pain grew louder. He closed his eyes, opened them again, and now saw the deflated airbag hung upside down from the steering wheel and was wet with blood and swayed gently. It felt like there was an optometrist clarifying his understanding of reality with each closing and opening of his eyes. The airbag swayed noiselessly, a drip of blood hanging from a corner. It occurred to him that the bag hung upside down in the same way he hung upside down from the seatbelt, and yet he was still compactly in his seat, almost squished in it, and he realized through a wave of pain – suddenly the hum of pain crescendoed – that moved up his abdomen and back and into his neck that the roof of the car had been collapsed in the accident, and he had almost been smashed. He felt his breathing get faster, shallower, trying to remember the accident, trying to not feel his body, which suddenly seared with heat and ache. The passenger seat, he could see by moving his eyes but not his head, was empty. He observed his body try to move almost without his will and then tried to think it into movement to get out of the car, as though getting out of the car would get him away from the pain, but he couldn't move his head or his left arm, which the crushed-in driver-side door had trapped somehow. He tried again to move his left arm and a ringing coldness radiated from his shoulder into his neck and back and chest and down, or was it now up, his arm into his fingers. He sensed himself thinking that his arm felt like it was his and not his at once, and behind this thought, he felt himself sensing that he was unsure he was thinking this thought, feeling this thought, or feeling feeling. He felt himself to be at some distance from himself, still falling into himself, as though he hadn't fully materialized yet, as though he was slowly resolving into physical manifestation – just as the car and physical world had done in his vision – like a slowly resolving and clarifying image on a screen. Cold air swept into the car and felt like thoughts from some other mind, which was watching from stillness: the symmetry of the cold air and the cold pain in his arm produced a strange synesthesia, as though his attempt to move his arm and the coldness he felt there had produced the cold air. He observed his mind think of this strange synesthesia, in order to get away from feeling the pain, feeling as though he hadn't produced the thought. Then the thought was gone as well as the synesthesia and he was just cold, shivering. He felt momentarily confused considering all this and his head involuntarily tried to tilt, cock, like a dog's head when considering human words, a habit which was completely mechanical, unthought, and that involuntary movement sent a flash of stabbing pain down through his chest and abdomen, which hit something in him and reverberated back up toward his head along his spine with the force of a physical blow, causing a heat to rush up into his head in a flashing that wiped everything to white.

Sometime later gathering through wide spaces of dark to his waking self again. Like spilled water collecting itself back into a toppled glass, which righted itself again. His eyes did the same slow readjustment to the dark. He closed his eyes hard and opened them wider in an effort to wake himself up. For a moment, he believed he had woken from the bad dream of the accident, but then realized that it hadn't been a dream. A lone cricket was now chirping in the forest among a sea of quiet humming sound. He could still feel a strange pulling into his body, as though parts of himself were still gathering back into him from the various places they had been dispersed to. This gathering feeling made him know that whatever was in him could be dispersed again and that he was about to die and this was his being gathering itself into him again in order to divest itself of his body – as though his being was one final inbreath and outbreath. It wasn't an entirely unpleasant sensation, but then the gathering into himself changed somehow, like he could hold what was gathering, and it made him know that he was just here in the car again. He squinted his eyes closed then opened them wide, trying to see and trying to stop from shivering in the cold dark. The shivering of his upper body made something in his neck pulse and hurt. He inwardly told himself to breathe, breathe, just be cold, and to his surprise, it helped some and lessened the shivering and pain in his neck, though then, through breathing cold air and steadying the shivering, he felt other pain more distinctly: a searing and pulsing in his left leg and left shoulder and along his chest, sternum, and neck, the different parts of his body individuated by pain, making it clear that something had happened to his left shoulder, maybe a broken collarbone, that maybe he'd cracked some ribs or his sternum, and the new pain in his left leg, which when he tried to look at he couldn't and when he tried to move he couldn't, something holding him there, the lower part of the dash collapsed or maybe the drive-side door pinning him somehow. His body was these individual areas of pain, shoulder and chest and neck and legs, and everything else, the rest of his body, felt like a blank white space, as though it wasn't there at all. Then with his one free right hand, he felt the stickiness of what he knew to be blood along his abdomen, and it was the blood that made him feel in real danger, and the thought arose again that he was going to die here, that he needed to get out. He searched his chest and stomach and along his ribs with his free right hand but couldn't find any lacerations or open wounds and knew that the blood that was soaking through his shirt must be coming from his legs, which were above him. Blood from his legs was seeping down his body. He pushed lightly on his upper body and felt that his shoulders and ribs and stomach were sore but okay. He was okay, he thought, though the blood was not good because it was still night and he couldn't move, so if he was still bleeding, that meant he would keep bleeding, he would bleed out, he would die here. He wanted to move his head to see the blood or its source and assess how serious the bleeding was and maybe put pressure on it with his free hand, but he remembered not to move his neck, that he'd already done that and it had caused him to pass out.

Then the dark was undoing itself again: out the frame that usually held the windshield there were the trunks of trees and further in the woods full trees and weeds and smaller plants on the forest floor, already, or still, green. Again not seeing April beside him and knowing without thinking that she'd been thrown through the windshield and then a wavelike pain, like an instant fever, ran through his body, making him convulse with shivers, which in turn made his entire body seem a clenched ball of deep discomfort. He felt himself sweating though he was freezing.

Something in him told himself to breathe. He recognized the voice, though it wasn't his voice, didn't seem like his voice, but he recognized it, a voice he felt he'd been hearing in glimpses intermittently as long as he could remember and occasionally came in clearly, like a suddenly tuned transistor radio, during his project on the mountain. It reminded him vaguely of a thing April had once done for him when he'd broken his leg playing soccer. As she drove him to the hospital, he'd nearly gone into shock, the muscles in his arms and legs stiffening, making the pain worse, and she'd told him he was hyperventilating and to breathe slower, slower, slow down, deep breaths – and this voice too had not seemed like hers, like he was hearing it from out of the depths of a cave – and he'd followed the force of those words then in the same way he did now. Eyes closed, steady in and out. He opened his eyes again. For a few minutes, lightheadedness caused his mind to move toward and away from waking consciousness and again he felt himself expansive and large: images of trees and dense wood and second growth timber and weeds and damp, decaying leaves, and the smell of mud, fungus, a burned rubber smell and gasoline or oil, the creak of the trees in wind, a sliver of moon through the trees and among the clouds, all as if being in a dream. He told himself to wake up, thinking it over and over like a chant – this is a dream, this is a dream, the thought stretched out and slow. Then there was a strange sensation – like a record player that had been lagging suddenly moving again at the right speed – and he felt his thinking accelerating, himself slipping back into himself fully, that gathering that occurred slowly and strangely before, now occurred instantaneously, and what for a moment was expansive compressed suddenly: he was in a car, trapped, unable to move, needed to get out.

He reached with his right hand across his body and put his hand on the driver-side door handle. He could see now that the door was buckled inward. The handle moved, but the door didn't. He jiggled the handle and shook it and pushed against the door, but nothing happened. He took a breath and pushed against it across his body with his right hand, pushed as hard as he could, but still the door wouldn't move. It was crushing his left arm, keeping him stuck in place, and wasn't going to move, wasn't going to open. He let the handle go and noticed that the digital clock on the dash was still working. It was nearly one thirty in the morning. He tried to remember the last time he noticed time, and he thought it must have been leaving the house where the party was, sometime around midnight. So he hadn't been passed out long. If he could get out, he could help April. He pulled at the belt and felt wrenched back into place, a screaming pain through his body, which was his own scream. Then, the pain pulling back like a wave receding back into the ocean, the voice telling him to stay calm, to breathe. He thought that he didn't want to be doing this, he didn't want to be in here alone, trapped in this car alone. He had the realization that he hadn't tried the seatbelt. It passed through his mind as a kind of boyish excitement, like a kid finding five dollars in his winter jacket from the previous winter. He reached down, or up, he thought, up, with his free and uninjured right hand and pressed the button thing but the belt didn't unlatch, or unbuckle, he thought, unbuckle. It was a thing his seatbelt did sometimes – he'd once had to slither out of his seat and then mess with the buckle until it'd come out of the latch – and now it was doing it again, sticking, and he pushed and pushed the button, but nothing happened, and in his right hand he felt a new hot pain from pressing, though the pain wasn't unbearable. He pressed the button again and again and the stinging pain in his hand dulled some and he pressed as hard as he could through gritted teeth and he heard a click and he felt a huge relief, like the process had begun, like this was the first indication that he wasn't going to die here, he was going to get out of this car. But somehow, though he'd heard, or maybe felt, the buckle click, the seatbelt was still in the latch, it wasn't coming out. His breathing felt freer, but when he tried to move his body he still couldn't, and he thought that he really didn't want to be doing this, he wanted to be doing anything but this. Then, as if conveyed to him by some reluctant god or alien being, he again thought of April. That this wasn't only happening to him. That this was happening, had happened, to her, too. And she was out there alone. He thought of her on the road. Or her body on the forest floor among the trees. Wet, maybe, due to the rain, which, he now registered, fell in a gentle humming static. Had it just begun to rain and he hadn't noticed? The sound of the rain made him feel as though he wasn't paying close enough attention, that if he just paid close enough attention, he could understand how to get himself out of this position. After a moment of listening, he thought of the rain covering April's body as a kindness, though he didn't know why, like the thousands of raindrops that fell on her were thousands of tiny hands holding her. He called out to her. Not loud the first time, then louder, like he had to gather her name in his mouth and try it first in order to make the action real. He called again and again, now shouting her name. He screamed it as loud as he could. He waited. Only the rain in response.

He pulled at the seatbelt, but it was somehow stuck in the latch, still holding him upside down, and it wouldn't move. Fucking shit, he said. Thinking of April made him think of Jack – that this was not only just happening to him and April, but to Jack as well – and for a panicked moment he tried to look in the rearview mirror to see the boy in his car seat – a sudden visual montage in his mind of Jack hurt in his car seat, arm broken, tossed about the car during the accident and lying motionless in the backseat, hurt or dead – but then he knew that Jack was with the babysitter, he was in bed, he would be sleeping until morning, which made Nicholas look at the digital clock again and see that only a few minutes had passed. He didn't know exactly how long ago the accident occurred, though it couldn't have been too long, and he didn't know how long he'd have to wait for help, how long April would have to wait but at least he did know that Jack was with the babysitter and safe, his little boy was okay, and in this inward expression he felt what he perceived to be a deep warmth and gratitude move through him, which he told himself to focus on, to stay right there with it. Jack in bed, asleep. Reading a book to Jack. Jack hiding his stuffed animals in the woods around the cabin. Nicholas finding them. Nicholas hiding them for Jack to find. But not too difficult, April said. Don't make them too hard to find, or too high. Nicholas looked out the car window and understood that when he and April weren't home by midnight the babysitter would attempt to call April. A phone call would be coming. The babysitter was going to call April. He knew for sure that a phone call would be coming – maybe he'd even hear April's phone, which he knew to be in her jacket pocket, go off, and he'd be able to locate her by sound – and when that phone call wasn't answered, people would know something was wrong, someone would find him, they'd know where he and April had gone for the night, they'd retrace where they'd been, they'd call friends, they'd find him on Smoky Mills Road and he'd be alive, and so would April, and they'd get home and Jack would still be asleep, as though none of this had occurred, and at the same time he thought this, he also thought that April might not pick up her phone again and might never speak to anyone, not to Jack, not to him, ever again, and he felt his heart nearly pushing against his ribs upside down in the car, and he shouted her name again, waiting, and when he heard nothing, he told himself to calm himself – though it was not the distant voice, he was aware, that spoke this, but his own mimicking it – and then he felt the ridiculousness of telling himself to calm himself when he was upside down in a crashed car and bleeding and cold in freezing temperatures and sweating and could die and April was in all likelihood not alive, she was dead, and yet there it was again, some competing voice in him telling himself to calm himself, this time distinctly not his voice, some voice from some distant place telling him to calm himself, to think of what he needed to do, what do you need to do, which after asking it of himself he knew was to do only what he could do, and to understand that Jack was okay and safe, that the babysitter would attempt to call April, was probably already attempting to call April, and was not getting April, and would eventually call the police, and he'd be found and then be back with Jack. But April wouldn't be, he thought. There was the competing urge to be both utterly honest with himself and to feel that she was still alive. He felt some knot of tension in his chest, which made his chest hurt, and then tears and he mumbled aloud that he didn't know anything to be true or not true, you don't know anything. He thought that maybe she was only unconscious. Maybe April was out there in a soft pile of leaves or maybe she'd been thrown in such a way that she'd rolled and had hit her head and was now passed out, though the delusional nature of this thought was almost too apparent, and his fight against what was actual felt almost stupid, like playing tug of war with a rope securely attached to a wall, though then he considered that maybe she'd walked away from the accident. Maybe she was on her way to get help. Maybe he'd been passed out, and she'd woken up, looked at him, tried to wake him, and then had left and was walking, or running even, jogging, right now into town. How long would that take her? If the babysitter fell asleep, she might stay asleep until the morning came, until her own parents woke and realized she wasn't there, so it could be hours before anyone found him, but if April had walked away from the accident, someone would find him. She'd turn off this old, isolated road, get onto one of the old farm roads where surely someone would be driving by, some farmer maybe, would pick her up, she'd call the police. Maybe she already had. Though none of that made sense. Her door was closed, her seatbelt recoiled, she'd left no indication that she'd gone for help, and if she was okay, why hadn't she just called the police? But maybe she was okay and looking for help and had called the police and they were on the way and had called the babysitter, what was she going to do, leave him a note, she probably rushed away as fast as she could to get him help, and if her cell phone had been damaged, or lost, she could still be walking and it could take hours to get back to town on foot, he thought. Maybe it wasn't such a ridiculous thought after all.

The rain increased, a near hissing sound off the forest floor, and now that his eyes had adjusted to the darkness, he saw both the rainfall and spray of rainfall as it hit the ground, as well as a soft mist moving between the trees. Because the car was on a slope, he could look down into the forest as it moved down the mountain. A scattered light reflected on the corner of the flattened windshield, and he couldn't understand what light it was, then knew it was the moon reflected there, fractured into glints of light. A single ant was walking along the cracked windshield. It seemed to rise up on its hind legs for a moment to survey Nicholas. He half wanted to ask it for help. He called April's name again, then again, louder, and heard only the rain on the trees and leaves of the forest floor. He felt afraid to say her name and then said it, quietly, and then yelled it. The rain seemed to increase as if in remorseful response. It was not helpful to think that April was alive and walking toward help in the same way that it was not helpful to think that April was dead simply because he couldn't see her or hear her, or that she couldn't hear him. He told himself that he couldn't know anything for certain. He grabbed onto the steering wheel with his unstuck arm and tried to pull himself out of the stuck seat and horrifying pain like ripping occurred in his left leg and he stopped immediately. In order to not feel the echoing pain, he made himself recall that he'd actually witnessed an accident once in graduate school when he and April had been driving to see her mother, they were driving on the highway, and in front of them, maybe two hundred yards, a truck's tire blew out and the truck flipped several times and he'd seen a girl inside the truck sort of fly out of a window like a crash-test dummy, her body seeming not real at all, and her body kind of did two strange rolls, half-summersaults on the side of the road into a sitting position. He'd barely been able to believe that the girl sitting there had survived. Like other people, he and April had pulled onto the shoulder of the highway and stopped and gotten out of their cars and rushed over to her. The girl's eyes had been glazed and she appeared to be looking down through some telescope at her hands and body, a little cross-eyed almost, her head unsteady, as though she was not in control of herself. But she was okay. They all asked, What hurts? Are you okay? And she'd looked up at them and down at her hands and said, I'm fine. I think I'm fine. Then she said to them when they asked if she was okay again, she said, directly to Nicholas, Where's Mark? Mark was her boyfriend and he was back in the truck, which was flipped over, and he too was okay except for a cut on his forehead, a bruised thigh. Nicholas thought now that maybe that was like a precursor to this moment, that maybe him witnessing that accident was proof not to be despairing now, that maybe April was okay, and so maybe was he, though he then considered the idea that another person's life, this girl, whose name he never learned, and this Mark person, they were not blue-prints for his life, they were not signs or symbols, they were real people, who didn't necessarily have anything to do with him. So maybe just take it as evidence that people survive, he thought. Then he wished he had a phone, wished he hadn't taken what now felt like a somewhat stupid stand against certain technologies, refusing to ever have a phone, and in this wishing, he looked at the center console, near the gearshift, thinking that's where it would be if he had a phone, but then remembered he and the car were upside down and his hypothetical phone could be anywhere, might not even be in the car. The digital clock said that it was just before two in the morning. Only twenty minutes, he thought. How long was this going to take?

The rain held a steady rhythm and he now began to feel some drops hitting his face and arms, which at first he didn't understand, how it could be raining on him, then realized the drops were warm, that he was bleeding on himself, from his legs. He was panicked a moment, desperately wanted out of the car, and he pulled with his free right arm on the steering wheel, pulling harder than before, pulling his entire body toward the open windshield. Pain throbbed through his still stuck left arm and in his legs. It moved up his body in a hot and cold light. It blurred his vision. He heard himself sort of whimpering and sobbing, breathing quickly, and saying, Okay, okay, I won't, I won't move, as though he was talking to his own body from outside it. He tried to make himself very still and breathed and breathed and tried to slow himself down, just like he'd been practicing on the mountain. He suddenly understood that this was an opportunity to view things as he'd been trying to view things, without any positives or negatives, but just to constantly be learning from his existence, and to be able to calmly approach all situations, and yet, despite this understanding, he felt himself trying to not think that he was stuck here, trying to not think that he was not only stuck but trapped and could die here, trying instead to allow the part of himself that believed that he could get out to take over his thinking. He'd just have to do it slowly, carefully. It couldn't be some rushed and unthought thing. He'd have to get his body out of this car with great care, he thought. In fact, he'd have to do it in stages, like with the seatbelt buckle. First free his left arm. Then one leg. Then another. With care for each part of his body in order to keep pain at a minimum. He could do it if he did it in slow increments.

His project on the mountain had been to slow his life down in order to teach himself to be content and easeful with all situations, with all life, even negative moments, to be always in aware repose, like a tree accepting its divestment of leaves every winter, and he thought this situation now couldn't be more negative and that his fighting against it was purposeless. He had to accept it, be with it, and with a calm awareness, he'd get himself out of it. But he couldn't hate it or fight it. He'd wear himself out, pass out, or, if he wasn't careful, he'd hurt himself more. He almost started moving his left arm, then stopped himself, and inwardly repeated to himself to wait, just wait. He needed to let the pain subside, needed to allow his body to get back to a sort of stable base of non-pain, or less pain, because freeing the arm would be excruciating, and he was still feeling a hot tingle in his spine and legs, sweat on his forehead though it was very cold. Rain began falling harder, and a little distance from the car, there was a spiderweb shimmering in the rain and wind and moonlight. The web had no insects in it, no spider, it looked abandoned. He could see where the web connected at several points to a branch of a small tree, and then on the other side, to the stem of a weed. A circular pattern at the center of the web. He didn't want to be doing any of this, he thought again, but he was, and next he had to figure out some way to free the arm that was stuck, and in doing so, he knew he had to feel that pain again, which was not something he wanted to do, then he would have to take a rest, then feel more pain freeing the left leg, he thought, then rest, then more pain, then rest. Again, something in him viewed this from some distance, something far from himself communicating to him that all things were this, suffering, then no-suffering, then suffering again. He told himself it was as simple as this: pain, rest, pain, rest, and he could do it now again, just as he did anything, even though he didn't want to and some other part of himself told himself that it was not possible, he was trapped here. So much of his life, he reflected now, was determined by what he wanted to do and how he wanted moments to be as good as they could possibly be. And he was dissatisfied by so much of his life, as though he had failed, over and over again, to get the message that his wanting to do something and make it exactly how he wanted it to be did not equate to any kind of satisfaction. In fact, this wanting was often starkly against his own satisfaction. He'd learned this in numerous ways, and he thought now, it was only in the last few years that he'd actually begun to try to live by it, in a slow, stunted manner, like an android first learning it was not a human but an android and speaking again, for the first time, its millionth word.

He thought that he'd wasted so many years wanting things to be different than they were, wanting himself, others, to be different than they were, and it was only Jack who he'd never felt this way about. But everything else, he thought, he was constantly wanting to be different. He closed his eyes and blinked several times in order to get sweat that was running down his forehead to stop pooling near his eyes. If he blinked fast, he could get the sweat to move around his eyes. The burning sensation from the salt slowly subsided, and he was again listening to the quiet rain. For a moment, the physical world – rainfall, woods, tree trunks, the slip of dark sky he could see, the rising crescent moon, damp mud and fungus-y earth smell, mist moving between the trees, the spiderweb vibrating in the rain – manifested itself as a stronger reality than his mind, and he tried to let himself go out into it, and he felt something in him pulling outward.

He told himself he needed to stop thinking and start doing something. He needed to get out of this car now, and with his right arm, he pulled at his left arm a little, felt a streak of hot-cold pain, and stopped due to the pain and felt cowardly. Then, he focused on his right leg, which he could move some, and he reached down, which was up, with his right hand and felt around his right thigh, then under his thigh, felt only a small amount of pulsing in his lower back, and then with his right arm pulled on the thigh. It didn't come loose, but he felt it move to the right. It was too dark to see up into the floor of the car, but he reached again, and grabbed his right leg behind the knee, pulled and wiggled it at the same time, and it wiggled, loosening, and he realized he needed to slide it. He slid it toward the center console, toward the passenger door, moving it along the seat and whatever was pinning it in place, and as he slid it, it suddenly lurched free and fell toward him. He waited a moment, then moved the leg, and he could. He could move it. He was doing it, he thought. He was getting out. Now, feeling that he had this under control, he knew what to do, he reached across his chest to his left arm, and tried to jiggle it like he'd jiggled the leg and when he tried that again the same stabbing sensation screamed through him, and he stopped and said, Okay, not that, not doing that. The stabbing pain slowly dissipated and he breathed, deep breaths. He thought, in what he knew was a self-pitying way, that if he just hadn't been driving on this road then this wouldn't have occurred – he wouldn't be trapped in the car, April wouldn't be on the road somewhere, Jack wouldn't be alone with the babysitter waiting for them. Images arose in his mind like a sort of indie movie cliché, complete with opening credits – his name playing himself, April's name playing herself – over the slow-motion capture of a simulated accident, and yet this was no simulation, this was not a movie, not a drama. He felt the force of the cliché's actuality, that if he'd just said no to the tenure party like he'd wanted to say no to it and not let that other part of him that wanted recognition win out, if he'd just said that he wouldn't have another beer and not let that part of him that told him to get drunk tonight, whatever, win out, if he hadn't listened to April saying that this was something his colleagues wanted to do for him and he should be both accepting of and grateful for their respect and kindness and then let the sincere part of him also have its say, as though he suddenly saw that he wasn't going for selfish reasons but because it was actually kind of him, a kindness and respect shown to his colleagues, if he and April hadn't been arguing on the way home about the fact that Nicholas had been talking to Nora Evans in the kitchen, an argument he hadn't wanted to have, but which he definitely wanted to win, then none of this would've happened. If he could just have been one person at any one moment, he thought, then none of this would've occurred.

He took several deep breaths and tried to roll his head. He tugged a little at the seatbelt and it slipped up his chest some, which allowed him to maneuver his right arm so that he could slip it out from under the belt, but the belt stayed in place, now wrapped around the outside of his left arm, holding him in the seat. He tried to get the belt around the outside of his left shoulder but couldn't. Shit, he heard himself say, even more confined than before. He pulled his arm across his abdomen, tight against himself, without moving his upper body at all, afraid that it might hurt his left arm if he did, and was able to slip the arm under the belt, so that it was back into the original position, free of the belt, but still the rest of him stuck. He then noticed that his freed right leg hung uncomfortably toward his chest. The leg pulled on his lower back and made something ache there, so he pushed the leg back down, wedging it under part of the collapsed dash. He made sure he could easily free the leg again, and he could, and then put it back in under the dash, which relieved some pressure on his lower back. He noticed himself breathing hard, like he'd just climbed several flights of stairs in quick succession. Not wanting to move his left arm, not wanting to do this at all, he thought again of the ride home, and suddenly understood with a kind of paralyzed horror that barely allowed him to fully form the thought and wouldn't, for a moment, let him go beyond the thought, that the argument he had with April might be the last communication he had with her. Momentarily unable to move, to think, to do anything, until his mind began again moving toward what he didn't want it to move toward, which was their argument, and more specifically what led to their argument in the car, he felt a deep shame and regret. The impression of the car ride home – like a kind of emotional signal from a distant star, not definable and clear until he was able to decode it – arose in his consciousness, and in that impression he recognized their worst selves: April at her worst, him at his worst. He felt nauseated and for a moment his mouth began to water as it did before vomiting and he told himself to breathe, breathe, and after a moment, the feeling subsided. In the car driving home, he recalled, April had said she'd noticed him talking with Nora Evans for quite a while in the kitchen tonight. She'd said it off-handedly, an affect he hated, like she didn't really care. But he felt it – her jealousy, a kind of held-in energy that she was ready to direct, negatively, at him, like a weapon. As soon as she said it, he'd interrupted her by saying that he'd been trapped there in the kitchen, he hadn't wanted to be talking to her, and anyway, Nora Evans was the one who was talking to *him*, asking *him* questions, *he* wasn't talking to *her*, and also she was mainly asking about the two of you, he'd added. As he was saying this, though, he was also aware that when Nora Evans had begun talking to him, he'd liked it, he'd wanted it to happen, he'd been happy this pretty woman wanted to speak with him, yet he didn't say this to April. He'd told April that whatever she thought had occurred with Nora Evans probably hadn't come close to occurring in the way she was thinking it had. He remembered saying to April in the car that Nora Evans had actually asked about April and Jack, saying that she so much liked the idea of all of us, you know, whatever she called it, living on a sustainable farm and attempting to go off the grid. There's nothing to be jealous about because Nora Evans was asking about you, he had said. And Jack. She wanted to know how you two both liked living in the woods. She said it like that, *living in the woods*. I mean, she was asking about you two, about our life. She said things like how she admired that we were making no small attempt to do our part, to live beyond the confines of late capitalist ideology, and that she admired it very much, our lives, and the way we were raising Jack to have these alternative values, and she'd said that she too had these values, that maybe they weren't even alternative anymore, what intelligent person didn't have them, we all wanted to save the planet and not hurt animals, but who actually lived it, and from her perspective, she said, no one really lived it fully but that we made a decent attempt at least. Nicholas remembered himself saying things like this, though they sounded better in his head now, and he couldn't be sure what was real or not, though he did clearly recall not wanting to engage in an argument with April, but also at the same time wanting April to try to argue with him so he could show her how wrong she was. He recalled that he had been a little drunk, that he hadn't wanted to get drunk, or to drink at all, but he had, he had gotten drunk, and now, upside down in the car, he realized that part of the reason his head was aching and his mouth was dry and he had to pee was because he was hungover and the little stream of water running by his face was tempting him, his own blood running copper through the water. He stuck his tongue out to try to reach the water but it was just beyond him. He tried to nudge his head forward against the ceiling of the car and though he moved, the water seemed no closer. He glanced at her empty seat.

He told himself to think of something else, of good times with April, with Jack, of how Jack was the present moment around which he and April moved and were pulled into. They'd discussed this maybe when Jack was a year old, the way in that first year he pulled them to immediacy and away from their own private lives with ease. He was a quiet baby, a good sleeper mostly, a good eater, though when he got constipated he had made strange faces that had scared both Nicholas and April, then made them laugh, faces like he was going to explode either himself or the room, like this little baby was actually some kind of magician gnome, but then, after some time of strange, wrinkled, occasionally evil-looking faces, they'd hear the poop, and then smell it, which caused Jack to smile tiredly, like he'd been making some enormous effort, which he had been, he had, and they then were brought into action. After already being in the action of laughing, they were now in the action of diaper change. They noticed that their days, which they had once categorized as good, okay, great, bad, boring, no longer could be contained in such a way. There was less time to judge, for one, but what they both felt was that any judgment couldn't contain Jack. Jack crying all night, which was rare, was not bad. How could it be? It was only exactly what it was. It was exhausting, frustrating, but the designation of 'bad night' didn't even have a chance to exist. In the morning, it was just another day. Jack playing quietly by himself for the first time was exactly what it was: Jack playing. His deep screams when he wanted food were just that: a screaming baby. And their own exhaustion was just that: tiredness.

Of course they got annoyed, frustrated, but it seemed to happen after the fact, later, upon analysis, and only ever at each other. In the evening, when Jack was asleep for the night, they argued about when he should be taking naps, when he shouldn't, when he should be going to bed, getting up, when he should be starting more solids, what types of solids, should he eat baby food, or the same food they ate just cut very small, they argued about how it was frustrating that one of them let him sit in a wet diaper too long, that's why he had a rash now, or one of them thought baths every other day were okay, or that they should be using organic disposable diapers less and washable cloth diapers more, though Nicholas couldn't now say which side he'd fallen on in any of these arguments, just that he had. Stupidly, they both had. They'd quietly argue, blame, judge, accuse, retreat, apologize, attack again, claim tiredness, claim confusion as excuses, apologize again, wait, get quiet, tell each other that this was where they were, they had to keep something for themselves, and it couldn't just be their exhaustion and frustration. Then, when Jack was with them again, it was as though their frustration had been some kind of game – unreal – and they were there for him. It was sad, Nicholas thought now, that they saved their annoyance for each other, though after a couple years, as the boy became more capable and independent, this frustration dissipated and they found space to be themselves again, to be there for each other, too, and not just for Jack. They'd almost forgotten what that was like, and Nicholas was glad to return to some version of it, him and April together, with Jack, yes, but together alone, too, once again getting to be just what they were. Nicholas thought that those first two years with Jack had taught him something indispensable. In any given moment with Jack, there was only what there was to do: feed the baby, put him down, be tired, burp him, change his diaper, clean his spit-up, talk to him, laugh with him, walk him around the yard, sing to him, be spit-up on, be peed on, be interrupted while doing work, listen to his cries, unrelenting and sometimes causing him to vomit, all perfectly as it was. There was no chance, April said, when with Jack to make analysis of how life was going and wish for something better or wish things were different if not better – there was no better, no worse, and even the one medical scare that year, they only did what they could do, which was take him to the doctor, give him the medicine, be concerned, be wary, hold him in a gentler manner, speak more softly. It was later that they thought and argued and complicated it all, but in the moment there was only what they were doing. How to make all life like that? Nicholas thought. To just do what one had to do.

Beneath this thought Nicholas felt the other thought about the argument with April and felt his mind wanting to go there, to think of the argument, but he didn't allow himself to do it. He tried to stay with Jack, and April too, and not find too much meaning in this one argument, though he felt the pull, wanting to analyze, wanting to see why it occurred, why it happened, why the fight came into existence, but he made himself think of when Jack played as a toddler. His little tongue stuck out in the corner of his mouth, at play with great seriousness, and it was the same when he got older and began reading little books and drawing and doing chores around the cabin. Everything he did was what he was doing right there, and though Nicholas and April had wanted to move to the mountain for the quiet and isolation, for the opportunity to find again the moment that they were constantly rushing from, it was their child who revealed what this actually meant, that even in rushing there could be presence, that even in difficult moments, there was immediacy, and Nicholas thought now in an effort to not think about his and April's argument, that what Jack revealed to him was that he'd mistaken being present for every moment being good. What he feared most for Jack was that he'd lose this, the ease of not living in any world except the one right in front of him. Nicholas thought of how he'd worked so hard to try to be able to do that again, to live without any obstructions, and it only rarely worked, or he only rarely felt the depths of where that might lead, but on the mountain he'd been moving toward it. There were small moments, glimpses, when sawing a table was sawing a table, not sawing a table and thinking about work, and worrying about an article he needed to write, and worrying about what April said earlier, or what to say to a male student he knew was gay, and who kept coming to his office hours with throw-away questions in order to flirt with him. He just sawed the table. There were moments when he just walked on the mountain path, just planted the garden, just played with Jack, just changed him, just fed him, just read him a book – this thing he'd wanted and was trying to access was only accessed through this other being, who he'd been afraid he could not be a good father to. Jack made things for both him and April simple again, even in the chaotic, exhausting moments of parenting, it was still simple, the focus of their life was simple, obvious, clear, what one needed to do was clear: be there for Jack, and even this formulation, he thought now, itself was lacking, didn't actually come into existence in the moment, it was only afterwards in analysis of the situation that it came into being, which made it an imperative, which it did not feel like. He, like April, didn't think, Be there for Jack. It just occurred, arose of its own accord, like a seed that had always been inside him manifesting itself as a tree, without any will. But with the exception of Jack, he rarely brought this same kind of awareness and attention to the rest of his life. Even now in the car, he thought, he wasn't living in the moment because he didn't want to be: because the moment meant pain, diffuse throughout his body, and it meant mental pain, the recollection of this last conversation with April, which he didn't want to think about, but which he could feel under his thoughts about Jack like a virus infecting his memories of his little boy, Jackie. Jackie, he'd say, gimme a big big nug-hug. Jackie, he'd say, what are the words on page four of *I Am a Bunny*? Jackie, he'd say, what do the bees who don't collect honey do, just to hear the ridiculous answer, which had something to do with being traitor bees who showed bears where the honey was located. With Jack everything was not easy, but easeful, whereas in the rest of his life there was some discord, some divide between how he wished things would be and how they were. As he was thinking this, he suddenly had the competing thought that maybe things with Jack weren't perfect or easeful, but were only that way in retrospect, and that he was idealizing his time with Jack, was doing it, right now, constructing a fantasy past, a delusion. The idea that Jack was some force of immediacy that brought him and April into the present moment and wiped away their delusions was maybe itself a delusion, in the same way that thinking about Jack now was avoiding this moment of pain and suffering that he didn't want to suffer through, deluding himself.

He closed his eyes and gritted his teeth and something distant in him told him to breathe. He opened his eyes and looked at the digital clock, which neared three a.m., and he wondered again where April was, why no one had found him yet, and how long he'd have to wait, and he felt a tiredness that was more than being sleepy, he felt weak and drained, literally drained, the blood in him going out still, and he wondered if someone didn't find him soon, if April wasn't walking to get help right now, who would take care of Jack, and like the thought of April and him arguing in the car, he didn't want to think of him and April not being there for Jack, and he willed the thought to stop, and what was waiting there behind it seemed to wake and come into being, and he again thought of what April had said in the car, Yes, I heard her talking to you. She was talking to you and being all flattering, Oh, Nicholas, what a brave forestman bringing his family to the forest to live a life of forest people among the bears, please show me what a big forestman does please, she had said. Nicholas remembered saying that he couldn't believe she was eavesdropping on his conversation, what a ridiculous and untrusting thing to do. I can't believe that after eleven years together you still don't trust me with a woman who you deem to be somehow above you. April had said that was the most ridiculous thing she'd ever heard, and yes, she felt bad she'd eavesdropped. Nicholas told her to just wait, just hold on a minute, because he wasn't finished, he wasn't going to, you know, he wasn't going to let this happen, he wanted to finish this fight before it began. Oh, you're going to finish it, big forestman, she said. Nora Evans wasn't interested in him, he had continued, and he wasn't interested in Nora Evans, it was all just happenstance, he'd said to April. April had said that she was going to interrupt him now in the same way he had interrupted her, and then she added, Watch the road. She was quiet for a moment, testing him, he knew, to see if he'd say anything more, if he'd fill in the silence with more explaining, which he knew was an indication to keep quiet and also a temptation: he wanted to speak. Then, when more quiet passed than he could stand, he said, Say whatever it is you actually think, feeling a quick anger in his body extending from mind to arms and chest and legs, which were clenched and tight. April said he just couldn't shut up, could he? You're drunk, he'd told her, you did that on purpose and I know you did. And yet you couldn't not talk for fifteen seconds, she said. Try it now. Fifteen seconds. I'll count. He'd waited, counting in his head in the same way he was counting now, then told himself to stop counting, annoyed at her. After a moment, she said she was just going to say one thing, and that one thing was that whatever Nora Evans had said in the kitchen with him, that's just what she was *saying*. What she was *doing* was giving you fuck-me eyes. And you were playing along. And what really bothered me about it, was she was using me and Jack, but mainly I was pissed that she was using *me*, *using* me, to do it. The comment caused Nicholas to say to April that that wasn't fair, that wasn't fair both to him and to Nora. He didn't think anyone would be that brazen about something like that. Nora wasn't a bad person. Upside down in the car, he recalled feeling a little insane when he was talking, as though the beers and drinks had loosened his mind enough to let it spill forth unreservedly: he recalled the clear feeling that much of what he was saying he didn't really mean and didn't feel very convincingly, it was just glancing thoughts, like the white noise of his mind, that he simply allowed to slip out without any real investigation or care.

Additionally, he remembered adding – unable to stop the random thoughts and words and seeming to view himself from outside himself, as though his words were tuned to some disparate source of annoyance and anger but his actual being was observing from some distant place in the cosmos, calm and dispassionate – that it annoyed him that if he was talking with a woman, any woman, the first thing April went to was that he was, in some way, flirting with said woman, a statement that he understood to be utterly false, and yet which he said in order to make April angry. April replied by saying that she hadn't said that Nicholas was flirting, she had said that Nora was, but that it wasn't the flirting that had annoyed her, and actually, she wasn't even that annoyed, she'd wanted to talk to Nicholas and instead he was being an asshole, but what annoyed her was Nora Evans was flattering Nicholas and using her and Jack to do it, like he was the big man of the family and took care of April and Jack and fended off bears and invested their money and taught them how to live in accord with nature, like I'm your little housemaid of a wife and Jack is going to take over the family one day and become an intellectual Navy Seal. It was gross. Nicholas said, Look, Nora was a gender studies professor. He didn't think she'd think that. April said that she didn't think Nora thought any of that shit was true – it wasn't the flirtation itself that bothered

April, it was the nature of it, which was to flatter his manliness. It was disgusting. And what was doubly disgusting, though mainly annoying, was how easily Nicholas got sucked into it, blushing and looking away in his deep flattery, swimming in flattery. That is really all that April wanted to say, why couldn't they just have a conversation, why was Nicholas defensive, which Nicholas recalled now had caused him to say that he wanted to go back a minute, to the idea that maybe it was just Nora flirting and not him, maybe that was the case, but then why bring it up? I understand now you're saying you just wanted to chat with me about it, but if she didn't suspect him, or if she knew that he wasn't participating in the flirting then the idea that she just wanted to have a laugh about Nora or whatever seemed weak, like why she really wanted to bring it up was because it really felt like she thought he was in some way participating and that she was subtly attacking him here, or wanting to fight or something. It wasn't him wanting to fight, it was her, she was the one doing it, he'd told her. He had tried to keep what he felt was a clenched anger – all his thoughts and energy compressed to a singularly dense frustrated point, which he was fighting to not let explode out, like trying to hold in a universe which would explode out from him only to create more anger and resentment and fighting – down and unexpressed. He had always been able to do this: to view himself and his anger and his emotions as though at some remove from them, both engaging in them and somehow some other part of him acting as the passive observer. April had replied that she wasn't attacking him, that she hadn't been, and wasn't now, but she felt jealousy, insecurity, and yeah, it was annoying, this woman, him giving so much of his attention to this woman, but what she didn't like now was that if Nicholas had nothing to do with this flirting, well, his defensiveness showed her that maybe that wasn't the case, that maybe he wasn't being completely honest here. Nicholas had gone quiet. He had paid attention to the mountain road, the slow rain, the slow wind, the trees slow in their rocking, in an effort to let his anger pass. He'd thought in the space of their quiet that April was right: he had in fact enjoyed the presence of this other woman. He *had* noticed, at some point, that Nora Evans was flirting with him, and while he didn't feel as though he engaged with the flirtation, he hadn't stopped it either. He didn't like this, he didn't want it to be the case, he was arguing with April as much as he was arguing with himself, for indulging in the flirtation. Yet, there was something more there, he knew. He remembered being in the kitchen, and in remembering it, he recreated it, being in the kitchen, whose faucet was dripping slowly, enjoying this other woman talking to him and possibly flirting with him and him possibly flirting with her, her being impressed by something he'd written in one of his books, which April maybe hadn't been eavesdropping on yet, her looking different than April, her face different from April's, her eyes not grey-green, but brown, her hair not sandy blonde, but dark, her face not oval, but round, her upper lip fuller, though her lower lip not as full as April's, the rest of her body different, slightly younger, maybe more in shape, maybe her breasts a little bit smaller than April's, her fingers slightly longer than April's, her breath different from April's, the recognition of her different body instantly manifesting as sexual attraction, him briefly wanting her (and, secondarily, annoyed that he was wanting her, annoyed that something in him was attracted to her, and annoyed that, once again, his biology was taking over, compelling him, this other side of him he associated as being the negative, selfish, probably more primitive side), her voice different, her opinions different, her thoughts and feelings different from April's, her interest in him newer and different and in all likelihood caused because she didn't actually know him. At the same time that he felt and sensed all of this and both enjoyed it and wanted her with some part observing that he didn't want her, and feeling a little repulsed by his own wanting, he also was listening to the dripping faucet. The drops of water spaced perfectly, like the metronome of his thoughts. Something about the slow drops slowed his mind, slowed Nora Evans speaking, slowed his occasional looking past Nora Evans to the party in the other room, everything moving slower, even his sudden wanting of her moving slower, so that he could see it. Suddenly a drop of water in the sink seemed to reverberate like a bell through his mind, rippling out and settling the surface of the water of his mind into a glassy stillness so that the kitchen and Nora Evans and the party and everything almost rippled to a stop, and while waiting for the next drop, the moment in the kitchen slowed so much that he suddenly saw, and saw again, his wanting this person as purposeless and selfish and completely biological and as only leading to dissatisfaction – which, in some way, was exactly what it led to: the fight in the car – and saw Nora as somehow being the same as April. That April's body was not new only to him. That April's voice, her habits, her actions, her interests, were only not new to him. That because he knew April so *fully*, this other person he didn't

know created some sexual attraction in him due to her newness, which when he allowed himself to see clearly, as Nora
Evans spoke, he saw as specter-like, and which he recreated
again now, recreating the moment, the thoughts of the
moment, the intuition and understanding of the moment,
and he imagined that her beauty and his attraction dispersed as a cloud might. The force of his attraction undoing
itself like a mist clearing, and in the space of the moment
before the next drop of water from the kitchen sink, he felt
this all clearly and simply, and then he observed April in a
surrounding room, talking to one of his colleagues, about
to eat what appeared to be a piece of cheese on a cracker.
He then saw April's immediate freshness, her always newness, everyone's, Nora the same as her, not the same person,
but both of their newness in each new moment complete
and whole, and what replaced the passing sexual attraction
for Nora Evans was a gentle and open seeing of Nora Evans
no longer as a sexual body, but just as a body. Which he
was too. Which April was. Each in their difference the same.
All of this had materialized in his mind, he thought and
reconstructed now, in the instant a drop of tap water fell
from the sink: he felt it all move through him and understood it with the intuition he'd developed over four years
living in the woods and living in complete silence for a week
at a time each year. He'd thought, standing in the kitchen,
that this moment wouldn't have been possible if he hadn't
learned to pull from himself the inner feeling that often got
covered over in his stupid and selfish wants: some distant
voice inside him that spoke as though from the depths of a
cave – your wanting isn't you. Yet, he hadn't been able to
tell any of this to April in the car on the way home, he

hadn't been able to explain any of it, it was too complex, the way his feeling about the situation with Nora Evans and how it had transformed was too complexly intertwined with his perceptions, his view of himself, his opinion of April, of Nora, of the water dripping from the faucet, of how he wished he was and how he actually was, how he wanted to be and how he actually was, and so he hadn't said any of it. Feeling an intense pain behind his eyes now, like a sudden migraine arriving, he hated that he hadn't said any of this and he tried to think if their last conversation had really been this ugly or if he or she had said anything more, and at the same time he tried to think if they'd said anything more, he also didn't want to think about it at all, and then he wondered what was more real: his attraction to Nora Evans or his sudden unattraction, his fight and annoyance at April or his care and concern for her, his thinking and recreating these moments in his mind in the car or his body in pain in the car. It was impossible to tell, he thought, what was real and what wasn't, and he thought that his problem was that he thought some moments were real and some weren't, that some moments appeared to be real and some appeared to be a dream that needed to be woken from.

His cheek was smashed against the roof, and his neck was bent and growing sore and stiff. He moved himself a little, readjusting his neck with careful movements, rolling his neck so that his face was off the roof of the car and his ear was pressed against it, muffling the sound of his breathing. It felt good to move and when he felt no pain, he thought he'd try again in a minute, feeling in this new position like he could go to sleep, though he was thirsty. The sound of thunder reverberated through the car. He felt it in the ground, and heard the rain increase, and then felt rainwater running under him, as though the thunder had loosened some pocket of water somewhere. The little stream went right by his face and he moved his neck to lap at it, his mouth so dry, and what he tasted was water mixed with his own blood, and he momentarily became lightheaded again and nauseated. A flickering of dizziness and nausea that made the world reconfigure: the trees and forest and interior of the car all blurred into a flattened visual field. His body and the pain in it pulsed and then seemed diffuse and amorphous and bodiless and not there, and his hearing became confused, as though the sound of the rain, breathing, the running rainwater, the wind in the treetops all became voices speaking an alien language to him in order to coax him from himself. He closed his eyes and breathed and tried to make it stop, and his senses gathered inside him again, and the pain that had dispersed momentarily returned, and his body was the different parts of his body again, pain in arm and left leg and neck, and he opened his eyes, grateful it was back, though now he felt an extreme exhaustion. He thought there was no way he was getting out of this car, he was so tired – he looked at the clock nearing four in the morning. Why hadn't anyone arrived? Why had no one found him yet? He reached down with his right arm and felt around his left leg. There was sticky blood there making his pants feel thick. He explored what he could of his thigh, knee, and when he moved his hand up his leg, maybe mid-thigh, there was a searing sensation that made him stop touching the leg for a moment, and then after the sensation faded, he reached down again and felt around the knee, noting that there was less pain. He reached across himself toward the outside of the left knee and then pulled a little, felt only a dim ache, and then pulled harder, and the knee moved some. Maybe that was it, he thought. Slide the leg toward his right leg, away from the crushed-in door, just slide it carefully. He took a breath and reached across his body again and grabbed the outside of his knee and pulled it. Instantly a stabbing pain in his thigh, but he kept pulling, and the knee and leg moved a little, and gritting his teeth and yelling he pulled hard one more time and the leg slid a bit more and then the pulsing and stabbing moved up his spine into his head and his vision flashed in and out and he stopped and breathed, breathed. More sweat dripped down his temples, he could feel some sweat getting into an ear, tickling it annoyingly. He breathed and waited, was so tired, so glad to not have to move the leg for a minute. He'd done something, he thought. It'd moved some. He felt his legs shifted, both aimed now diagonally toward the opposite side of the car, away from the crushed door. He could still get out. He was doing it. He was getting out, untrapping himself, slowly, just as he pictured it. Take your time, he told himself. The leg would come free. It was nearly free. He could feel it under the dash, the dash still holding it, but looser. It was just the arm now that would hurt. Take your time. Take a little break. Rest.

After a moment of getting his breath back, of hearing the rain outside and the wind in the trees, he suddenly had the feeling that he was more alone than he'd felt in a long time, maybe than ever before, as though he was experiencing loneliness again for the first time. There was no one else. Just rain and wind, just this crushed car, his body. He tried to think of when he had felt the least alone, or when he didn't even consider loneliness, when it didn't even enter into his being, and knew that the answer was when Jack arrived, when it felt like the first time in their lives that their life was not about them: the force of the sleeping baby's presence on his chest, the connection of the baby to April's breast, milk and spittle on their clothes, soupy diarrhea in cloth diapers and on Nicholas's own clothes, washing the boy's clothes and hanging them on the line that the mountain wind dried crisp and fresh smelling, the baby growing from a baby into a toddler, slowly learning consonants: Nicholas thought that these bas and das and mas were the complete expression of this little, helpless being, stating exactly what it was: I'm here, I'm here, I'm here. But not only that. I'm with you. You're here. You tell me, what is that, what is that, what is that, like a mind awakening to everything and everything in turn inviting it to awaken. At nine months, pointing to everything: ba. I'm here, you're here, what is that. April sitting on the floor in the small family room, the windows of the cabin open, rolling a ball toward the baby. Jack reaching for Nicholas by constantly grabbing the air and flapping his hands toward Nicholas. Reading books in the low, yellow lamplight. Holding objects for the baby, slinging him over his shoulder. The baby crawling toward Nicholas as he worked on an article, as he cooked dinner, as he vacuumed, swept, cleaned, and everything pausing for the immediacy of Jack. The first time Nicholas felt a warm energy move from his head to his heart and expand through his chest like a kind of gentle electricity, he'd been holding April in a parking lot after an argument. In the parking lot, it occurred to him that the thought of Jack, of April, of both of them, of him with both them, made him aware that this energy – not an emotion and not a conceptual feeling, but a sensation in his body, his chest – had always been there and was only waiting to be awakened.

Upside down in the car, not wanting to move again but knowing he had to move, he suddenly felt this vacillation between not wanting and having to as a principle of existential import: if he didn't do this thing he didn't want to do – move his arm – he wouldn't live. Trapped in the car, he suddenly saw a strange convergence of what he deemed the two competing sides of himself: he wanted to live, but he didn't want to experience any pain. This, it suddenly seemed, this being trapped in the car, sweating and cold, his own blood occasionally falling on his face, this moment felt symbolic, as though his life itself was metaphorical, the convergence of a story, as though there was some abstraction behind the reality he was experiencing, but that the abstraction was just reality itself, no abstraction at all, that wanting and avoiding were not two separate things, that death and life were not two separate things, that he would die. He felt confused and fought against this thought with the suddenly urgent need to get out of the car and he pulled hard on the steering wheel, so that his neck lifted momentarily off the carpeted ceiling, and he took a breath and tried to extract himself like extracting a deeply embedded thorn from a toe, from the seat. He felt hot pain in his left arm, which pulled and wrenched him back in place, making him yell in pain. He stopped and sat and felt sweat running down his face and his body breathing. Something in him telling himself to breathe, keep breathing, calm down, and after a few minutes, his breathing steadied, though there was still a searing pain in his arm. That was so stupid, why'd you do that, he thought. Now he'd have to wait again until the pain subsided and try to get out slowly, you moron, do it in steps. Another rumble of thunder through the ground and up through his body. Another moment of thinking of the last conversation with April. The thunder moved through the ground, the vibration holding him momentarily. He told himself to breathe and watched another rivulet of rainwater stream by his face, watching the rivulet grow larger, waiting for it to get big enough again so that he could take another drink, and through breathing he told himself to rest, to let his eyes close, he was so tired, to think of something else, to not reduce his entire relationship with April to one argument, to think of the good moments, cooking dinner with her, talking with her, hiking with her, being Jack's parents together with her, think of something else, he inwardly related to himself, which caused him to remember the days that he and April used to smoke lots of marijuana when they were both in grad school and then sit around and self-analyze in order to figure out things about themselves and their relationship. He opened his eyes as though what was there might not be there, as though he might only be in bed, but he wasn't, and he remembered how they'd have these discussions, very stoned, as though they were holding each other up for the other to look at, and they knew it was a kind of indulgence, a privilege to have the job that gave them the money that allowed for the time for them to do this, not to mention to have been educated in a way that allowed them to do this, but Nicholas remembered that at least they were doing it, maybe that analysis was better than no analysis at all, maybe, though privileged, they were using their privilege to at least attempt to better themselves, they asked each other. Was that what they were doing? They agreed that they felt they were sculpting their lives into the shapes they wanted, the figures they wished to be, and that it was their view of it that was important, and Nicholas accepted that. He could feel them somehow becoming intertwined, as though their minds in these discussions became one mind, as though they were two cells on a slide under a microscope that bump each other, for a moment separate, and then slip inside one another, a whole new existence, two and not at the same time, a new life. And yet he'd never, no matter how aware he was, and no matter how aware April was, neither had been able to end this feeling that there was division in them, between them, and now, Nicholas thought, what did any of that feeling of connection matter if he was going to pass out of existence here alone? And then the immediate competing and contradictory thought that all that he had just thought had only been possible because of April, because of Jack: they were inside him, they were him. He felt he could let himself fall into this thought, this feeling, a warm dark – he was moving toward it, it enveloping him, it was happening slowly, gently, moving toward it, it moving toward him – and then he opened his eyes. No, he thought. He couldn't do that. Don't fall asleep. He opened his eyes wide, and wondered how much time had passed. He blinked hard several times, waking himself, telling himself to wake up, to stay awake.

In the periphery of his vision he saw what at first was only a flash of shadow moving quickly, he thought at first a person, but he heard wings and a small noise, and he knew it was a bird. Out the passenger-side window where

April's profile should've been, shifting his head ever so slightly, he saw, on the road, directly in the middle of the road, what appeared to be a hawk. He closed his eyes and opened them and looked and saw the bird was not a hawk, but an owl. He saw the animal in profile, its round head, wings like hunched shoulders, claws on the ground, all visible in the moonlight. The owl stood and slowly rotated its head with its hooked beak and large eyes like a cat's. It looked into the car at him. The owl's entire body turned, though its head stayed facing him, and it seemed to lean over and stretch forward, to see him. He didn't know if this was real, or if he was dreaming, and the owl's head seemed to move in response, as though it was confused by his thoughts, and then his eyes and the owl's aligned and he felt a rushing toward the animal and it moving toward him, though the same space separated them, as though the animal's eyes were pulling him out of the car and himself, and for a moment he seemed to see his own face, the eyes with which he watched the owl the same eyes with which the owl watched him. Then the owl lifted its wings and flew to a branch of a tree, its body completely in silhouette against the moonlit sky. He couldn't tell if it was still watching him or not, or what it was doing here, or why it had landed on the road and looked at him. It was now a two-dimensional figure on a tree branch, completely quiet, and its silence reminded him of his own failed attempt, of the cultivated quiet and isolation in his family's life that he hoped would allow him to see clearly what he was trying to do. To change the narrative of his thoughts, to see through the seeming validity of his personal fiction. But he hadn't changed anything, he thought.

Nicholas closed his eyes in an effort to stop the pulsing in his head and his continuing thoughts, which he both wanted to stop and wanted to keep having, because what if these were his last thoughts? He opened his eyes again and saw that it was nearing five in the morning. What if this cold air here was his last breath? What if this heartbeat, this view out the frame of the car into the forest was the last thing he would see, the last sound the sound of the gentle rain? He wanted to keep seeing and experiencing and thinking, he wanted to apologize to April and feel her body pressed to his, he wanted to pick Jack up from his bed and carry him into the kitchen and share a bowl of organic Sunny-Os, he wanted to bite his lip and be annoyed while eating too fast, he wanted to pop a perfect whitehead on his chin, he wanted to take a piss or crap in the morning, he wanted to have a fever and feel himself changed after it, he wanted to hold Jack's hand crossing the street or surprise April with a kiss, he wanted to fight with her, manipulate her, feel her manipulating him, feel bad for manipulating her, attempt to be sincere, feel her wanting to be sincere, apologize, begin again, he wanted to keep being alive no matter if he was confused or clear or selfish or mean or kind or dumb. He just wanted to keep doing it, he just wanted to keep being himself and wanted the pain to stop. He didn't want to think of freeing his stuck left arm. Being stuck in the car, shivering with cold, no longer sweating, he felt an enormous force in him explaining that in every moment he was deeply divided between what he wanted and what he didn't, as though what he'd always thought about himself was being confirmed now, as he was dying, that yes, he was a deeply divided person, and now that he was not going to live anymore, he was going to experience that divide on the most physical and painful level: he didn't want to die, yet he was. The pressure in his head that had been increasing for some time, both from being hungover and from being upside down, and from, he thought now, the loss of blood, began to make him see spots of flashing white, as though the material world was de-pixelating, coming apart. He again had an urgent need to pee and felt himself clench down there and it hurt. At the same time, again the thought arose to move his arm, to do whatever he had to do, he'd moved his legs, it was just this last thing. He was so tired, he told himself, and then something in him told him it didn't matter if he was tired, he had to free the arm. The drips of blood that had been hitting his face and cheek and nose at what felt like random intervals were now hitting him more frequently. He tasted his own blood again, though he couldn't tell if this came from dripping down his face into his mouth or came from inside him, and that made him afraid. It was time to try the arm, he told himself. He told himself it was time to free the arm, over and over in order to make the action one he was prepared for. What he knew would be pure pain. The rivulet of water running through the car still wasn't close enough, and in complete exhaustion, he thought he needed to move his arm, get his left arm free, and when he pulled it now he felt a wave of pain, and he stopped again, feeling the effort was futile, watching the rivulet of rainwater become larger and larger, until it was so close that he could drink it, lap it up finally, a great reprieve. He drank the water with his tongue and sort of sucked at the rivulet moving by, coughing occasionally due to the dryness of his throat. The water in his mouth was momentarily just the water in his mouth and everything in him was this drinking. He drank and drank, the water tasting of dirt, but it was lovely and clean somehow. He tried to push his face into it even though he was very cold and shivering. He wanted the blood off of his face. No, he thought. You want to free your arm. You're getting tired. You have to do it now.

He observed that the pain in his arm had lessened, he was breathing steadily, he'd rested for a while, the pressure of the blood in his head because he'd been flipped over for so long now was constantly intensifying. He pulled with his upper body, pulling his left shoulder forward and seemed to be able to feel a string of pain along his arm and into his neck, but it wasn't unbearable. His left arm, which was behind him a little, jammed in place by the door, he pulled forward gently, and when the arm didn't move, he pulled more forcefully, then he jolted forward, in frustration, and he heard a horrific cracking sound, then a bell-like ringing of hot energy that quickly morphed into excruciating pain, and he said aloud fuck fuck fuck, jesus. He tried to focus on his breathing, but couldn't: shallow and halting and quick breaths, which his heart followed. There was no sweat on his brow now, his mouth was dry even though he'd just had water, his eyes felt sunken in his face, and the ringing pulse in his left arm made it feel as though the arm was inflated and large, made of shattered ice. After a few long moments, it settled, his body quieted its shivering. And while the pain was still intense and the arm still stuck, he thought the arm was looser, not quite as stuck, and he told himself good, maybe he'd broken it, but it was looser, he could get it out, and he breathed and inwardly related to himself to calm down and try again and just wait a little and then try again. He tried to regulate the pain through his breathing. Then, in attempting to re-shift his upper body in order to reach his left leg, he moved his left arm and a ringing pain moved up his spine, causing a lightheadedness, his vision flashing white, like a camera's flash right in his face, and then the world slowly resolved again. Stop, he told himself. Don't pass out now. You can't pass out now. He breathed, breathed in again, as deep as he could, little points of pain firing all around his body with the deeper breaths. He breathed in again, slowly, and tried to let it move through him and then out of him, then breathed in again. He moved his head against the ceiling of the car. He didn't experience the same sharp pain in his neck, and he felt a brief reprieve, being able to move his head, adjusting his neck and right arm, and though the pressure of the blood in his head made him dizzy, it felt so nice to roll his head like this even against his own sticky blood. For a moment, just from being able to move his neck he thought that he'd be okay, that there wasn't something seriously wrong with his neck, it was just sore from being in the same position – and in this lack of pain, the momentary feeling that he wouldn't die here, he'd get out, he'd talk to April again, he'd get another chance. He moved his head again, kind of rolling it against the ceiling of the car in order to stretch his neck, feeling sticky blood pull away from his face and hair when he moved from the ceiling, and then stopped, breathing heavier, resting. The dim thought that it was just the leg now, just that that had to be completely freed from under the dash.

More rainwater passed by his face, and he drank for a few minutes and stared thoughtlessly, exhaustedly into the dark forest, which was now in a heavy fog. It made him think that morning was approaching, the world beginning again. Maybe April was near town, but that thought was stupid, he knew. She wasn't walking anywhere, and the last conversation they'd had was one in which they'd argued. He stopped drinking and closed his eyes hard and opened them and the urge to pee became too strong and he allowed himself to pee and felt it warm running down his stomach and chest and down his neck and he turned his head so that only a little got on his chin and face. The warmth was momentarily comforting. It made him sleepier and he told himself to rest for a minute, just a few minutes, and as he closed his eyes he again reconstructed the scenario, standing in the kitchen with Nora Evans, her talking to him, him talking to her, and eventually a strange space opening that allowed him to recognize this Nora Evans person as a person, in which he'd felt clarify in him the simple intention to go find April, which was what he had done, telling Nora Evans that it was nice talking to her. He remembered after the party driving home in the car with April, thinking that he'd wanted to convey all this to her. That he'd come to find *her*, and what had allowed that to occur was the confusion of his selfish wanting to flirt or be near this other person, that the dispersal of the wanting awakened the actuality of this other feeling, which was not a feeling, but a self, another story: not wanting April, but just being with her, just being there. But to be able to explain that properly, he remembered thinking, he'd have to admit the sexual attraction first, which had led him to this other feeling, this other intention, this clearer recognition of the others around him and himself, and he didn't want to have to do that because he knew it'd both hurt April and make her angry and cause an argument. Though they'd eventually argued *anyway*, in the car, the argument he'd wanted to avoid somehow manifesting itself, and the most painful part of the argument was that the clear intention he'd thought he'd found in the kitchen was once again lost, was once again dispersed in his feeling that April's implied accusation was unfair, unjust, mean-spirited, and that he didn't want to be doing this, and in feeling that he didn't want to be doing this fight with April, he felt clearly he was against April and her fighting, fighting her, trying to wrestle through words to his own rightness and to the end of the argument, and he had then thought, hands on the wheel, that the only thing he really knew now with any certainty was that he didn't want to be doing what they were doing, which was arguing, he only wanted to stop arguing, though he also felt he wasn't wrong, there was nothing wrong with his actions at the party, so he kept arguing with her, explaining to her that she was simplifying the situation in a way that was frustrating, and that she'd be frustrated by it too if she really thought about it. Then he remembered, at the sort of climax of the fight, that she'd said that she was upset not because of the flirting and not only because Nora Evans was using April as part of her flirtation method, but because Nora Evans had said something about Nicholas bringing the family off the grid, and he hadn't corrected her. In fact, he'd gone along with it. When the whole thing was my idea, she had said. It was my suggestion to get you out of that job you hated. My suggestion to move some place quieter, slower. My suggestion to get out of the city. I know you remember that I told you that maybe you needed a place where you could see what you were doing again, I know you remember that, but what I remember thinking was that I was getting sick of you bitching about how everything was wrong, the fast pace was wrong, driving in cars was wrong, TV, social media, publishing, your job, and I framed it like that, move to some place quieter because I was sick of hearing you complain. That's not fair, Nicholas had said. You were just as annoyed with the traffic, the commute, the loss of our time getting to some place we didn't want to be, don't give me bullshit about how you did it because all I do is complain, to which Nicholas imagined her saying in his memory that of course she wanted something different, too, but that, see, what he wasn't understanding even now was that she had to frame it in this particular way, she had to frame it like maybe doing this would help his work, would help him do what he was always saying he needed to do, live in the present, and you took that and ran with it, but really I just wanted you to stop complaining about everything, and now you're talking to this Nora Evans woman like you dreamed up another way of life for me and Jack. Such bullshit. Nicholas thought of how he'd shaken his head, saying that it'd just been easier, he was just moving the conversation on, and to please think about it, and April had said, Oh, I'm thinking about it, she'd said. And what I think is you're a selfish asshole. She had gone quiet on the ride home but in the continued conversation in his mind, she said, What I think is that you're a selfish asshole, and what I think is you've always done this shit, why would it be any different now? You always eliminate Jack and me. You always say, I live in the mountains of North Carolina. I live off the grid. I took my family off the grid. But you wouldn't have done any of that had I not shown you the books and the websites and introduced you to some people to help us do it. It was *my* idea and you make it seem like you grew a beard, put on a flannel, grabbed an axe, and created the entirety of our life by hewing thatch huts for us to live in. Nicholas imagined himself saying that that was all maybe true but that he really wasn't even trying to do that, he wasn't trying to eliminate her and Jack, it was just easier in conversation to talk in this way, and he knew that April would say that that was exactly her point, it was easier to talk about him, it was easier to make everything about him, it wasn't malicious, she realized, she wasn't saying he was evil, she was calling him an asshole, and that's what an asshole was, a person who made everything about himself, and that was exactly what he did, she thought maybe Jack arriving would change it, and to some degree it had, but after Jack grew up some, Nicholas was back to being the way he'd always been, which was self-concerned with his own self-improvement or investigation or whatever he was calling it these days, his project, she guessed that's what he was calling it now, his project, and it left her and Jack out, except when it was convenient for Nicholas.

He opened his eyes. Listening to the rain, he wondered if this was the last word she'd spoken to him. They often reached a point in their arguing when they'd stop, and they'd both relent, and then both claim that they'd attacked the other, that the attack wasn't really how they felt and thought about the other, but this time there had been nothing more. In remembering the argument with April, Nicholas now wondered if everything he'd ever done had been a selfish delusion, if nothing in his life was truly done for another person, but was always done with some thought of self-gain: make a nice dinner for April and she'd massage his back later, play and sing with Jack because he wanted to be seen as a caring and attentive father, publish articles and become slightly well-known in his field to impress his colleagues and parents and old friends, live off the grid to show his moral superiority to everyone else, thereby impressing them. It made him feel self-pitying and ashamed at his self-pity, just another selfishness, another way he put his pain before anyone else's. In an effort to not keep think-ing in this painful, though possibly true way, he decided it was time. One more pull and the arm would be unstuck, then he'd do the legs. Do it now, he told himself. He thought that he had to move in order to at least have an attempt to correct this last conversation. He wanted the chance to make it so that his last interaction with someone on this planet was not one of meanness and ugliness and selfish-ness. He breathed in and breathed out, steadying himself, waiting for the moment, and in the waiting he thought the last thing she'd said to him was that he was an asshole – the word like an echo – and he thought that this couldn't be the last conversation they'd have, then, in a kind of hor-rified understanding, realized it was, knew it was, and attempted to think of what else he'd said, what else she'd said, had either of them said anything more? The conver-sation couldn't have ended with April saying this and him feeling angry and guilty and mean. He couldn't remember anything else though. He remembered not talking after that, and he feared for a moment that this was maybe the actual expression of who he was. That this last thing that April had said, maybe it was the truest thing, the realest thing about him, was the most banal and stupid thing one could be. Maybe the universe had designed his living to inevitably lead up to this moment when he had nearly died and April presented to him what he actually was, as though through April's mouth, the universe had said: selfish asshole. And in hearing this message from either the universe or April, he thought now, he had no choice but to face the idea that he was an asshole. Was essentially an unkind, uncaring, selfish, idiotic person despite whatever intellectual successes and understandings he'd had. Then he thought that he was turning April into a message for him, another selfishness, and he made himself stop. Was life a designed teaching or was it happenstance? Were there real messages behind things or were things things themselves, or were they not even that? What was real and what was delusion? Trying to keep breathing steadily and deeply and to let go of the pain that was pulsing in his arm and shoulder and dully in his neck and back, he thought that what he felt he'd been doing in supposedly cultivating clarity, in coming to the mountains, in attempting to live in a sustainable way, in attempting, with April, to live again in balance with the world, in attempting to extricate their lives as much as possible from the patriarchal, materialistic, corporately driven, consumerist, competition-based culture that inundated everything in their country and was oppressing not only minorities in the States, but was exploiting people in other counties, the poor and indigenous, as well as exploiting land and plant and animal, maybe in moving to the mountains and in building the little cabin and taking it off the grid and attempting to create a garden they could live on, maybe what he'd been doing was actually nothing. Maybe what he was actually doing, maybe all he was really doing, rather than getting rid of his stupidities, rather than seeing into and listening closely among the quiet to his better self, rather than dropping what he had come to see as cultural selfishness, he had become, as April indicated, selfish in a different way. Maybe they both had. Maybe they'd just created a little island of selfishness. Maybe what he thought they'd done in order to be less distanced from each other and the nature of things was merely create a space where they could more easily fight one another, more easily see how they were in the same room and yet were not, were there and not there, were with each other and somewhere else. Maybe all they'd really done was given themselves a space to see just how alone, how distanced from each other, from their family and friends, from society, and from even themselves they were.

Out the open frame of the windshield, the now gentle rain continued falling in a pattering rhythm that seemed to regenerate itself through sound. He thought that it was probably raining where Jack was sleeping. He looked at the digital clock nearing six in the morning, and out the window through the trees, the small space of sky he could see was just lightening. In his exhaustion, he thought that he'd never say goodnight to Jack again, never get to sing him a new song, never show him the movies and albums he wanted to show him when he got older, never argue with him when he became a teenager, never feel like he was losing him when he left, never feel old himself due to the youth of his kid, never have a falling out and reconnect, and his little boy would always be the little boy whose parents had died, and someone else, over time, would become Jack's real parents, and what had been real for Jack would become unreal.

Just like it was doing for Nicholas now. What was real became unreal and what was unreal became real. He hoped it'd be Nathaniel and Stefanie, and he thought for a terrifying moment of April's mother wanting Jack and how he and April had never made a will, and the poor boy being fought over by the entire family. He tried to think of Nathaniel and Stefanie, like thinking of them taking the boy could somehow create the reality. He closed his eyes and tried to construct the thought from some sourceless depth inside him in an effort to make what was unreal real. When he opened his eyes, viewing the dark woods in the rain, he didn't know why someone hadn't found him yet, why someone hadn't called April's cell phone and realized something was wrong, and he began crying, and said in his mind to Jack that he hoped he would be okay and he was sorry for not being there, for the fact that he might not be there again, he was sorry he'd been stupid and was stupid, he apologized for not being able to say goodbye, he apologized to April, though he knew she was no longer alive. He apologized to his parents, to his brother. He apologized to the rain falling in the woods, and felt his consciousness slip toward the woods, move away from his body, and he seemed to be looking at himself, his face a pale light in the dark of the upside-down car, staring out, but not seeing out of his own eyes, seeing into them, and then he seemed to be viewing himself from up on the branch of a tree, like he was seeing out of the owl's eyes and viewing himself from above, feeling himself move away from his slumped and upside-down body, now above the car, and a part of the woods, the rain, the mist moving through the forest, and he felt as though he was the mist, as though he was gently moving over the earth, and in watching himself grow smaller (he could somehow see himself through the bottom of the car) and now that he was more distant from himself through the trees, he felt a gratitude for his life, and instead of apologizing, he thought the words thank you to the same people he apologized to a moment before and then said thank you to what was everything else. Then there was a sharp pain in his ribs and he was back in his body in the car, looking out. The owl was there looking in at him through the opened frame of the car. A brief moment of feeling dispersed and bodiless slipped away, and was replaced by utter fear, which in turn was replaced by the thought that he needed to understand right away if he and April had said anything else after this argument they'd had. Then, in both fear and awe, he observed his mind slow down and his thinking become abstract, as though his identity was dropping away and he was a representation of one half of the universe, male, though he felt also female, and the female in him was April, was his mother, was other women he knew, and the male in him was his father, Nathaniel, Jack, that existence was divided, that everything was separate and alone so that it might know itself, divided on some vast continuum between male and female, divided between myriad other forms, plant, land, water, animal, air, and myriad other forms of mind, clarity, confusion, boredom, excitement, lust, love, greed, giving, kindness, hate, each complementing each, each forming each, nothing its own existence, selfishness and selflessness, all the same thing, all in him, and his face became some other face that he both knew and didn't know hovering right behind his own face. He didn't see the face so much as become it, which made him breathe in shallower, shorter breaths. Not even become. He was it. This other face that wasn't other. Then he perceived the female face, that also was not fully female. Both faces were looking unwaveringly at each other, and in his fear at observing these faces that were his and not his, he began crying, at the understanding that these thoughts he'd been having were not him, they were not April, not Jack, not his mother, father, Nathaniel, that all of them and everyone were beyond his thinking of them. He closed his eyes to make the faces go away and opened them again and saw them behind the rainy forest. It was as though his mind had become intermingled with the forest itself, had become a physical thing. He could not tell if it was his mind or the not speaking faces that he lightheadedly perceived that conveyed to him that what he'd been learning on the mountain with April and Jack was that what he knew was insignificant compared to what he didn't know, both about others and about himself. He didn't know himself or anyone. Everything was shining beyond knowing. I'm dying, he thought. The lack of knowing was a gift that he'd always been hesitant to accept, afraid to accept.

His vision darkened from the outside in, making a sort of tunnel of looking out the empty frame of the car into the rainy woods. He closed his eyes – a bright pulsing star of light behind his lids – and opened them. The seatbelt suddenly slipped off his left shoulder and hit his ear as it slipped around his head and jolted, retracting back into place, and in an equal and opposite reaction, his body lurched forward and he fell from his sitting position and his right leg came unstuck, and all except for his left leg was loosed onto the ceiling of the car and heard himself yell in pain. The moaning understanding that he'd unbuckled the seatbelt, but it had remained latched, and it had suddenly let go fully and retracted. He was splayed across the ceiling of the upside-down car, his left arm broken and limp above him, his right knee coming down, and the left leg was still stuck beneath the dash, but the entire leg now outstretched, his entire body pulling on it, a burning, pulsing pain through the whole leg. He reached up and tried to move his left arm into a more comfortable position but there was a stabbing jolt against the side of his body and he stopped moving. He felt warm liquid hit his face and knew it was his own blood and knew that he needed to get the stuck leg out now. If he could get the stuck leg out, he could then get out the car – an image of him crawling out from under the car, through the open windshield, over the cracked glass, into the rain and ditch, free. He reached down across his body with his right hand down below the dash, to his left knee, and he felt up and down the knee and thigh, the lower part of his thigh smashed by the dash, and he reached down again to the knee, in the space between seat and some part of the dash, and pulled hard against the outside of the knee, sliding the leg under the dash, the thigh resisting, and he pulled harder and the entire leg slid along the seat, between the seat and dash, a fire burning up and down his leg and up his back and into his neck – the faces behind and beneath everything hovering in his mind and vision. When he closed his eyes, the faces were there, and when he opened them, they were there. He whimpered in pain, heard himself whimpering, half crying, then breathing deeply, trying to make his shallow breathing deeper. Rainwater was now gathering in pools inside the car, on the ceiling of the car, and running over the windshield in small streams. He waited for the burning pain in his leg to settle and he breathed and breathed and told himself to breathe deeply and he heard his breathing quivering. It was just a few more inches, he thought, it must be, slide the stuck leg just a little further, and it'd fall on top of him and he'd be able to get out. He could look at his legs now, he noticed – the faces behind everything seeming to be watching him with distant and neutral curiosity, as though they were the filmmakers of the universe – and he moved his neck and head, and through streaks and sparks that filled his vision, when he looked into the dark below the steering wheel and blood-soaked airbag, he saw his pants ripped and left leg bent strangely at the thigh under the dash, and for a moment he felt he might vomit and then did, watery bile, onto the ceiling beside him. He looked away. The seat where he'd just been was soaked in blood and now he felt the stickiness on his head as well and again thought that this couldn't be the way he died. He couldn't die in a ditch trapped in a car after arguing with his wife about some stupid moment at a party. The faces in his mind, or that were his mind – he was trying to understand – were there. He could not tell if he thought it or if the faces conveyed that he was nothing, was not even a he, and he fought against this and said aloud that he was getting out of this car, he was just drained and tired and hallucinating and told himself to not pay attention to anything his mind was making up and he shifted on the ceiling of the car, moving his torso and trying with his good right arm to reach his stuck left leg, but he couldn't reach it now without a new, sharp pain in his back, that made him take quick breaths, and then he forced himself to do it and through screaming pain pulled and slid his left leg beneath the dash and felt it come loose when he pulled sideways and then the entire leg fell on top of him – his vision bursting in sparks and stars of convulsing energy that was pain – almost feeling as though it was dangling right above the knee, and he had his left thigh in his right hand, his entire body flipped on itself. After a moment, he propped the leg against the steering wheel so it wouldn't fall, and then he looked out the open frame of the windshield and pulled with both arms toward the opening and scooted his upper body, his legs falling down, his left leg on fire, and pulled his body out from the car and then out from under the hood, pulling himself and almost growling through a clenched jaw, pulling onto wet leaves away from the car, and then he was looking back at where'd he'd been trapped and saw something like the impression of his body in blood in the upside-down car seat. He moved himself to lie on his back and had to hold his left thigh to do it, and he felt, in his thigh, bone coming through muscle and skin and jeans, and newly moving blood. When he had flipped onto his back his body remained a pulsing center of pain and for a moment he didn't register the rain, until he did, and told himself to breathe, and took a deep breath, which eased his body momentarily.

Rain was falling gently through the forest onto his body, and he saw now, looking back about ten feet, that the car had gone into the forest some, was actually beyond the ditch near the side of the road, and had broken a tree. He looked around for April, but didn't see her. In exhaustion he let his head fall back on what he assumed were wet leaves, and again took a deep breath, which seemed to come into him slowly. Being free of the car made it feel as though his body was not his and was expanding, and with a slow-moving in-breath, the rain falling on his body slowed, and he looked up on the out-breath, which proceeded from him even slower, and he could see each raindrop that was falling and behind each drop of rain another drop, his eyes barely open, and the warmth of blood running down his leg, the brief vague thought that he shouldn't have moved it, that it was pinned and something had been stopping the bleeding, but nothing was stopping the bleeding now, and the faces he'd seen in the car emerged again more clearly and force-fully, behind the trees and mist and rain, and then the rain stopped and the paused rain was now a ladder, each drop a drop proceeding up, outward, and each drop led toward the faces, which were both of his faces, his face merely an aspect of these other faces, and felt himself go into them, which was himself, but not himself as he knew himself, and so he was no longer he, and he saw time moving beyond him, time that was no longer his time but was Jack's, Jack with him and April on the mountain, then Jack with Nath-aniel and Stefanie, Jack amid conversations and argument between the family members in the cabin, the entire family discussing and questioning and propositioning and debating in the cabin, Jack alone in his room, Jack crying, a decision finally made, promises and compromises and intentions presented, to include all, to allow Jack to know both sides of his family, and Jack leaving with Nathaniel and Stefanie, Jack in an apartment, Jack in a new room, Jack crying, Jack going to a new school, Jack alone, Jack sitting with Nathan-iel, with Stefanie, Jack watching TV, Jack playing soccer, Jack running around the house while Nathaniel chases him,

Jack sitting in a chair while Stefanie cuts his hair, Jack helping Nathaniel make bread, Jack helping Stefanie in the urban garden, Jack having friends over, Jack spending weekends away, Jack sitting between Nicholas's father and mother and watching a movie, Jack playing with Tammy, who'd moved across the country, Jack doing flashcards with her, Jack showing her videos of Nathaniel cooking online, Jack growing taller, Jack with his friends, Jack moving to a new house in the suburbs, Jack with new friends and girl-friends, Jack through his life thinking of Nicholas and April, Jack missing them, Jack wanting them back, Jack seeing his father in Nathaniel, his mother in Tammy, Jack missing his mom and dad, Jack wondering who they were, where they were, if they could hear him, if they couldn't, Jack talking to them, Jack no longer talking to them, Jack forgetting them, Jack becoming Jack, Jack's life moving in a slow bloom outward like a flower opening and all the people around him doing exactly as he and April had done, trying, despite their selfishness, to be there for him, to be there for him in his sadness at losing his parents, to be there for him at his first soccer game, to be there for him when he hated them, when he loved them, when he felt cared for, when he didn't, when he wanted them, when he didn't, when they thought he was being difficult, when he was, when he wasn't, when they were too busy to be there for him, when they weren't, when they held him, punished him, thought they knew how to raise him, didn't know, when they judged, blamed, accused each other, when they didn't, when they needed each other, when they each wanted to do it alone, when they were right, wrong, open, closed, considering Jack, considering themselves, when they gossiped behind each other's backs and Jack heard and felt alone amid the fighting and arguing, when he felt the family members, on a car drive, on a walk, while eating pizza, subtly suggesting that this person was not good enough, that this other person was, when they relented to each other, when they all saw beyond themselves, when they failed to, when they remembered that they had all agreed to do it together, when they all did it together, for Jack they all did it together, whether they wanted to or not, when Jack felt it, when he didn't, all their concern and neglect and selfishness and judgment and greed and delusion and kindness and care, all exactly as it was, his face and all of their faces merging into the two faces in his mind and Jack's face merging there, too, all held by each other. His breath still slowly moving out from him and breathing them all out, up the drops of rain, up through the mist, beyond the mist up through the treetops with just sprouting leaves, up beyond the treetops – his body lying on the ground bleeding – up into the raincloud, a grey growth on the sky, up beyond it into the dark blue night and beyond the moon swiftly passing by, planets, beyond the solar system into some deep darkness and then a galaxy and the faces behind it and further – the flashing image of the body on the ground – a gaseous cloud that was passing through faster into the blackness toward the two faces which slowly merged into one expressionless and calm face which at the same moment dispersed into being the web of the universe which was a mind and every mind and yet also there was the body on the ground trying to hold a hand though there was no hand to hold watching the rain fall from the treetops and being afraid the neutral and calm mind itself afraid through the wet trees a crescent moon in the now lightening sky beyond and moving so fast that galaxies and stars passed by in streaked light, the light also rotational, the streaking light seeming to rotate or spiral inward and outward at once to the neutral face and mind which was the face and mind that was also on the ground feeling an enormous fear that was the fear of itself inviting itself to be itself and then again breathing on the ground feeling the rain hit the body and in each breath the raindrops fell on the body as the face and mind of everything moved up into the body and breathed in and out and this mind that was everything rose up through the body and breathed in just as it ever did and that mind despite its calm acceptance of everything it gave rise to felt fear and awe and foolishness and gratitude as it once again breathed in and out and collapsed in on itself once again, and the first flashing blue lights lighted the treetops.

ACKNOWLEDGEMENTS

Thank you to my family, my mom and dad, former teachers, and friends, who have offered support over the years, in particular Eric Kocher and Patrick Whitfill. Thank you to Seren Adams for seeing something when no one else did, for her brilliant editing, and for all her hard work and kindness. Thank you to my publisher, Picador, in particular Gill Fitzgerald-Kelly and Ravi Mirchandani, for caring about this book. Most importantly, thank you to Emily Rossi, for never failing to see me, even when I haven't been able to see myself, and for all that she has given - her endless and unconditional support, kindness, advice, and time – so selflessly: this is for you.